YOU NEVER FORGET YOUR FIRST

AND HE JUST MIGHT BE THE DEATH OF ME...

MILLIE PEREZ

Edited by Britt Taylor
Cover art by Sam Palencia

CONTENTS

For all the little girls who dream beyond their circumstances...
Sí se puede.

PROLOGUE

Amelia
January

I'D NEVER THOUGHT ABOUT WHAT IT WOULD BE LIKE TO stare at a dead body. With the countless Dateline episodes I've watched, I would have thought I'd be terrified, stunned, or at the very least running away as fast as possible. But no. I stood still, caressing the still-warm left hand of the dead woman that lay in front of me. Slowly removing the simple gold wedding band off her ring finger. Keeping my eyes on the green veins that coursed through her slightly wrinkled hand. The hand that belonged to my mother, Anna.

I'd known this moment was coming. We had time to prepare for the inevitable. I mean let's face it, you didn't see many fun 5k's hosted for pancreatic cancer.

Two months ago, when we were given the diagnosis, it was as if the doctor had given us her time of death, rather than the information regarding this disease. What made this moment even more unsettling, was that the doctor was my father. A man who had dedicated his life to his wife, family and medicine. Yet now, after decades of practicing medicine, wielding his power and knowledge to save endless lives, it seemed as though it was all in vain as he could not save the love of his life.

Being an expert in his field meant knowing that there was no sugar coating what would happen. My mother, who had been with my father since she was eighteen and had sat through endless dinners with medical chatter, had known once she heard the words "stage four pancreatic cancer" that there was no course of action for her to cling onto hope.

Me on the other hand, I like to consider myself as a healthy balance of stubborn and optimistic, and maybe a little sprinkle of delusional. So of course I'd gone down the rabbit hole looking for any and all clinical treatments available around the world. Unfortunately, when I presented my parents with my erratic research, they just gave me a look that let me know I had clearly missed the memo that we weren't fighting this, but rather "making arrangements" with the time we had left.

You would think my job as a financial risk analyst would help me understand the data and the cold hard facts that the likelihood of my mother surviving were slim to none. Yet no matter how many medical reports I read, my brain refused to accept the inevitable result.

The last two months had been the most gut wrenching of my life. Not because my mother was withering away, but quite the opposite. She'd seemed relatively healthy to me and everyone around her, even though we knew that there was a silent killer living inside of her.

No, the worst part of it all was that my mother, my best friend, had still walked side by side with me, but it felt as though she were already a ghost.

Even in the midst of the impending doom, my mother had been keen on preparing for all the moments she would miss in the future. She wrote letters and left video messages to her future grandchildren. Arranged gifts to be opened on certain birthdays and holidays, and even took me wedding dress shopping.

Yes, wedding dress shopping for a wedding that had no groom at the time. My mother said she didn't want to miss out on the experience, and to be honest, neither had I. The appointment started out awkward since there was no wedding date, location or groom to consider, but I should have known that my mother would come prepared. She pulled out a photo from her purse and asked the bridal consultant for a specific dress.

"Mami, what was that about?"

"Mija I saw this dress on Eva Longoria, and knew it would look great on you since you two are about the same height and body type."

"Eva Longoria?! Mom, we can't afford a dress like that! Plus, I don't plan on wearing a black dress on my wedding day."

"No, no. It's the new Oscar de la Renta collection, you know he was Dominican right? Anyways they've reimagined the same dress with a few minor variations with women of different body types and sizes modeling it. Creates a whole different look. I heard that they made a bridal version, and I just need to see it on you. Just humor me." She smiles warmly.

"Okay. I admit it looks stunning, but again, we can't afford to be spending that kind of money for a wedding that may never happen." I say grimly.

"Ay, none of that. Your time will come, when you're ready. I'm sure of it. And in terms of the cost... consider it your inheritance." She winks.

"Wow. That was super morbid. Lovely reminder for my future nonexistent wedding day," I mumble, but before I can push the matter, the bridal consultant pulls me into a changing room to try on the dress.

I walk out to meet my mother's instant watery gaze.

"Ay Amelia." She covers her mouth with her shaky hands.

I clear my throat. "Yeah. I know," I respond, wide-eyed as I look *at my reflection in the mirror, then at my dying mother sitting behind me.*

This is the dress.

Even if I never find a husband. This dress, this moment with my mother, it's all worth it.

"Amelia, it's time to go," my brother Antonio said, snapping me out of my trance.

I finally placed her hand back on the bed and risked one final look to her face, the reality seeping in that she was really gone. I walked over to my brother and he pulled me in for a hug.

"Now what?" I muffled into his shoulder.

He sighed. "Now we go home and pretend that there is a life worth living after mom. And hopefully sometime real soon, we can actually start to believe it."

∼

The next few days are a blur. No matter how many end-of-life conversations and family cry sessions prior to her death, there is no way of protecting my heart from completely and utterly shattering.

I thought I would sob, throw myself at her bed, or even scream when it was finally over. Instead, I had just looked at my mother quietly as a nurse went about turning off every machine that was connected to my mother as a lifeline. It's mind boggling to think that these machines work to keep people alive, and once someone dies, they just get turned off like a light switch. For weeks I'd heard the beeps from the machines, giving notice of signs of life, and now I am engulfed in the silence.

Ah the silence, now that she's gone, the silence is definitely the worst part.

Friends and family surround us during the funeral. The funeral that my mother planned herself. It sounds so morbid, but given that there was nothing we could do to save my mom, my parents did what they do best; they planned. My mother was very adamant about wanting a celebration of life versus a depressing funeral. She'd even hired a merengue band to play during the entirety of it to make sure that people were at least swaying back and forth on their feet while discussing her life.

No matter how many brightly-colored tulips or upbeat music that surrounds us, it's still her funeral, and there are only so many times a person can hear, "Sorry for your loss," "I'm sure she's in a better place," and "At least we know she's no longer in pain."

I am aware that people are speaking to me, but I can barely look anyone in the eye. I just repeat, "Thank you for coming" on a loop and hope that after I'm bestowed with the generic pity look, I am left alone.

I find myself constantly smoothing over my long dark hair, making sure my side bangs stay tucked behind my ears and not in my face. I pick invisible lint from my conservative black dress. The only one I own that doesn't make it obvious that I have thick thighs and a booty that doesn't seem appropriate to make an appearance at a funeral. My usual big brown eyes are slightly puffy, even though I've tried to keep the crying to a minimum today, and my full lips are adorned with nude lipstick that keeps getting reapplied since I can't seem to turn down any of the Dominican appetizers that are brought to me every few minutes by well-wishers.

Then finally, I spot them. The cousin crew. We gave ourselves that name when we were kids. We're children of immigrants, so none of us had extended family to grow up with. And in true Hispanic fashion, it was just easier to call ourselves cousins, instead of explaining to friends who everyone was. And as I see them make their way towards me, I'm forever thankful that I have my chosen family.

The oldest are Vanessa and Luciana, or Lucy as we all call her. Their parents are the other Dominican immigrants, Dr. Ricardo Ortega and Lourdes Ortega. Vanessa is the total mama bear of the group and has always been in charge of corralling the crew during holiday parties. Which seems to come in handy now that she and her attorney wife, Abby, have adopted five siblings whose parents died in a car accident last year. Vanessa is a social worker and caught wind that these siblings would have to be separated in order to give the younger ones a chance of being adopted, leaving the teenagers to filter through various foster homes to fend for themselves.

Vanessa and Abby had already been in the agonizing process of adoption when the opportunity presented itself, and instead of adopting one kid, they ended up with five. Three boys and two girls, and they wouldn't have it any other way.

Lucy is a pediatrician and is married to Bill, an OB/GYN. They love to joke about Bill catching babies and then tossing them to Lucy to care for. Doctor jokes are weird. Lucy's currently pregnant with a baby girl and due any day now.

Xioana and Roselyn are the twins, and their parents are from Puerto Rico, Dr. Manuel Astacio and Isabel Astacio. I became close to them when my parents and I moved to Puerto Rico for my last two years of high school. Antonio stayed behind because he was already attending college at Fordham. It sucked to be the new girl in a new place, but the twins rallied all of their island friends to befriend me, making the experience one I remember fondly.

The twins are always fun to have around because they're always bickering, yet can never go anywhere without the other. They're both married, and somehow convinced their spouses to buy apartments in the same building in Brooklyn. They're both teachers at the same school and their students absolutely love them, especially when they pull the 'twin swap' prank every semester.

Then there are the Cuban immigrants in the group, Dr. Francisco Mejia and Maria Mejia's daughters, Priscilla and Danielle. Danielle is in her second year of residency at Lenox Hill and will be specializing in neurology when she's done. She and her husband Luis are like the Cuban doctor versions of Barbie and Ken, and some of the sweetest people you will ever meet.

Unlike her antichrist sister, Priscilla.

Priscilla is your quintessential *peaked too soon* cautionary tale. Grew double d's by the time she was a freshman in high school, and hasn't worn a top that fully covers the upper part of her body ever since. Also, she's a massive bitch.

For some reason, she's derived nothing but pleasure by teasing me for as long as I can remember.

As kids, she would always exclude me from any fun games or activities, and blame it on not wanting to play with little kids. As we grew older, her favorite pastime became critiquing my outfit or makeup choices. Then in a condescending tone would loudly offer her styling services so that I could hope to leave high school with at least being asked out once.

But enough about her.

Last, but not least, is Evan Cooper. Evan isn't an original member of the cousin crew. He joined when he was fifteen and I was ten. His mother, Maggie, was a nurse at the same hospital my dad and Dr. Ortega worked at. My dad overheard Maggie talk about how her husband had walked out on her and her teenage son, so she needed to pick up more shifts to be able to cover rent. That meant leaving Evan home alone during the holidays since they had no other family in the city, having just moved from Boston. My dad and Dr. Ricardo weren't letting that slide, so they offered Maggie and Evan an open invitation to any and every holiday that our families hosted. They both also put in requests for Maggie to be put on their rounds, so that she would always have hours on her schedule, and a more stable paycheck.

My brother Antonio was grateful to have another guy join the group, since he was the only teenage boy of the cousin crew. After that first Thanksgiving, Antonio and Evan became best friends, which meant that I saw Evan more often than just the holidays. He was always nice to me, and even ignored Priscilla when she tried to exclude me from the group.

Which is probably one of the many reasons that Evan Cooper

was my first crush. Ever. But now is not the time to rehash that string of events as he and the crew make their way towards Antonio and me.

The first to reach me while standing by the casket is Priscilla. Instinctively my guard goes up. "Amelia," Priscilla croaks. "Wow, I don't even know what to say. I'm sure you've heard it all today. We all loved your mother. You guys don't deserve this, I'm so sorry." She pulls me in for an embrace.

"Umm, yeah. Thank you," is all I can muster up. Sure, this is a funeral, so I should have assumed that she wouldn't come here guns blazing, but that's just always been my experience with her. Feeling her act warmly towards me caught me off guard, but actually made me feel better.

Before I know it, it's hard to keep track of who comes second or third because the ladies of the cousin crew surround me with hugs and kisses. Promises to feed me and offers to stay at their respective homes whenever I don't want to be alone. I smile and nod sincerely, because even though we are all first-generation Americans, at that moment, they are all acting like frantic Hispanic mothers, something I no longer have.

It takes me a minute to catch my breath and welcome the light-heartedness that these women have brought me. I even giggle a few times.

Then my eyes lock with a man hovering more than a foot above any of our heads. Evan Cooper.

He closes the distance between us, never breaking eye contact with me. "Amelia," he sighs.

"Hey Mr. Big Shot. Thanks for coming." I offer a timid smile, and he pulls me into a hug. His right arm slides around my waist while he places his left hand behind my head, keeping my cheek pressed into his chest, right by his heart. I slide my arms inside his suit jacket and sink into his hug.

"I'm so sorry. I should have come back to the city more and

visited you guys once I found out she was sick. I should have been there for you guys," Evan laments.

I take a deep breath. And instantly become consumed by Evan's scent. It somehow has a calming effect on me, and I feel myself melting more and more into his embrace.

"Trust me Evan, my mom didn't want anyone around her besides dad, Antonio and me. And we never left her side. We're just glad you're all here now."

He kisses the top of my head and I close my eyes to steady my heartbeat. "I can fly back and forth from California any time, Amelia. Will you please let me know when you guys need me? Even if it's just for dinner and some company. I'm serious," he mumbles into my hair.

I chuckle against his dress shirt. "I hope you have a lot of air miles then."

"I have a jet, you know this," he groans.

"Yeah, I know. Just wanted to hear you say it again so you could hear how ridiculous that sounds. Which reminds me, I remember lending you fifty cents so you could buy an Italian ice once. How much do you think I've earned in interest at this point?" I squint my eyes.

He slowly leans back to look at me with feigned shock in his eyes. "Amelia Nuñez, is this a shake down at your own mother's funeral? I knew you were a force to be reckoned with, but damn that's cold." He laughs, and I do too.

I can't remember the last time I had a full belly laugh. And once it starts, I can't stop. Then one by one, each of the ladies of the cousin crew start laughing too. They have no idea why we're all laughing, which is what probably makes the moment even funnier. I'm now wiping away tears of laughter instead of grief, and it feels like the breath I hadn't realized I was holding since learning of my mother's diagnosis, is released. All thanks to Evan Cooper.

But the table has countless glasses and dishes, which means I've still got time to keep going.

"You, on the other hand, can't tell me the last time you were in a relationship because it's probably been over a decade. Now I wouldn't be so rude as to make an assumption about your love life, but since you so callously made an assumption about mine, let's have at it."

Xioana chimes in. "Amelia, maybe it's time to go. We can walk you to the train station—"

"You're a coward Evan. You don't let anyone in, and yet somehow feel entitled to belittle my relationship."

"Maldita sea," Roselyn groans.

"I know some of you still think of me as the baby of the group, but I'm a grown ass woman, and I've been through hell and back these last few months. So if I decide that I don't want to waste any more time and finally marry Sebastián, then that's exactly what I'm going to do!"

"Amelia come on, let's grab an Uber instead, Roselyn and I have to go home and change for a date with our husbands," Xioana pleads.

Evan pierces me with his eyes, and I swear I can feel the fury pulsating off of his skin. "It's ok ladies, you can leave. You see, Amelia here is a *grown ass woman*, as she just mentioned, and therefore can hold her own." He turns back to face me as the twins eye one another in confusion.

I turn to the twins. "No need for that Uber, my *fiancé* will be picking me up a few blocks away from here, near his favorite sandwich shop soon," I sneer.

The twins seemed satisfied enough with my answer and slowly exit the pub.

"So why don't you answer this little question for me," Evan begins. "Where is he Amelia?"

"What?" I say, caught off guard.

"Your fiancé. Soon-to-be husband, goes by the name of

Sebastián or so I hear. Why isn't he here with you announcing your engagement?" He pins me with his relentless stare.

"W—what do you mean?" I clear my throat and try to steel myself. "He's not my shadow, Evan. I'm allowed to go places without him. Plus, he's a very busy man, he's running errands all around the city today. And even so, he should be picking me up any minute now," I scramble.

"Bullshit," Evan spits out. "You mean to tell me that you're here with people that you consider family, and he's too busy running *errands* to celebrate with us?!" he barks.

I open my mouth to respond but words have seemed to fail me at this very inopportune time, so he continues.

"Oh, and that lovely engagement story you told us, are you fucking kidding me? You came to a mutual agreement that constantly breaking up sucks, so the next logical step is to legally commit yourselves to each other. Really, Amelia? Wow, I mean I didn't know that was the fairytale you were banking on, but I guess I should say congrats instead of pointing out the painfully obvious?" Evan spits.

"Which is what, Evan?" I yell. The whole pub can probably hear us, but I'm so livid that I can feel my pulse on the tips of my ears.

He huffs out a breath and lowers his voice so only I can hear. "That you deserve better."

Huh. That is not what I was expecting.

Calling me a loser, maybe. Saying that I was a delusional bride-to-be, perhaps. But saying I deserved better ... not the response I was expecting.

"Well since you seem to know everything about me and relationships, why don't you enlighten me, Evan? What is it exactly that I deserve that I am not getting?" I say as I lean back into my chair, emotionally exhausted from this unexpected conversation.

He runs his hand through his short, light brown hair in frustration. He looks down at the table, then back up to me.

"First of all, if this guy had any sense to him, he would have never allowed that first breakup to ever happen, because he would have known that a woman like you isn't something that comes by very often."

Gulp. What the hell.

"Also, when you announce your engagement to your loved ones, you shouldn't have to second guess what anyone's reaction will be, because it should automatically be a given that whoever is with you is the luckiest man alive.

I think about interrupting him, but a part of me is curious to see what else he has to say on the matter, so I stay quiet.

"Amelia, I don't care if you're the type of girl who is into grand gestures or not, but that engagement story ... yeah that's not the story you want to tell your kids about, it's not the once in a lifetime experience that you deserve."

I look down at my engagement ring and move it side to side. I can feel tears starting to well up, but I don't let them fall. I won't let him see me cry.

"And one last thing. Let's say that for some reason he really couldn't be here today. Fine. But what is stopping that man from picking you up here, in this bar, and saying a quick hello to your loved ones, even if it's just for a minute. Not at some stupid sandwich shop a few blocks away. It's not about him physically being here for you, but rather showing up for you. There's a difference. And THAT, Amelia, is what you deserve." He smacks the empty glass on the table, nearly shattering it.

I slowly nod my head and take a deep breath. I hop off the high stool and push it back into the table, while gathering my purse and phone.

"Is that it? You're leaving? You have nothing? No rebuttal to what I have to say?" Evan scoffs.

I hook my purse on my shoulder and take a step towards the exit, but stop and turn back to Evan.

"Actually, I do have one thing to say." A single tear escapes and I quickly work to wipe it away. "I hate you, Evan Cooper."

I exit the pub, and at that moment, no truer words have ever been spoken.

By the both of us.

2

AMELIA
AUGUST

"Hurry up, we're gonna be late!" I shout at my best friend Nikki who's currently trailing behind me carrying an absurd amount of balloons.

"Tell me again how you roped me into coming to the east side of town to help set up your apartment for sexy time with Sebastián?" Nikki says, out of breath.

"It's not sexy time, it's a romantic dinner for two as an early birthday surprise. He's going to be working during his whole birthday weekend, so I thought we could celebrate early ... and have sexy time." I wink at Nikki as I push open the apartment building's front door.

"You guys live together, how is he not supposed to see us set this stuff up, Einstein?" Nikki groans as we start climbing the stairs to my and Sebastián's fifth floor apartment. "And when is your hulk of a brother showing up to help put up all these streamers and banners? I know for a fact you don't have a ladder and Antonio will find a way to pin any injury of yours on me." She huffs.

"I told Sebastián I was staying this weekend at my dad's place so I could help him with a couple things around the house, and have some father/daughter time. But it was my cover for getting all my party supply packages delivered over at my dad's so he wouldn't suspect anything. Once he knew I'd be gone, he decided to pick up an extra shift at the hospital, like he usually does when I stay with my dad. I texted him an hour ago and he confirmed that he was still at work. I swear I could work for the FBI if I wanted to, ya know," I say with a grin. "And Antonio already texted me that he's on his way, so simmer down."

I met Nikki at college in Miami, and we've been inseparable since. She's got the whole *girl next door* vibe going for her, with fair skin and blonde hair. Today the tips of her hair are pink. She's adventurous like that. Whereas I've probably sported the same hairstyle longer than Lisa Rinna. But don't let her looks deceive you, that girl probably has more degrees in psychology than Freud.

We may be complete opposites, but she is my person. She's petite like me, but that's where our physical similarities end.

I'm the brunette, and she's the blonde.

She's got the boobs, and I've got the ass.

I'm the hopeless romantic, and she's the maneater.

The yin to my yang.

We finally made it to my apartment door, and I set down the boxes I was holding on the floor. "Ok let's try to get this done within an hour so I have time to shower and get ready for when he gets home tonight. Good thing I thought ahead and ordered takeout from his favorite steakhouse so I don't have to cook," I say as I turn the key in the lock and open the door.

Once inside, it takes me a minute to realize what I'm looking at.

A pair of strappy heels by the entrance, *not mine*. Two red-stained glasses of wine on the coffee table in the living room ...

Nikki's mind seems to be able to piece everything together before I can. "Amelia, wait by the door, I can handle this," Nikki whispers to me.

"I'm confused, handle what—" And then I hear them. "Oh

God. This can't be happening, Nikki please tell me this isn't happening," I say as I hold on to her arm for dear life while hearing faint moans in the background.

Before I know it, Nikki is hauling ass to my bedroom, and trailing me along behind her. I plead with her to stop, and say that this must be some weird misunderstanding. It's quite pathetic that my first instinct is to try to preserve Sebastián's integrity when I'm 99.9% sure I've figured out what I just walked into.

I stop her as soon as we reach the door, my brain scrambling to figure out my next move, when I hear another familiar voice moaning Sebastián's name. No, it can't be. Now I really must be hallucinating. But before I can finish that thought, I find myself pushing past Nikki and turning the door knob, the bedroom door flying wide open.

WHAT THE FUCK.

Christine Villanueva. My co-worker and frenemy, clearly more enemy than friend, is riding my fiancé like it's her last goddamn rodeo.

"Oh shit! Amelia, this isn't what it looks like!" Sebastián screeches as he bucks a very naked Christine off of him.

"Oh really, cause it looks like this chick was riding your dick into oblivion, you asshole," Nikki yells as Christine makes her way off the bed and pulls the bed sheet over her head. Yes, over her head as if I magically can't see her.

It feels as though all the blood in my body has pooled at my feet, and I am frozen in place. I sense my throat clenching shut, leaving me unable to speak. My eyes are brimmed with tears and a look of bewilderment is plastered on my face taking in the scene that lays before me.

"¡Amelia, mi amor! Don't cry. I'm sorry, I made a mistake!" he says as he fumbles to put on a pair of dress pants and wobbles his way towards me.

"Don't you even think about getting near her you asshat! And how about you focus on Casper the friendly ghost over there?" She points at Christine, who is still standing like a statue with a sheet covering her whole body. "Hello, yoohoo, we can see you, lady with the mermaid tramp stamp!" Nikki croons.

Just as Sebastián is closing the space between us, I muster up the ability to speak for the first time.

"W–why? How long?" I sniffle, tears now streaming down my face uncontrollably. "And for fuck's sake Christine, take that stupid sheet off your head before I do it myself!" I scream.

Christine slowly pulls the sheet down until her face is revealed. I'm surprised when her facial expressions show annoyance, rather than embarrassment.

"You said she wasn't supposed to be here this weekend, I knew we should have gone back to my place," she whisper shouts at Sebastián.

This bitch ...

I hear a thud by the front door and we all turn to see Antonio with a confused look on his face. He takes the scene in for one more second, and I see it all click in his mind. "You're a dead man!" Antonio charges towards Sebastián, making it to our bedroom in three purposeful strides.

My brother Antonio is a beast. He's like a Dominican version of Dwayne *The Rock* Johnson, but with hair. He's an NYPD officer and practically lives in the gym. And he also likes to box and practice mixed martial arts for fun. So yeah, Sebastián just might meet his maker if I don't intercept.

I put myself between them to prevent turning this nightmare into a murder scene. "Antonio, stop!" My voice cracks through the tears.

Antonio tries to push past me, and even Nikki realizes that the bloodshed would be bad, so she helps me block his path.

"Listen to your sister Tony, don't think your friends in blue are gonna like seeing you in lock up," Nikki warns.

I grab Antonio's face with my hands and force him to look at me. "Por favor. Stop! Let me handle this! I can't lose you too. I can't let you get fired, or worse—arrested," I plead.

Antonio pants like a bull, eyes looking up to Sebastián who is cowering by the bed behind me. "Fine. But I need him out of this apartment. NOW!" His shout shakes the small apartment.

Nikki is able to grab Antonio's hand, causing his attention to shift to her. "Come on big boy. Let's stand by the kitchen and give the sleaze bag a clear path so he can leave with his skank." Antonio rolls his eyes at her absurdity then nods, allowing Nikki to guide him away from Sebastián.

"Okay. You heard him. Get out," I say with venom in my voice.

He is clearly dumber than I thought, because he takes a chance, and grabs my hand to plead for forgiveness, one more time. "Amelia. I'll go, but please, can we just—" Oof.

I tap into the self defense training Antonio taught me last year, and give Sebastián a nice knee to his crown jewels. Followed by a sharp elbow to the back of his head, causing him to plummet to the ground. Christine shrieks in the background.

"On second thought, I'll leave. I'll be back in an hour to pack my stuff. With Antonio. So make yourself scarce unless you want to go for round two. And I'm not referring to your bimbo booty call," I say to a withering Sebastián on the ground.

Sebastián moans in pain, while in fetal position, holding on to his privates. *Good luck with those now, Christine.*

"Come on, let's get out of here before I ask for my turn," Nikki says as she locks her arm with mine.

I walk out the front door and stop to give one final look into the catastrophe I just walked into. In a matter of minutes, my love story came crashing down.

Sebastián will no longer be my husband, or the father of my children. I will not be married or a mother in the timeframe I have always imagined. And my mother will never get the chance to meet my future husband.

Goodbye old life. Hello rock bottom.

3

AMELIA
NOVEMBER

THE LAST COUPLE OF MONTHS I LIVED IN A CONSTANT daze.

I moved in with my dad the night I caught Sebastián cheating. I hate how heartbroken he was for me. The man has suffered enough by losing the love of his life, and I hate that my poor choice in men added another reason for him to be upset.

Nikki's uncle is the landlord in her building, so they were able to pull some strings and get me a studio apartment, ready to move in two weeks after the scandal occurred. It was definitely tight quarters, but better than commuting to work from my dad's place every day. Plus, I needed my own space to be able to cry freely without worrying about raising my dad's blood pressure.

I went from happily engaged, living in a two-bedroom apartment in the Upper East Side, to a publicly embarrassed singleton living in a classic NYC shoebox in the Upper West Side.

Still a great location, just shitty setup complete with life changes.

I don't know how, but the news of my broken engagement was met with minimal murmurs from the cousin crew. I'm pretty sure

Instead, in the wise words of Biggie Smalls, "Mo money, Mo problems."

I will admit I have come a long way from the kid who grew up in South Boston. I had the cards stacked against me the second my dad imploded our lives by leaving us to fend for ourselves. My mother is an angel who supported my dreams as a single mom. Which is why I love the daily photos I get from her at her Boca Raton home, relaxing by the pool.

I set her up with a fund with enough money to last her ten lifetimes. I called it her retirement present. She wasn't keen on accepting my financial help, but once she fully understood that I was basically a billionaire, it seemed silly for her to refuse the things that I've always dreamed of giving her. She also complained that the home I bought her was too big for just her, so she moved her sisters in, and now they're spending their retirement hitting up all the happy hours and flirting with the locals.

I keep her in mind, and try to remind myself to be grateful while spending most of my time during these meetings staring at memes, checking Twitch to see which of my friends are currently gaming, *lucky bastards*, and scrolling through Instagram. I'm not a big social media guy, but some recent activity has unfortunately piqued my interest.

Amelia Nuñez's profile.

During one of my endless meetings with my finance team, I noticed that some pictures were missing from Amelia's profile. And yes, I noticed because I look often, even though I know I shouldn't torture myself. The pictures in question are the ones with her fiancé. Some sick part of me keeps hoping that it means trouble in paradise, but that would mean Amelia would be heartbroken, and she's had enough of that to last a lifetime. Yet something in my gut tells me that this is more than just a lovers quarrel over wedding planning.

Usually, news like this gets to me quickly via the cousin crew group chat, but Amelia is also on it so I doubt anyone would bring it up there. I really need to meet up with them in person soon because I know within the first five minutes of saying hello, one of the women will give me a full unsolicited deep dive of the *chisme* that I've missed while I was gone.

Just as I'm about to close the app and try to feign the least bit of interest in what my head of finance is saying, I notice that Amelia has just posted a story. I click on it and panic turns in my stomach.

5

EVAN

"BAD DECISIONS WILL BE MADE TONIGHT!"

I read these words over and over again while watching a boomerang of Amelia and her friend Nikki taking shots of God knows what while wearing ... *Jesus Christ* what is she wearing?! The photo is angled from above, but I can make out a shiny material with a very low cut. Too low cut.

I refresh the story again hoping to see if there's a follow up to these "bad decisions," but come up empty.

Close the app, leave it alone. It's none of your business.

"So, we'll pause here and hand it over to Evan. Anything you would like to add to the Q1 projections?"

Shit.

"Thanks Peter. No, I have nothing to add. You guys seem to have covered it all, it's as if you don't even need me here." I smile and the team lightly chuckles. "Speaking of which, you can all continue without me. Some pressing matters have come up that I need to tend to. Feel free to CC me on all future emails on Q1 projections and we can touch base on Monday. Goodnight, everyone." I stand and start making my way out of the conference room.

And that is how I've survived the corporate world. You use the most amount of words to give an answer with the least amount of new information. Then receive nods from your colleagues, and find the nearest escape route.

Except this time, I'm not rushing home to game with my friends. I'm now on a mission to find where these "bad decisions" are taking place, so I can have a long overdue conversation with *Little Miss Amelia.*

6

AMELIA

"I can't believe I let you convince me to leave the apartment looking like a hoochie," I say as we get out of the Uber and start walking to the warehouse hosting the elusive party Nikki has been amping me up for all week. Thank God I forgot to charge my phone and it died on me. That way drunk Amelia won't make an appearance all over my social media.

"Oh stop, that dress was literally made for your ass, my flap-jacks could never fill it out the way you do!" Nikki laughs.

"Can you please stop talking about my ass? Especially in public. People might get the wrong idea. Wasn't the point of tonight to *get my groove back*? Whatever that means."

"Ha! Never! I would gladly use your tush as a pillow every night, but you eat cheese like everyday and refuse to accept the fact that you're lactose intolerant."

"Nikki!" I yell.

"Oh come on loosen up! You're dressed like a sex kitten, you've taken four shots of tequila with me so far tonight, and you're about to set off boners all over this party. I'm already proud of you for taking my advice and putting on that sexy underwear!" Nikki exclaims.

Nikki can sometimes have a bit of an online shopping problem, and in this case she bought a very nice lingerie set from La Perla, and didn't even bother double checking the sizes when she ordered, now saying it's too late to return it.

"Somehow I creepily feel like you bought these for me to wear knowing I wouldn't turn down luxury goods," I say as I eye her suspiciously.

"Oh my God I really didn't, although that would be a genius idea. I would love to invest in your future sex life. Who knows, maybe you get some mileage on them tonight." She wiggles her eyebrows at me.

"Can you please remind me again why you made me come out tonight to hear you guys talk about lactose intolerance and Amelia getting in some sex mileage?" Justin pipes in, looking at Nikki as we finally make it into the club after waiting in line. Poor Justin is always roped into our girl chats, and even though he and Nikki have been dating for a year, he clearly is the third wheel in this arrangement.

"Sorry Justin. Please tell your woman to behave tonight, I feel like she's keen on having me go home with a stranger, and I would like to remind you that we all live in the same building. So I would have to run over to your place in the middle of the night and ask you to get rid of the guy once I start telling him my sob story about my dead mom and cheating fiancé."

"Uh Amelia, I don't think you'd need me to get rid of him, I'm sure he'd run for the hills on his own accord." Justin laughs.

"Sheesh, I'm such a gem. Can we just go back home now?" I say as I reluctantly hand my coat over to the coat check.

"Hell no. Look, you obviously don't need to go home with anyone tonight. But I do need you to realize how hot you are and that your douchebag ex-fiancé's inability to keep his penis in his pants has nothing to do with you," Nikki starts. "I mean for fuck's sake Amelia look around, we haven't even made it to the bar and it's starting to look like the hunger games in here," she says, grinning.

I slowly take in the ambiance of the party, feeling much smaller and cozier than I had imagined for a warehouse, and then one by one begin to notice the men looking at me. A lot of men. Holy shit this is uncomfortable, I must look naked.

"Ok now I remember why I had to come tonight. Bodyguard reporting for duty. Amelia, this isn't your first rodeo at a club, you did go to college in Miami and all. Stay close to us and let me know if anyone is making you feel uncomfortable," Justin says as he surveys the room.

Justin is such a teddy bear and puts up with our girly brunches and at-home mani/pedi's that I sometimes forget he's a 6'2 tatted man who probably spends more time in the gym than at his actual job.

"Thanks Justin. I really appreciate you coming and keeping us safe." I smile.

"Our fucking hero," Nikki says as she bats her eyelashes at Justin. She may come off as a flake, but Nikki is one of the smartest women I know, and she is total mush for Justin. Her sass is just a front for the rest of the world.

"Ok, now let's get some drinks and get those bad decisions taken care of crew. Quick selfie!" she says as us three gather close and smile in front of the neon sign that glared BAD DECISIONS NIGHT.

7

AMELIA

HELL MUST HAVE FROZEN OVER, BECAUSE I AM ACTUALLY having a good time. I'm smiling and laughing like I haven't in what feels like a century. I feel lighter as I dance with Nikki and Justin, and not only because I've consumed three drinks in a short time span.

Even though I feel like I'm dressed as a porno disco ball, the men at this party have been surprisingly respectful, and actually seem nervous to approach me.

Me.

I even struck up flirtatious conversation with someone while in line for the porta potty.

I know, real romantic.

Tonight has turned out to be exactly what I needed. I now understand what Nikki meant about me getting my groove back. After so much loss and devastation this year, I feel like I completely forgot how to function in society. My world came crashing down, but the rest of the world kept moving forward, making me feel like I lost my place in it. But tonight, I've been able to finally jump back in a little, even if it means dancing to 2000's throwback music and drinking too much tequila.

"You're totally having fun! Don't lie to me. Let's take another pic!" Nikki yells into my ear. Followed by her planting a big smooch on my cheek that forces me to close my eyes while laughing. I'm sure that one won't be pretty, but none of my family follows Nikki, so I'll be saved from embarrassment once she inevitably posts it on her story.

"Yeah yeah, you were right. Bask in all your glory now because we're probably going to be feeling this hangover for three days. Cheers to the newfound perks of turning 30 next month!" I say sarcastically. "Oh well, we're already going to be hurting tomorrow, so screw it, next round's on me!" I shout as I bolt into the crowd and off to the bar.

Ok, even I can admit I'm feeling a bit buzzed now. Ok a lot buzzed, but we have a perfect game plan to eat frozen pizza, mozzarella sticks and leftover takeout chicken parm when we get home, so all this booze should be absorbed soon. Or hopefully most of it?

Anyways, now that Justin has agreed that this place isn't a total sleaze fest, he's relaxed a bit on the bodyguard front, but every twenty minutes or so gives me a look to make sure I'm still good.

Just when I think I'll start to slow down for the evening, I hear the DJ start playing Ashanti and Fat Joe's *What's Luv*. I am immediately flooded with silly memories of jamming to this at my fifth-grade school dance.

Geez, was that really something I needed to know all the lyrics to at the age of eleven?!

I look for Nikki, but see that she's making out with Justin. Before I know it, my feet are taking me to the middle of the dance floor, and I am dancing like I don't have a care in the world.

The way I'm rolling my hips, shaking my ass, and running my hands over my body while singing the lyrics to the music is definitely something that sober Amelia would cringe over, but she ain't here. Drunk Amelia at your service!

I see everyone on the dancefloor smiling at me and dancing along. Out of the corner of my eye, and probably hazy vision at this point, I catch someone standing still in a room full of swaying people. I almost don't give it a second thought until—

"AMELIA!"

Oh fuck.

8

EVAN

"She's gonna be the death of me," I mumble to myself.

"You say something Mr. Cooper?" Teddy asks. My driver, a tall, African American man in his fifties, who is often either too polite, or too nosy, but always nice to be around.

"No, Teddy. And I've told you a million times to call me Evan."

"Sorry sir, force of habit. You sure this is where you want me to take you?" Teddy asks with an arched eyebrow.

"Don't judge me Teddy, just planning on picking up a family friend from this party. Clearly she's lost her mind," I say while rubbing my hand down my face.

"No judgment from me sir, I mean, Evan. This car is a vault. You can say or do as you please, and you won't hear a peep from me," Teddy promises as he looks at me in the rearview mirror. "Also because I signed an NDA, but even if I hadn't, your secrets would be safe with me," he says with a grin on his face.

"Thanks." I offer a forced smile. Best I can do given what's on my phone screen.

I've lost track of how many stories Nikki has been posting all night.

Yes, I saw that Nikki was tagged on Amelia's story and then found my way onto her friend's page. God, I'm cyber creeping.

I push away the creep vibes and refocus on the fact that I've basically had a front row seat to Amelia's night thanks to Nikki's Instagram. I'm going to have to talk to them about online safety at some point. I mean Nikki's page is public for fuck's sake, anyone could be doing what I'm doing right now.

Fuck, what am I doing?

As soon as I figured out the location of this party, I immediately had Teddy reroute us there. I've been playing detective all night trying to find them, and it's just dawned on me that I don't exactly have a plan as to what I'm going to do once I see Amelia.

Hey, haven't seen you since I yelled at you at a pub, but I'm here to take you home because you're dressed way too sexy for my liking. Also, are you still engaged to that douchebag by any chance?

Jesus Christ, what am I thinking?

That's it, I'm not thinking at all.

One flash of Amelia on my screen when I'm anywhere within driving distance of her and I just bolt for the door. Although it isn't exactly the first time I've done something like this, but now isn't the time to think about that spontaneous trip to Miami.

"We're here, boss," Teddy says as we pull up to a hipster-looking spot.

"Gosh, I'm thirty-five, but I might as well be seventy-five. I can hear the music from inside the car, I fear for the headache I will inevitably get by just walking in there," I dryly say.

Teddy laughs, "Go on and handle your business, I'll be out here waiting."

I step out of the car, and a couple of college-aged kids barrel out of the club looking like they're on their way to Coachella. Which reminds me that I'm in my usual boardroom attire, a three-piece suit and tie. "This should be fun," I say out loud.

I walk into the club and immediately feel knots turning in my stomach. There are a lot more men than women here, and Amelia has been here all night. According to Nikki's incessant social media updates, I know that they had four shots before leaving the house, and they were cheering in a group selfie thanking Amelia for a round of drinks.

I fear for the state I'm going to find Amelia in. I know first-hand how special her mother was. I know that her death has forever changed her, and I'm just praying that I don't see her curled up in a corner crying, because I don't know if I would have the strength to not pull her into my arms and hold her there until the sun comes up.

Finally, after weaving through the crowd for a few moments, I spot something that resembles the glimmer from Amelia's outfit. I get closer, and freeze.

Nope, definitely not crying.

It takes my brain a few seconds to come to terms with how the woman dancing in the center of the crowd, moving her body in the most joyful yet sinful manner, is Amelia. Once I get a better look of her side profile through the crowd, I can tell that she's singing the song out loud.

Of course she is.

I dare get a few feet closer, and all I can feel is the heat rising in my chest.

I get a full unobstructed view of Amelia, and I see ALL of Amelia. The front of the dress is asking for a wardrobe malfunction, with her cleavage on full display. Her breasts rise and fall with every move she makes, highlighted by her hands running all over her body.

Fuck, I'm never going to get this visual out of my head.

She then sways her body and my hands balled into fists. Her dress is hugging her curves in a way that leaves very little to the imagination, and trust me, I've had a long time to—imagine—many things about Amelia. But what stands before me doesn't even come close.

Also, the fact that one of her booty shaking moves can easily ride the dress up and give everyone a peek of that scrumptious, thick ass—

Stop. You don't need an erection while yelling at Amelia...
Too late.

At that moment, I realize that every man in that room is salivating over her. Where the hell is her fiancé? Where is Nikki? What the hell is she doing? Before I can ask myself another stupid question, I see her turn in my direction. Releasing the rage that's been burning in my chest since I first saw her face flash across my screen, I shout, "AMELIA!"

9

AMELIA

EVAN *FUCKING* COOPER.

For a split second I think I may be hallucinating. That the alcohol and booty shaking combo has somehow managed to make me start seeing things. But Evan closes the distance between us, and the realization that he's actually here hits me like a freight train, and instantly starts the process of sobering me up.

"Amelia, what the fuck are you doing?" Evan yells.

"Training for the New York City Marathon. You?" I say casually.

Evan snarls. He knows that I have quite the mouth on me, but I assume he at least expected me to be embarrassed at being seen like this.

"I don't have time for this, get your coat, I'm driving you hom—"

"Is there a problem here Amelia?" Justin shouts while staring directly at Evan.

"Nope, no problem at all. Evan here was just leaving," I say as I put my hands on Evan's arm and attempt to turn him towards the exit. He doesn't move an inch, while I get a handful of his biceps.

Sheesh.

We both stay locked in a staring contest while I make pitiful attempts to move him.

"Wait, wait, wait. Evan? As in Evan *Fucking* Cooper?" Nikki screeches. "My my my have I heard stories about you, Mr. Cooper!" Nikki grins. "Babe, Evan and Amelia have known each other since they were kids. No need to break any necks tonight," she chuckles as she playfully rubs her hands over Justin's chest.

"Actually, the jury is still out on that one, so please standby." I give up trying to push Evan out of the door, but I still have my hands on him. Evan looks down at the point that connects us, and I quickly drop my hands to my sides.

"Amelia. Outside. Now... Please," he says through gritted teeth. *Woah.*

Nobody tells me what to do. *At least not anymore.* So why would Evan barge in here yelling at me? Why is he in New York? How did he find me? Where the hell has all this tension come from? Too many questions I need answers to, and I find my curiosity starting to get the best out of me.

"Stay here guys. If I'm not back in five minutes, that means I'm gonna need an alibi," I say as I walk towards the exit, avoiding Evan's searing gaze and bypassing the coat check altogether.

Time to match some fucking energy.

10

EVAN

As soon as she hits the sidewalk, I realize that she probably should have made a pitstop for her coat on her angry strut out of the club.

"For Christ's sake Amelia." I groan as I take off my suit jacket and attempt to put it on her. She quickly snatches it out of my hands, and begrudgingly puts it on, crossing her arms over her chest.

"Explain yourself. What are you doing here?" Amelia demands.

"I was about to say the same to you." I scoff. "What the hell has gotten into you Amelia? If your brother saw you right now—"

"NO." Amelia cuts me off, poking her index finger into my chest. "You don't get to do that."

Poke.

"*No one* gets to make me feel anything I don't want to feel anymore."

Poke.

"My need of being perfect died with my mother."

Poke.

"I now do what I want, when I want, and I answer to no one."

Poke.

I grab her hand on the last poke and keep it on my chest. I look down, quickly realizing she's not wearing her engagement ring. She follows my gaze and I watch her eyes widen and begin to mist.

Fuck. Here come the tears.

She rips her hand out of my grasp and immediately turns toward the street's curb. Before I get the chance to pull her in to me, I watch as she bends over, throws her hair over her shoulder and begins to vomit.

Nope. Still definitely not crying.

Teddy appears immediately and hands me a fistful of napkins. He must have been watching the whole debacle. "I'll go grab some water from the bodega on the corner. Be back in a second!" he offers a sheepish smile.

"Here. Take these." I offer the napkins to Amelia.

"Ughhhh please just go away now," Amelia pleads as she grabs the napkins and tidies up.

"Woah, clean up on aisle five!" Nikki teases, walking over to us with Justin tailing behind. "Did you get any in your hair?" Nikki asks, rubbing Amelia's back as she starts to vomit again. "I got you girl. Let it all out, you'll feel better in a minute."

"How much has she had to drink? Do I need her to get her stomach pumped at the hospital?" I scold.

"Calm down there cowboy. We drank water throughout the night, but this one insisted on a street dog after our second round of drinks here, so that's most likely your culprit. Besides, my girl here is in the market for a different kind of pumping." Nikki winks.

"Nikki!" Amelia shouts as she stands up straight. Evidence of her projectile vomit nowhere to be seen on her face. My Tom Ford suit jacket on the other hand hasn't gone unscathed.

Teddy reappears and hands the bottle of water to her. "Here you go, miss." She looks at Teddy suspiciously, then takes the bottle.

"Amelia, this is Teddy, my driver. You can drink the water," I say as I rub my eyes, feeling a headache coming on.

"Thank you so much for the water, Teddy. Hope I didn't traumatize you back there." She offers him a sweet and sincere smile.

Great, now I fucking hate Teddy.

"My pleasure miss. No need to apologize. We can stop by and get you some Gatorade on the way home. This place only had the gross flavors," he says with a scrunched up nose.

"Thanks for the offer, Teddy. That's very kind of you, but I don't need a ride home, I'll be leaving with my friends tonight," she says while glaring straight at me.

"Actually, about that..." Nikki starts. "We just got a call that Justin's baby brother Jason got into another bar fight. In Brooklyn this time, so we need to head over there and bail him out." Nikki shoots Justin a stern look. To me, it looks like he's trying to cover up a laugh with a cough. "And you refused to bring a purse tonight, so that means that you left your keys at my place while getting ready soooo ..." She gives me a look, urging me to take the hint.

"You can stay at my place for the night," I say way too quickly for my own liking.

"Ha! That's funny," Amelia muses. "It's okay Nikki, I'll tag along to the precinct with you guys, then we'll head home when we've bailed out Justin's brother." Amelia rolls her eyes.

"Ummm Amelia. I love you and all, but I just watched you barf twice all over New York City garbage. We can't shlep you to another borough and have you up until God knows what hour they'll let us take Jason out of there. He's probably in a drunk tank for all we know. And then we'll probably be summoned to Justin's mom's house to hand over the prisoner. I'm sorry babes but I think maybe it's just safer to crash at Evan's until we get back home in the morning." Nikki winces.

Amelia stands with her mouth gaped, staring at Nikki. Before she can protest, Nikki asks Amelia for her coat check ticket. "Hand it over before you freeze all your bits off."

Amelia slowly closes her mouth and sighs. She opens my suit jacket that she's been clutching onto and pulls out a coat check ticket out of the depths of her cleavage. Leaving me to wonder what other treasures lie under that dress top.

Teddy takes that as his cue to hop back in the car.

The drive back to my apartment is agonizingly quiet. Amelia sits so far away from me while facing the door, that she's practically straddling it.

Teddy stops by a pizza joint to grab us a large pepperoni pizza. After she eats two large slices, the only sound echoing in the vehicle is Amelia sipping the last ounces out of her fountain drink, incessantly raising and lowering the straw, as if the cup is going to magically refill itself. My only saving grace is that my apartment building has finally come into view.

II

AMELIA

I HATE THE UNIVERSE.

How did I go from *living my best life* to *living my worst nightmare*?

Ok, maybe that's a little dramatic. Younger Amelia may have been doing cartwheels at the idea of Evan swooping her up and taking her back to his apartment. But this version of Amelia, whatever pieces are left, not so much.

I've spent most of the car ride trying to plaster myself as far away from Evan as humanly possible. I can't stand to think that this is another situation that is out of my control. I mean, sure I don't *have* to stay at his place, I could call my brother or dad and crash with them. But truthfully, I would rather spare them from seeing me in my current state, and I hate that even Evan knows that.

"We're here." Teddy's voice pulls me from my thoughts as I look around and realize where we are.

"You live on the Upper West side? Aren't you supposed to live on Park Avenue or something?" I gaff.

"Yeah, I had my heart set on a place, but was outbid by one of your Real Housewives of New York." He smirks. "Kidding, I just got back last week and I'm not sure where I want to buy yet, so I figured I would stay somewhere that's at least familiar." He shrugs.

I want to roll my eyes, but I'm a bit stunned to see we are only two blocks away from my childhood home. The tiny two-bedroom apartment where I was raised and where all of my favorite childhood memories are held.

Teddy opens the door for me and guides me to the sidewalk. I'm surprised I'm still feeling a little wobbly from tonight's shenanigans. Really thought that the puking would have reset me, but guess not.

"It was nice to meet you, Amelia. Look forward to seeing you in the future. Hope you guys have a good night." Teddy smiles warmly.

"Thank you, you're too kind. Don't know how you drew the short stick in driving this grump around, but I hope you get a big fat promotion soon and a less barbaric boss." I give him a side hug, making sure it's the side that I'm pretty certain doesn't have any puke on the bottom of the jacket.

"Goodnight Teddy, see you Monday," Evan says as he puts his hand on my shoulder to guide me towards his building. I jolt at the feeling of his large hand unexpectedly on me, and he removes it quickly.

"Relax. Just trying to get you in the building in one piece. You're walking like a newborn fawn at this point." he grumbles in my ear, causing me to roll my eyes as far back as humanly possible. "And don't worry, I'll try my best to keep the *barbaric* in me at bay," he mutters.

We make our way into the lobby of his building, and then into the elevator. He presses the number 15. "You know, you never really answered my question," I say as I cross my arms over my chest.

He chuckles, "Oh Amelia."

Oh Amelia? What is that supposed to mean?

We exit the elevator and enter one of the three apartments on this floor. It's not the penthouse I would expect *new money Evan* to live in, but it certainly isn't modest for New York standards.

First of all, this building looks brand new. Also, we rode in an elevator instead of trekking up countless stairs. I realize that my list is only going to get longer the second Evan opens the door to his apartment and yep—I'm reminded that even though he might consider this apartment a place to crash at while he decides which Soho apartment to pour his millions into, this place is probably every New Yorker's dream apartment.

Open floor plan. State of the art kitchen, floor to ceiling windows in the living room, and multiple doors which either means more than one bedroom or closet space. Each just as unattainable in this city as the other.

"Ok quick tour before you go to bed. Kitchen, living room, and dining room are pretty obvious. On the left is the guest bedroom and bathroom. Feel free to shower and use anything in there. And before you ask, no I didn't set this place up myself, someone else did." He sighs, as if already tired of whatever comment I was about to make. "I'll get you some clothes to wear tonight and then I'm going to shower and head to bed, it's been an excruciatingly long day for me," Evan says as he makes his way to another door.

"Well hold on! You didn't give me the full tour now did you?" I smirk.

"I'm not sure why you need to see my bedroom, Amelia," he protests.

I wave him away and walk into the room he was about to enter.

"Well, last I checked you literally interrupted me from having a good time, potentially cock-blocked me, caused me to have an exorcist-type vomiting session due to your presence, and then kidnapped me," I say, listing each offense with my fingers. "I'm pretty sure that allows me some snooping privileges, don't cha think?" I ask as I walk into his room running my hands over any surface I can reach.

I look over my shoulder and see Evan at the doorway, looking every bit as uncomfortable as I'd intended. Stiff as a board, shoulders almost up to his ears, hands balled into fists at his sides.

Actually, for the first time since he showed up tonight, I'm feeling like I have the upper hand somehow. It's making me way too giddy, but I make sure not to show it.

I make my way to his nightstand drawer and open it. If I'm going to snoop, I'm going to be thorough. I make a fake gasping sound and look him straight in the eyes, "No condoms, Mr. Cooper? Tsk tsk tsk. A man like you needs to be careful and use protection. Too many gold diggers out there looking to trap a man with deep pockets like yours," I say with an exaggerated southern accent.

"Are you done having fun?" he asks as he makes his way to me, closing his nightstand drawer harshly. "I need to go to sleep, and so do you. And for the record, I just moved in last week like I already mentioned. Condoms weren't the first thing on my shopping list, nor on my mind," he huffs.

I dramatically put the back of my hand on his forehead, "Oh dear, are you sick? You must be. A man saying he doesn't have sex on the mind? We should call a doctor. Maybe my dad could squeeze you in for an emergency appointment." I grin.

Evan grabs my hand and holds it between us, marking the second time that's happened tonight, come to think of it. "Amelia. Stop fucking around. Get in the shower and I'll get you some clothes."

I am having way too much fun now. Evan and I have never really been in a setting that allowed us to be alone like this. Even in Miami, when we were partying with all of my college friends, we were never truly alone.

But now, I'm getting such pleasure by getting under his skin. I think it's time to up the ante.

"You know, I think my Bambi legs are still a little too wobbly to jump straight in the shower. Do you have a ginger ale or something to drink so I can get some more sugar in me before bed?" I say innocently.

Time to catch him off guard, and nothing seems to be more important to Evan tonight than making sure I live to see another day.

"Yeah, that's probably a good idea. I have some ginger ale in the pantry and some baked goods on the counter." He motions to the kitchen.

"Perfect. Why don't you head off into the shower while I snack a bit, then when you're done hand me some clothes and I'll be out of your hair for the night." I smile.

He eyes me suspiciously, but nods and heads to his bathroom and closes the door. A shot of adrenaline runs through me instantly. I'm about to do something a little crazy, but just the right amount of crazy that I can live with. My life may be in shambles, but I am about to put on the biggest tease of my life, and who better to torture than my first childhood crush.

12

EVAN

SHE'S GOING TO DRIVE ME INSANE. I CAN FEEL IT.

Why have I put myself in this position? I should have left well enough alone, but here I am taking a shower with half a hard-on because *Little Miss Amelia* is in my apartment.

I should be pissed that she seems quite pleased with herself from her little snooping session, but truthfully, I didn't mind seeing her in my room. Although now it's all I can picture. And all that talk about me not having condoms, what the fuck was that? Was she insinuating that I should have condoms to use with her? Or am I reaching? Fuck. I need to stop thinking about this before I get a full hard-on. I still need to see her one more time after this shower to give her some of my clothes. I should probably throw them at her and run into my room because I am certain there is no sexier image than Amelia wearing one of my T-shirts to bed.

I finally get out of the shower and get dressed. I want to get this over with as soon as possible so I can put this night behind me and possibly find some goddamn sense to my actions tomorrow. I grab one of my favorite T-shirts, because I'm a glutton for punishment, and some sweatpants.

"Just hand her the clothes, say goodnight, and go to sleep. Simple," I say to myself in the mirror.

I open the door to my bedroom with the clothes in my hand and head towards the kitchen, where I assume Amelia will be. I make it three steps out of my doorway, but it takes a few beats for my brain to process what my eyes are seeing.

My refrigerator door is wide open and digging between the lower refrigerator shelves is Amelia. Not just Amelia, but bent over Amelia in nothing but her lingerie. And by lingerie, I mean a lacy black bra and thong that disappears into the holy land.

Is that what she was wearing under her fucking dress?!

Amelia slowly straightens up like she has no care in the world and opens a can of Peroni beer. She's still in her heels, and I'm pretty sure my jaw is on the ground the second her eyes connect with mine. She leans against the refrigerator door and takes a sip without breaking eye contact with me. "Gosh, don't you just love an ice cold beer? Nothing like it," she says with a breathy tone.

I think she's waiting on me to say something, but words are literally incapable of coming out of my mouth.

"Oh come on Evan, you've seen me in a bathing suit countless times," she says as she makes her way towards me. My two remaining brain cells help me out and let me close my mouth and try to poorly cover up my reaction with the weakest cough known to man. "Besides, according to Deux Moi's Sunday Spotted stories, you've been seen with countless models in LA, so little ol' me shouldn't bother you one bit." She pats my chest and grabs the clothes out of my hand and puts them on the dining table next to us.

I put my hand on one of the dining chairs, discreetly bending forward, slowly putting one foot in front of the other. As you probably guessed, that hard-on is in full effect now, probably will be for the rest of my life. Amelia has most likely broken my penis without ever having sex with me.

She's eyeing me while taking a dainty sip of her beer. "You

want some? You look a little off. Guess you did have a long day. Me on the other hand, I was hoping to have a long night as you can see. Too bad this getup went to waste," she says as she waves up and down her body. "Evan Cooper, have you taken a vow of silence or is this the kind of hospitality you show all of your guests?" She taps her shoes on my hardwood floors, and I can tell she's trying to get a rise out of me, but that ends now.

"Amelia, I don't know what you're getting at, but it's late, and I don't have time for whatever game you're playing, so go to your room and go to sleep."

She leans in close and whispers in my ear, "Whatever you say... Daddy." She immediately chuckles.

I'm about to utterly lose my mind when she turns around, and my eyes drop to the most perfect ass cheeks I have ever even seen in my goddamn life.

"I'll be out of your hair in a minute, but I'm having a little trouble with my bra clasp. You see, it's brand new, and I haven't figured out how to finagle it quite yet. Don't worry, I won't scar you by letting you see my boobs, I'll hold up the bra cups so your virginal eyes won't be put through such horrid torture." She moves a little closer to me, and now her back is almost touching my chest.

She continues. "The sooner you get to it, the sooner you'll be able to drift off to your sweet dreams Mr. Cooper," she croons.

I let out a painful grunt and get to work on the clasp. She wasn't wrong, it's not as simple as it seems. Just when I can feel that I'm about to figure the damn thing out, Amelia takes one more step closer to me, and now my erection is very clearly digging into her back, and she lets out a little gasp. We both stand stone still, until she has the audacity to step onto her tip toes and give her ass a little wiggle on my crotch.

"For fuck's sake Amelia!" I give up on the clasp and grab both of her arms, keeping her in place. We're both panting now.

"Seems like we have a little party crasher there, Evan," she says with a smug grin as she turns her head slightly.

"What's your angle here Amelia," I growled into her ear.

"Me? No angle here. But if I were to guess, you angle a little bit to the left—"

I drop my hands to her waist and pull her so close to me that my erection is settled right between her ass cheeks. She lets out a small yelp. "What's your angle here, Amelia," I repeat, panting into her ear.

It takes her a few breaths, then finally, "Just proving a point." She turns her head further up so we're making eye contact. "You spent all night looking at me like I should be appalled by my appearance, even so much as insinuating that I should be embarrassed." She still has made no attempt to leave my grasp.

"And yet here you are, with a boner poking my ass, and probably ready to fuck me with no condom in sight." I drop my hands and take a step back. She turns around and faces me with her chin held high, her anger clearly rising.

I, on the other hand, interlace my fingers and place them in front of my erection, trying to at least to make it look like I'm not pitching a tent in my pants.

She takes a deep breath, "You know, I had no interest in going out tonight, much less while wearing a dress that had almost as much coverage as wearing dental floss. But I did, and you know what, I was actually enjoying myself. I wasn't Amelia *the doctor's perfect daughter*, or Amelia *the one with the dead mom,* or my new not-so-favorite title, Amelia *the woman whose fiancé couldn't keep it in his pants.* And you know what, I can logically acknowledge that what Sebastián did to me was not my fault, even though at times I question it. But tonight Evan—tonight I had you swoop in and take me away from that dance floor. It's like you set off some alpha signal that let every man at that party know that I was off-limits. And you know what else? I'm so over not feeling in control. I'm also over letting people's perception of me rule my life, and I'm sooo over pining over my first crush and hoping that he is capable of anything besides getting a hard on for me when teased obnoxiously!" she roars.

Did she just call me her first crush? I know she said a lot of important things, but I'm still a little caught up on that little nugget of information. Before I can respond she pushes past me. "I'm using your shower and sleeping in your bed! Might even masturbate while I'm at it. And I'm locking the door so don't get any ideas!" She slams the door, and I'm left questioning all of my life decisions up to this point.

13

EVAN

WHAT THE FUCK JUST HAPPENED?

How did I end up in my guest bedroom holding my breath in case I hear Amelia touching herself?

This night has definitely taken me by surprise. I mean, that vision of Amelia in my kitchen will forever be ingrained in my mind. I should commission an artist to paint it, going off of my memory. Any other work of art would never compare. The Louvre would be knocking down my door and begging to swap it with the Mona Lisa.

I have no idea how long I toss and turn, but sleep finally wins after hours of restlessness. By the time I wake up it's eight in the morning. It takes me a few beats to realize that last night wasn't a dream, and that Amelia did in fact spend the night in my apartment. The realization jolts me awake and I throw my legs over the bedside while I try to come up with an appropriate morning greeting.

Good morning, did you masturbate in my bed last night?

How'd you sleep? Are you still wearing that lingerie?

Hey there, can you tell me more about being your first crush?

First crush.

The confession that kept me up most of the night. Amelia Nuñez has a crush on me. *Had.* First crush means she was just a kid, but what about now? To think that the woman who I've had embedded in my heart for the better part of a decade, at one time had feelings for me.

I have a million thoughts swirling through my mind, but I know I need to get up and check on her this morning. I clearly don't know Amelia as well as I thought I did. I have no clue as to which Amelia will be greeting me this morning. The versions I met last night were angry, hurt and sex kitten. The last one was my favorite but for now I need to focus.

I open the door to the guest bedroom slowly and peek around the hallway, all is quiet. I step out and notice that Amelia's left the door to my bedroom open. She must be awake now.

Knock Knock.

I clear my throat. "Amelia, are you awake?" I pause and wait for a response. When I don't get one, "I'm coming in, I think we need to talk—"

Empty.

I walk around my room and spin as if I will somehow find her hiding in a corner. If there wasn't a dent in my pillow and an unmade bed, I would think that I really did hallucinate the last twelve hours of my life.

If she left, she must have taken her coat.

I head towards the entrance of my apartment, but I stop when something catches my eye. Two items lie on my kitchen counter that leave me speechless. The first, a note.

Thanks for the hospitality.
I'm stealing your clothes, so I don't have to do the walk of shame in last night's outfit. I left something behind so it's an even trade.

You're still an asshole ☺
Amelia

I would be laughing at this note, if the second item she left behind hadn't been her thong.

14

AMELIA

UGHHHH WHAT HAVE I DONE?!

Those massive cojones that I grew last night are now shriveled into tiny worry warts. Sorry for the visual. Now that I'm alone in my own bed, I can't stop replaying every moment on a loop.

By seven AM, I was pounding on Nikki's door demanding to get my keys back. I let her know that she would be on the receiving end of my wrath once I got some sleep and painkillers in my system. She hardly looked fazed by my threats as she eyed my outfit, clearly Evan's clothes, and let me know that she would swing by my place at eleven and take me out to brunch, on her.

I should be sleeping now, given I barely slept a wink in Evan's bed. Breathing into his pillow like a full creep. I can't believe he actually let me take his room. I half expected him to be so over my shit and throw me over his shoulder and off to the guest room. At least that way he would have to touch me again.

God last night was insane.

I was insane.

Completely unhinged. And as if that wasn't enough, I just had to be extra cheeky and leave my thong behind this morning. I'm certifiable coo coo for coco puffs. I can't imagine what Evan must be thinking of me right now.

I pull my covers over my head as if they will push these thoughts out of my mind.

As much as I'm mortified, I'm no dummy. That was a full-on boner I elicited from Evan. Which means that no matter what he thinks of me, he at the very least finds me attractive.

Wow, way to have standards Amelia.

But now comes the inevitable. How am I going to face Evan as we head full swing into holiday season? I probably should have thought about that before I started handing out pieces of my underwear as souvenirs.

That answer will have to come at another time, because pure exhaustion prevails and I finally fall asleep, still dressed in his T-shirt.

"YOU DID WHAT?!" Nikki gasps as the piece of waffle falls from her fork midway to her mouth.

I shrug, "Yep, that's everything. I was mortified this morning, but this mimosa is making me feel much better about my current life choices," I say as I lift the glass up to my mouth for another sip. Nikki rips it from my hand and sets it down on the table, causing half of the contents to spill.

Thank God for bottomless mimosas I guess.

"Ok, I'm gonna need a little bit more than a *shrug and sip* as a response Amelia! This is better than if you guys actually had sex. You totally mind fucked him!" She starts to dab fake tears away from her eyes. "I'm so proud of you I could cry."

I swat her hand away from her face and take my glass back. "I mean yeah, it was a huge deal. I mean, it's Evan for fuck's sake. The person who not only has become more of a God in my mind, but to the rest of the world as well." I sigh as I lean back in my chair, but then feel a slow smile unfold across my lips, replaying the feeling of Evan pressed against my back.

"Oh God are you having sexy thoughts right here and now? Am I gonna have to ask for a mop? Clean up on aisle 7?" Nikki laughs.

"You know what's even crazier about this whole thing? As mortified as I am, I don't regret it. Not one bit. I feel like a part of me has been wanting to be bold with Evan ever since I first laid eyes on him. Which I know is pathetic, I'm almost thirty. I know I shouldn't still be hung up on my first crush, but Nikki you just had to see the look on Evan's face. It felt as if I were having an outer body experience with a front row seat to our interaction." I look out the window and chuckle. "I'm sorry for ditching your thong by the way."

"That thing needs to be put in the Ripley's Believe It or Not Museum." She smiles as we clink our glasses together.

"Anyways, at least I have almost a week until I have to see him for Thanksgiving. Which will give me plenty of time to figure out how I want to play this. Feigning amnesia is on the table." I take a big bite out of my French toast. "But seriously, we need to hurry up and eat. We're supposed to be at my dad's at noon to start decorating and setting up for his birthday party. It's his first one since... you know... and I want to make sure it doesn't turn into another memorial service. Today we are showing grieving boomers how to have fun!"

15

EVAN

I'VE SPENT THE LAST TWO HOURS AT THE GYM, AND I still feel just as wound up as when I first got here. I keep looking at my phone, thinking about texting Amelia, but what would I even say? I keep hoping that she'll text me, but she obviously won't. She already left me a handwritten note this morning, along with a special little something. I should be embarrassed that I'm a grown ass man that can't keep from blushing every time I think about her leaving her underwear at my place. Was she sending me a message? Am I supposed to dry clean and return it? Is it meant to stay at my place for her to wear? Is it a taunt?

Of course it's a taunt. Only Amelia has the power to get under my skin like this, but that was a well kept secret until last night. Now she knows, and I'm terrified of how she plans on abusing that power.

I'm about to call it at the gym, when I get a hard smack on my shoulder. I turn around and see Antonio with an exaggerated angry face. I panic for a minute, did Amelia tell him about last night?

Then he says, "You don't call, you don't write..." We laugh and I bring him in for a sweaty hug and pat on the back.

"Sorry man, got back last week, still getting acclimated to being back in the city."

"Acclimated?" he asks.

"Yeah, I'm officially here full-time. Surprise," I say with a tilt of my head and a half grin.

"What the hell man, you move back to the city and don't even give your best bro a heads up?" he complains.

Guilt creeps up on me. I know I've been a shitty friend the past few years. Letting work take up all of my time and energy. But this move will change that.

"I know, I'm sorry man. That's on me. I've been worked to the bone lately trying to get a business deal and this move done. But I'm here now, and I'm making it a point to have a life outside of my office now." Antonio is still giving me the side eye. So I continue, "Let me make it up to you. I'll have friendship bracelets made, and I'll take you out for beers."

This makes him laugh and he concedes, "Ok, hard pass on the bracelets, the guys on the force would never let me live that down, but absolutely on the beers."

"I'm free later," I say. "You on patrol tonight?"

"No, I'm off today, but I've got to head to my dad's birthday party later." He pauses. "Actually, you should swing by. Everyone will be there. They'll be happy to see that the prodigal son has returned," he says with a deep chuckle.

I pause before I answer. Amelia will be there. Obviously. I need to be careful; Antonio is Amelia's brother and my best friend. Plus, he owns a gun and knows how to use it.

I still don't know how she'll react to seeing me, but maybe that's a good thing. Maybe I should try to reclaim a bit of that power that Amelia took from me last night.

"You know what, that sounds good. Wouldn't miss it for the world."

But before I go, I just need to make one phone call, and set my new plan in motion. I'm about to make this one unforgettable holiday season.

.

16

AMELIA

THANK GOD FOR CARBS AND PAINKILLERS.

I'm moving around my dad's apartment as if I weren't a complete hot mess last night. Nikki is actually being helpful by setting up the Dominican catering that just came in. Seems like she can be extremely efficient when she knows we're in the presence of my dad and therefore, cannot badger me about any more information on my night with Evan. Thankfully, dad's currently holed up in his office completing his notes before our guests arrive.

"How many people did you say were coming? Because I'm pretty sure you can feed about 50 people with this amount of food," Nikki says as she peeks under the aluminum foil at the mini yaniqueques in the foil tray.

"There is never enough food at Dominican parties, trust me. The usual suspects are coming, probably 20 to 25 people coming including Vanessa and Abby's kids. Plus, whatever isn't inhaled by this crowd, gets dispersed into makeshift take out bags for everyone to bring home. I thought ahead and bought cute little colorful party favor bags. Thought my dad might get a kick out of it."

"Usual suspects? Does that mean Evan is coming too?!" Nikki whisper shouts excitedly.

"Hate to break it to you but Evan has never come to any of my dad's birthday parties. The official kick-off to the holiday season with this crew is Thanksgiving. Plus, the past few years mom and dad have taken trips for their birthdays instead of having parties. The main reason we're even having everyone over and throwing a party is because it's his first birthday since mom died. He's obviously not going on a trip, and we wanted to make sure we could keep his spirits up today."

"Yeah, that makes sense," Nikki offers a sympathetic smile. "But you never know, maybe Evan has the same thought and decides to swing by?" she says wishfully.

"I know that you would love nothing more than to be front row and center to my awkward interaction with Mr. Cooper. Unfortunately, you're gonna have to wait a few more days until I let you know how Thanksgiving goes, and that's if I even go to Thanksgiving this year," I say with a teasing wink.

"Ohhhhh do you call him Mr. Cooper?! That is so hot Amelia. You know I am a taken woman, but sheesh you sure know to make that man sound even more attractive," Nikki says as she fans her face with her hands and dramatically rolls her eyes. "And what do you mean *if you go to Thanksgiving*? You can't just ditch your family over the holidays to avoid Evan!"

"I'm not! It's just that I usually know by now who is hosting and what dish to bring. But none of my Tías have mentioned anything lately which would be odd, but I don't know if they just haven't clued me in because of the year I've had."

Truthfully, over the past few years our holiday gatherings have gotten smaller and smaller. We're all grown up now, and some of us have spouses and kids. Which means holidays get split between more families, and the surrogate family we've created is no longer the main priority for gatherings.

"Besides, I'm actually looking forward to the possibility of having a low-key long weekend. I feel like I need to get out of the city and clear my head for a bit. Maybe I'll book an Airbnb and read a book. Go on mental health walks or drink coffee at a café with actual mugs instead of to-go cups. I know, wild." I chuckle. "I mean, I'm leaving underwear as parting gifts nowadays, so I should probably reel it in before I start leaving bras behind, that would be a very expensive habit to pick up."

I move around the counter and take inventory of all the dishes that were delivered. Mangú, queso frito, salami, arroz con habichuelas, sancocho, plátano maduro, tostones, yuca, pasteles en hoja, and mini yaniqueques. You'd think that this would be enough food, but I'm sure everyone invited will bring something extra. I know for sure that my Tía Lourdes is bringing the Dominican cake, which is the best cake known to man and I will die on that hill.

DING DONG.

I open the door and find a bouquet of white roses in a simple clear vase.

"Did someone send your dad flowers?" Nikki asks over my shoulder.

"I guess, let me check the note."

Amelia

Happy birthday to your father.

Hope to see you soon.

Huh?

"Wait, that's it? It's not signed by anyone. Who the hell does that? And why is it addressed to you and not directly to your dad?" Nikki asks.

"Yeah, that is weird. Maybe when ordering the flowers online, the note box cut off their name?" I suggest.

"That fucker." Nikki groans, realization seemingly consuming her face.

"What? What fucker?"

"Don't you get it? Who else would direct the flowers to you Amelia? Think!" She taps her temple aggressively.

Evan? No Amelia, not everything is about that man.

"Ummmm."

"Sebastián, you idiot!" Nikki exclaims.

Shit.

"That bastard knows the importance of today and is trying to butter you up. Don't fall for it Amelia!"

"Sheesh, calm down. No need to get your panties in a bunch. I have no plans to ever speak to him again. Plus, he stopped calling and sending flowers months ago. I doubt this is a ploy to get back together with me." I wave her away.

"Regardless, what a shitty thing to do. Make you think of him on a day that's supposed to be about your dad. A true narcissist if you ask me!"

DING DONG.

I set the flowers on the kitchen counter and head to open the front door. "Hola, Amelia bella. ¿Como estás?" my Tío Ricardo says as he leans in for a hug and one kiss on my cheek, traditional Latino greeting. Tía Lourdes followed closely behind.

"¡Con permiso, steer clear! I have the cake!" Tía Lourdes hollers as she bypasses me and heads straight to the kitchen.

"¡Bienvenidos!" my dad roars at the sight of our first guests. They greet one another and head off to the dining room where I've set up a bar area with cups, ice and various booze options. My brother arrives and immediately hides his sacred beer stash, never one to share his precious IPA's with the family. Then, he stuffs an incomprehensible amount of tostones in his mouth. I tell him to go easy and leave some for the guests, and he grunts.

The next hour is the same cycle of the doorbell ringing, loud greetings and shuffling of cold bodies into dad's warm apartment. Nikki helps me play host and takes everyone's coats and purses and sets them on the guest bedroom mattress, the unofficial Latino coat closet in New York City.

Tía Isabella has me cornered, telling me about her friend's son that she wants to set me up with, when Tía Maria intercepts, "Ay mi bella Amelia. Such a pity to be single at this age." She shakes her head side to side. "Are you sure you can't forgive Sebastían and give him one more chance? You know good men are hard to come by, and everyone makes mistakes." She waves her hand dismissively.

"Tía, por favor." I try to stop her, but she talks over me.

"I'm just saying you're about to turn thirty, Amelia. You've spent so much time going back and forth with that man, and now you've lost valuable time. Just think about it before you scare him off for good. I would hate for you to miss out on having a family because of your stubbornness." She cups my face in her hands and offers me a pity look.

Finally, some of the cousin crew arrives, and I use that as my excuse to escape the conversation from hell.

I spot Vanessa and her wife Abby, along with their kids. Vanessa gives me one look and I already know I should immediately take out the private stash of fireball and discreetly serve her a shot. Going from zero to five kids is not for the faint of heart, but I know she and Abby wouldn't have it any other way.

"God you're a lifesaver," Vanessa whispers as soon as she takes the shot from my hand.

"Should I pour one for Abby, too?" I ask.

"No! I was on duty for all the Halloween activities this year while she was working. I still have a few more 'non-designated parent' nights left to even consider calling us even. Hit me again," she says as she dramatically slaps the counter as if she's in a bar and I'm her enabling bartender. I serve her one more shot and then figure it would probably be better use of my time to just leave her the bottle and walk away to check on Nikki.

Nikki has attended many of my family parties, and has even picked up a little bit of Spanish. I once suggested we invite one of my coworkers to my mom's Easter Brunch and she almost took me out right then and there. Proclaimed that she would be the only *gringa* at our parties. "If we just start letting any ol' white girl join the fun then I will lose my allure with this crowd!" were her exact words. The only exception is Abby since she's married to Vanessa, which is who I find her chatting with. They both look like they're up to no good.

"What are you two scheming up over here? And before you try to deny it, please know that I caught you both giving me overly dramatic evil grins from across the room," I warn playfully.

"Oh no scheming here, just thoroughly enjoying Abby's company. Oh and hearing all about your insane Thanksgiving plans." Nikki giggles as she silently claps her hands together. I can already tell I'm going to need a glass of wine for this.

"Ohhhh do tell. Am I being whisked away to Paris? Or are we road tripping to Montreal? Or better yet, I got it. Tucked in my bed watching endless hours of Netflix while eating Chinese food." I sigh dramatically as I pour myself a glass of Sauvignon Blanc. "Living the dream."

"Well actually, we're all being whisked away ..." Abby starts but Nikki can't seem to hold in her excitement.

"Oh my gosh so you guys are so lucky, you're all going to stay at a cabin in the Berkshires! And by you guys I mean the cousin crew!" Nikki exclaims.

I blink a few times and look at Abby. Before I can get a word out Nikki continues.

"The best part is that all the parents will be out of town. They're all flying to Punta Cana and using it as a belated birthday trip for your dad, isn't that so incredibly sweet and thoughtful?!" Nikki swoons.

"Um, what?" I look at Abby again as she tries to hide her smile behind her wine glass. Before Nikki can start again I speak up. "Ok, ABBY and ABBY only. Can you please explain what Nikki is referring to? She's clearly had a lobotomy since I last saw her twenty minutes ago."

"Ok, but I was sworn to secrecy so you can't be mad at me, promise?" Abby pleads.

"Ugh ok fine, spill," I say.

"So, for the past few weeks some of the doctors were trying to come up with a good birthday gift for your dad, and decided that they wanted to keep up the birthday trip tradition, even though your mom has passed. It's obviously tough for them to all coordinate their busy schedules, so they all agreed to push the trip back to Thanksgiving weekend, since they always take that time off every year no matter what. It's supposed to be a surprise for your dad tonight, which is why we had to also keep the secret from you. I'm so sorry, please don't shoot the messenger!" Abby pleads.

"Wait a minute, so you mean to tell me that the whole cousin crew knew and nobody told me or gave me a heads up?! What the hell Abby," I scolded.

"Umm Amelia, you know I love you, and you have many wonderful traits—"

"Wow, can't wait to see where this compliment leads to," I say sarcastically.

"But...You're really shitty at keeping secrets. It's a well known family fact. Like seriously. And if you even try to deny it, I am prepared to give at least fifteen different examples of when you spilled the beans to somebody in this family."

"Ughhhhhh. Really Abby?" I sigh.

"Lucy's pregnancy, Tía Isabella's surprise birthday party, our adoption being finalized..."

"Ok ok. Fine, you made your point! But for the record nobody told me that Tía Isabella's birthday was a surprise party and I just called her to make sure there wasn't a certain color I shouldn't wear to clash with hers. You know how anal she is about color aesthetics," I hiss. "And yes, it was really sweet of them to do that for my dad, but that still doesn't explain what your fellow gringa comrade is yapping about. The Berkshires?" I ask.

Abby smiles wide. "Well that's the best part! We hadn't really thought about what we would all do for Thanksgiving until today when—"

Nikki cuts in, "—When inspiration struck, and all the cousins thought it would be a great idea to getaway together without the old geezers holding you down!" She laughs nervously.

"Ok...so a cabin in the Berkshires? That can't be cheap. How much is it gonna cost to split—"

I'm interrupted by Nikki. "Well, that's the best part, it's free! I mean free for you. It's only fair, right? Your dad gets an all-expenses paid vacation and so do you!" She wiggles her fingers at me.

I turn my back to Nikki and completely ignore the annoying demon that has apparently possessed my best friend. "Abby, I'm not a charity case, I can pay for myself. Or better yet, you guys can go on without me. Like I said, Netflix and Chinese food awaits me." I shrug.

"Oh c'mon Amelia that's not fair. Nobody said you were a charity case. In fact, you yourself said that it was sweet for everyone to rally around your dad and gift him a trip," Nikki says into the back of my head while playing with my hair. "Plus you also said earlier today how you would love to get away and do all those fun self-care things and drink coffee out of mugs, the real dream if you ask me!" she squeals behind me.

I roll my eyes and face them both. "Ok fine. I'm not going to put up a big fight when I know I probably really need to get out of the city, and money is tight since I threw it all away on non-refundable deposits for a wedding that isn't happening." I take a deep breath. "So, when is the check-in date?"

Abby looks like she's not quite sure how to answer the question, but before Nikki can butt in, she says, "Well it's a flexible check-in process. We're heading over there on Thursday, the day of

Thanksgiving, but if you want to arrive sooner you can let me know what day you want to arrive, and I'll make sure you're able to check in yourself," she says, nodding her head.

I don't give too much thought to her half-baked answer. Her poor brain is probably fried, running after five kids and working for a successful law firm.

"Ok...well then do you think I could check in on Wednesday? I'm working from home that whole week and it would be nice if I could get there early before all the kids get there. Sorry, no offense." I offer a fake wince at the confession.

She laughs. "Trust me, none taken. My own wife has abandoned me until further notice. She thinks I can't see her taking fireball shots from here, isn't she adorable?" She smiles lovingly. "But yes, Wednesday should work just fine. I'll text you all the details in a day or two."

"Am I allowed to speak again?! Yay this is so exciting! If this weren't my first holiday meeting Justin's parents I would totally ditch my Thanksgiving plans and leech off of you guys. This is going to be so much fun," Nikki says, beaming.

I've somehow managed to survive the party with minimal whispers about my failed engagement. That is, until Priscilla arrived a minute ago.

"Prima Amelia, how are you?" She hugs and kisses me. "You look like you've lost weight, please tell me your secrets for that body! Or do I have to go find myself a fiancé to dump to get that killer ass." She laughs maniacally.

"En serio, Priscilla?!" Vanessa shouts from the kitchen in her scolding mom voice.

"Oh I'm just teasing. We all know that Amelia here knows how to take a joke, right baby cousin?" She smirks.

Match. That. Energy.

"Priscilla, you do know I'm turning thirty in a couple of weeks. I think it's time to retire the *baby cousin* pet name. Oh, and while we're at it, how old are you supposed to be now that I'm thirty? Since you've been claiming that age for the past four years now." I smile generously.

"Toma pendeja!" Vanessa laughs followed by a hiccup. I let Abby know it's time to get her wife some water and release the fireball bottle from her death grip.

Priscilla is still giving me a full body scan. You see, I've never so much as engaged in friendly banter with Priscilla. So my comment about her age for sure has her thrown off. Maybe this New Amelia attitude will have more victims than just Evan after all.

"Tell me Amelia," Priscilla starts as she follows me into the kitchen. "What are you looking for in a man these days? I'm assuming successful doctors are off the table?" She bats her eyelashes innocently.

I'm not exactly proud of what I say next, but I guess I'm just in the business of watching people squirm now.

"You know, I'm not really sure Priscilla. If you could give me the names of the men you haven't dated in Manhattan, I'm sure I can work off of that shortlist. And while you're at it, leave out the names of the married men. That's more your speed than mine anyways." I don't even give her a chance to respond. I walk away to answer the front door, winking at my Tías standing by the kitchen island busying themselves as though they hadn't been eavesdropping.

It feels good to finally give her a little bit of the shit that she's been throwing my way ever since we were kids. I don't know why I never felt as though I could push back, but damn am I glad my cojones from last night decided to make a quick appearance.

"Amelia, la puerta!" my dad shouts over the merengue music.

"Ya voy, I got it Papi!" I yell back, facing the living room while I open the front door.

"There she is," a familiar velvety voice speaks from the doorway. I'm stunned, but slowly turn to face the man who has lived rent free in my mind for longer than I'd like to admit.

"Um. Evan. What are you doing here?" I say as I close the door slightly, keeping him out of view from the party goers.

"Kicking people out of their own beds...not letting them into family gatherings? Tsk tsk." He gently pushes past me and into the entryway, then leans down and whispers into my ear, "Remind me to teach you some manners later tonight."

Holy shit. I'm screwed.

17

EVAN

THE LOOK ON AMELIA'S FACE: PRICELESS.

I would have lingered longer at the entryway, but I could see every woman over the age of sixty hightailing it towards me.

"Evan! What a surprise, we didn't know you were back in town!" says Mrs. Mejia as she comes in for a hug and kiss.

"Actually, I've just moved back." I glance over back to Amelia who looks like she's in the middle of an existential crisis, still holding the front door open. "So you're going to be seeing a lot more of me," I say as Amelia locks eyes with me, closes the door, then quickly walks off to busy herself in the kitchen.

"Ay Dios mío Ramón did you hear that? Evan moved back to New York!" shouts Tía Isabella.

"¡Pero mijo! What an amazing birthday surprise." Dr. Nuñez gestures for me to come into the living room after giving me a bear hug.

"I heard it was your birthday and couldn't think of a better person to celebrate. I brought you a bottle of Brugal and some champagne. Where should I drop this stuff off for you?" I ask.

"I'll take that off your hands... Mr. Cooper." Nikki comes out of nowhere with a mischievous grin. "And I can take your coat for you as well."

I hand her the bottles of alcohol and my black structured wool coat. "Hello Nikki. Nice to see you again." I hear her whisper, "*What the fuck, this is Prada?!*" under her breath and I stifle a chuckle.

"Oh, so you've met Nikki before?" Dr. Nuñez asks. Before I can come up with a lie that will cover up how I met her last night while his daughter was throwing up drunk, he cuts me off. "Oh, of course all you kids know each other, what am I saying." Nikki takes this opportunity to walk away with the gifted liquor and my coat. Hope she doesn't steal either items.

"Evan, what would you like to drink? Is your palate a little too refined for rum now?" Dr. Nuñez teases.

"Never. Especially since Antonio and I spent our late high school years stealing from your supply."

Amelia has been avoiding me like the plague.

Any time I catch her looking at me, she jets off to a different spot in the apartment. I can also see Nikki flanking her everywhere she goes while whisper shouting into her ear. Quite the scene.

Crazy how much can change in twenty-four hours. Like for instance, Amelia's outfit. She's dressed in an ivory long sleeve sweater dress with black tights. Funny enough, we're matching since I'm wearing an ivory cable knit sweater and dark jeans with black boots. If she would stand within an arm's length of me, we might even look like a real couple.

And although she may be trying to exude a vision of innocence, it's obvious how that dress hugs her in all the right places. Her makeup is simple, but emphasizes her beautiful large brown eyes, caramel skin, and her plump full lips. She keeps toying with the hair hanging out of her high ponytail, and my fingers itch to touch it. I force myself to not steal too many glances at her body, since it wouldn't be the right time or place to be turned on by Amelia. Which reminds me of something I came here to do. I stand up to make my way toward Amelia, only to be stopped by my new shadow. Priscilla.

"Well hey there big boy. I thought I told you to call me whenever you were in the city." She playfully pushes my bicep, only to leave her hand there and squeeze it. "Jeez Evan, do you live in a gym now? Good looking, successful, and ripped. Are you trying to be my dream man?" Priscilla sighs.

Priscilla has made her feelings for me known ever since we played spin the bottle during my senior year of high school. I gave her a small peck on the lips, and she carried on acting as if we were lovers in another life. I'm careful to avoid bruising Priscilla's ego, because we all know she can have a mean streak.

"I work behind a screen all day. Got to get some exercise to make sure I keep my mind sharp, and yes, my body fit. If you'll excuse me, I'm going to grab some tostones," I say as I try to side step around her.

"Oh don't be silly, I'll join you. Although I can't have any of the food here really. I try to make an effort to keep my body nice and... tight." She winks.

Seems like my shadow has won this round. I make it to the kitchen island and try to make small talk with Dr. Ortega about the new Dominican players on the Yankees' team, hoping this topic will help me fend off Priscilla. But no such luck.

Out of the corner of my eye, I spot Amelia heading down the hallway to the guest bedroom. I'm assuming she's going to use the ensuite bathroom, so I excuse myself from my conversation and head in her direction. Clearly stating that I need to use the restroom after eating too many tostones. Hopefully the idea of me having to take a shit will give Priscilla the hint to give me a five minute break.

When I reach the doorway to the bedroom, I spot Amelia

fixing her lipstick in the bathroom mirror. I enter the room and close the door behind me, and she nearly jumps out of her skin.

"What are you doing in here? I'm clearly using the bathroom. You can't just walk in on people like that you know?" she whispers nervously.

I arch my eyebrow and make my way towards her. "Are we really going to talk about being appropriate with one another? Because last I checked, we crossed that line last night. Speaking of which ..."

I put my hand in my front jean pocket and with my index finger pulled out the lacy fabric and let it hang in the air between us. Before I can say a word, she snatches her thong out of my hand.

"Are you fucking insane?! What are you doing with that thing, and here of all places?!" She takes the thong and throws it over the shower curtain into the bathtub.

"Hey!" I chastise playfully. "I thought that was a gift. I just brought it back to make sure you weren't still wandering the streets of New York commando." I give her a menacing grin.

"What do you want Evan? Huh. An apology? An *I'm sorry for stripping down, giving you a boner and then leaving you my underwear in the morning*? Well tough shit, because you aren't getting one from me!" she fumes as she starts to make her exit. Once she makes it to the bedroom door, she pauses, takes a few breaths, then turns and gives me a look that would make any guy go weak in the knees, me included.

"And for your information, you were right to return my underwear to me, because I'm still not wearing any." And with that she leaves, taking along with her my sanity.

18

AMELIA

THE NERVE OF THAT MAN.

Bringing my unmentionables to my father's home. I mean sure, I kind of started this little raunchy war, but I didn't think he would continue it! And of course I'm wearing underwear, but I wasn't gonna walk out of that room letting him feel like he won that round with me.

Deep breaths. Sing happy birthday, cut the cake, and we're in the clear. Nikki and I will be taking a few bottles of whatever wasn't opened tonight and catching up on The Real Housewives of Beverly Hills. Just the thought of booze and Bravo eases my soul. I make it back into the living room and announce that it's time to cut the cake.

"Espérate mija," my dad calls out. "I was actually thinking we could watch a few minutes of one of our old home videos. Maybe a Christmas one," he says.

The room grows silent.

My dad sighs heavily. "Mira, I appreciate you all coming here to celebrate my birthday, and for taking me on a trip next week, gracias familia. Pero I want you guys to know that we don't have to pretend like I didn't lose Anna. We all lost her. And I don't know what birthdays or holidays will feel like, now that she's not here, but I don't want to act like she still isn't a part of this family," he declares.

"Papi, of course. That's actually a great idea. Why don't we pick one from the early 2000's or something? That way you can laugh at how we all looked during our awkward prepubescent stages," I suggest.

Antonio shouts, "Don't pick the years that I had braces!"

"Or the years when I didn't have boobs!" Priscilla squeals.

Classy.

"Ok then, I'm going to pick a random home video without looking at the date, so no complaints," I say.

"Coño Ramón. You still have those videos on VCR? En serio?" Tío Francisco chuckles.

"You know I don't know much about technology and converting these things." He shrugs.

"Ok everyone, here we go. Don't know if we have to rewind or not, so I'm just going to play it from wherever it's paused," I caution as I step away and take a seat next to my dad on the couch.

Christmas of 2003. Of course the first scene is eleven-year-old me obnoxiously saying hello to my dad recording behind the camera with the biggest gap between my two front teeth. My parents should have started me on braces sooner, damnit.

My constant badgering for camera time makes everyone laugh, and I don't dare look in Evan's direction as he's leaning against the wall that opens up to the living room.

Next, my dad pans over the room of dancing couples in the living room, then makes his way to the tiny kitchen. That's where we get the first glimpse of my mom, looking young and more beautiful than ever. She's fussing over some rice dish and explaining what she's doing to a young Evan. *Wait, Evan?*

I don't remember ever watching this part of the video. Next to my mom is a tall and lanky Evan following my mom's orders in the kitchen, and moving around the rice in the *caldero*. I can hear her explaining why you have to move the rice around, and the best way to make *con con*. My dad calls her name so she turns around, sporting a magnificent smile. *Damn I miss her smiles.*

Next to me, I hear my dad sniffle, and notice that he has tears running down his face. I give Antonio a look and he goes to stop the video.

"It's ok Papi," I whisper in his ear. "I miss her too."

"Ay I'm sorry everyone. I didn't think I would cry," he says, looking bashful.

"Sorry Ramón, next time I won't get you the expensive stuff. That kind of alcohol will make any grown man cry. Next time we'll stick to Presidente beer only," Evan says playfully from across the room.

Everyone erupts in somber laughter, and it eases the mood a bit. I send him an appreciative smile and he nods at me.

"Actually Ramón, if you don't mind, why don't you give me this home video. Or better yet all your home videos, and I'll have them converted for you. My birthday gift to you." Evan smiles.

"Oh wow, really Evan? That would be amazing, thank you so much. I appreciate it." My dad beams at Evan and I mouth a *thank you* to him. He responds mouthing a sincere *you're welcome.*

"Ok enough of that, let's hurry up and sing happy birthday before these kids poke my cake!" Tía Lourdes complains. And with that, some background bachata music starts playing and the group disperses into the kitchen.

I stay back and retrieve the VHS tape.

"I'll take that," I hear Evan say behind me. I turn and face him. "If that's okay with you," he adds.

"Oh, right. Here you go. The rest of the tapes are in the clear container inside the tv stand."

He nods and makes his way to retrieve the tapes. With a container full of tapes propped under one arm, I stop him before he rejoins the group in the kitchen.

"Evan," I say as I place my hand on his free forearm. "It's really sweet of you to do this for my dad," I start. "I've always promised to convert them myself, but I either forget or work gets in the way and..." I sigh. "I just wanted to tell you that I really appreciate you doing this, and jumping in to salvage the night without giving my dad a chance to feel self conscious about crying in front of everyone."

"Don't sweat it," he says without looking at me as he's about to brush past me, but I hold a tighter grasp on his forearm.

"Evan." He finally looks me in the eyes underneath his full dark lashes, and for a moment I forget why I'm holding onto him.

"Yeah?"

I shake my head and hope my words come out coherently. "About last night... And today." I wince. "I don't even know what kind of explanation to give you if I'm being honest. But since we're going to be seeing each other this holiday season, and I don't want to make things more awkward than they are, how about I offer a truce?" I offer my hand for a handshake.

Evan looks at my outreached hand for a couple of beats, then takes it in his large hand. Instead of shaking it, he uses his grip to pull me in close. "That was a nice sentiment. Kudos and all. But the Amelia I've recently been introduced to wouldn't lay down the sword so quickly. So I'm going to chalk up this interaction to you feeling sentimental due to it being your father's birthday." He releases my hand with a devilish smirk and leans back.

I'm taken aback by his remarks, and before I can respond, he leans in one more time. "Oh and for the record, I'm looking forward to spending the holidays with this new Amelia. See you at Thanksgiving, babe." He places a goodbye kiss on my cheek and is off to the kitchen with the rest of the guests while I'm left with my jaw on the ground.

It's official. Evan Cooper is a fucking asshole. A very sexy asshole.

19

AMELIA

I SPEND THE NEXT COUPLE OF DAYS TRYING TO COME UP with a good excuse as to why I won't be making it to Thanksgiving this year.

I can't fathom the idea of having to share the same space with Evan after everything that's happened between us this past weekend.

My one little temptress act on Friday has now turned into a full blown battle of wills between us, and I need off this ride as soon as possible. Just as I'm deciding on whether mono is a plausible excuse to even use nowadays, I get a text notification on my phone. I check and see that it's a message from the cousin crew group chat.

Evan: Hey guys, looking forward to spending Thanksgiving with everyone this year. Since we're going to the Berkshires, I've booked a car service for each of you, so no one has to worry about renting one. Pick up time is 8AM on Thursday so we can all be at the cabin by lunchtime. Amelia, since you're arriving a day earlier, please text me what time you would like to be picked up.

Pfft. Of course he got us all private cars. How showy ... and kind of nice of him. Whatever. Ugh and did he have to single me out in the text? Was that a ploy or was he really just trying to nail down the details? I'm sure he has an assistant that could be doing this for him. Either way, it's now or never to back out of Thanksgiving. I need to use this opening to announce that I won't be able to make it. Mono it is. I start typing in the group chat when another message comes through.

Vanessa: OMG!! Evan that is so sweet of you! We were just looking at renting a sprinter van, because there is no way our kids and all their crap were going to fit in a sedan hahaha. Thank you so much! I also just want to say how excited I am for this Thanksgiving. It will be Abby and I's first as parents *crying emoji* This is also the first Thanksgiving that our kids will have without their birth parents, and while we will always honor their memory together, they are so excited to create new memories with you guys!!! Thank God you're arriving a day early Amelia, I hope it's because you plan on making your infamous flan!! I've told the kids about it, and they can't wait to try it. Anyways, love you all, can't wait for Thursday, woohoo!

Well. That just proper fucked my plans of backing out.

Danielle: OMG Vanessa you just made me cry at work! This will be the best Thanksgiving ever! Thanks for the ride Evan!

Lucy: My nieces and nephews will have the best holiday season and I will be broke by the end of it but that is my duty as an auntie! We may all be fake cousins, but we are real aunties to these kids, so we all better go broke together.

Thanks for the ride Evan, I'm gonna have a roadie so be ready for tipsy Lucy!

Priscilla: No need to go broke Lucy, don't you see we have our very own big spender in the chat *Winky face emoji* Anywho what kind of wheels are we talking Evan? Rolls Royce?? LOL.

Xioana: Thanks Evan! Do we need to bring anything? Food? Drinks?

Roselyn: Gracias Evan! Vanessa, those kiddos are so loved, it's going to be the best weekend!

Antonio: Sweet man. Works for me.

Evan: Just a normal car Priscilla...No need to bring anything ladies, I made sure the cabin was fully stocked. Even have a hidden stash of IPA's for you, Tony.

Antonio: Sick! Thanks man!

Lucy: Fully stocked you say...

Evan: Enough booze and food to last us a month, Lucy.

Lucy: *Dancing baby gif*

Xioana: Awesome! This is so exciting!

Evan: Amelia, time???

Ughhhhh. Come on Amelia. Think of Vanessa and Abby's kids. Fully stocked booze and food. Magical escape from the city.

There'll be so many kids and activities that I'll barely even notice Evan, right? Ok, I got this. Here goes nothing.

Amelia: Wednesday at 8AM works fine for me. I'll get those flan ingredients and make it with your kiddos Vanessa!

See. That wasn't so bad. Nothing to worry about here. I get one more message notification and immediately open it thinking it's Vanessa responding to me.

Evan: Perfect *smile emoji*

One word. One emoji.
Apparently that's all it takes to know that I'm screwed.

20

AMELIA

I CAN'T BELIEVE I'M DOING THIS.

Goddamn Vanessa and her unintentional guilt trip. It's eight AM and I'm making my way out of my apartment building when I see a familiar face waiting by a large black SUV.

"Good morning, Ms. Amelia."

"Oh, hi Teddy! I didn't know that you would be picking me up today, what a pleasant surprise," I say as he takes my luggage from me.

"Glad to see you again. Mr. Cooper requested that I be the driver to escort you to the Berkshires, since you and I have already met briefly," he says as he opens the back passenger door for me. I settle in my seat, and he closes my door, then rounds the vehicle and gets into the driver seat.

"So Teddy, about that night. I want to apologize for my state of ... pukiness. I'm not typically a raging hot mess, but you just happened to catch me in rare form that night." I wince.

"No need to apologize, Ms. Amelia I—"

"Just Amelia, no need to remind me of my marital status, which I'm painfully aware of." I chuckle.

Teddy smiles in amusement as he pulls into the street and

starts our three hour journey. "Ah, alright then, *just* Amelia. Although I'm sure there is no shortage of young men in the city that would love to be in your company."

I look at him through the rearview mirror and raise an eyebrow playfully.

"Oh no, not me Amelia, although I'm flattered you would even assume an old guy like me." He laughs. "But if you are interested in some respectful gentlemen to take you out, I do have five nephews!" He chuckles.

I laugh at his earnestness. "Thanks Teddy, I appreciate it. If I ever decide to give the male species another shot, you're my first call."

"Oh I'm sorry, I shouldn't have assumed—"

"Oh, no no! I'm straight. Unfortunately. Just going through your typical *hate all men* phase. I'm sure at some point I'll find a decent guy. Like in a decade or so." I shrug.

"Ah. I see. Let me guess. Someone broke your heart recently?"

"We only have a three hour drive Teddy, there just isn't enough time to cover it all. But I could have my therapist send over her extensive notes about our sessions if that helps." I tease.

"My apologies, I live in a house full of chatty women and I find myself more often than not being a bit nosey. Would you like me to play any music during the ride? Podcasts? Or would you like to use headphones, I have some up here. Also feel free to dig into the snack basket next to you. There are sodas and water in the cooler as well."

"Wow. Fancy shmancy. Evan's just living the life with you isn't he now? I'm probably just going to listen to a true crime podcast, so I'll use my headphones. That way you don't get creeped out."

"Would it happen to be the Crime Junkie's podcast by any chance? I saw that they dropped a couple of new episodes and I'm behind."

"You listen to Crime Junkies?!" I shout. "Oh man, I think you just restored my faith in the whole male species ... by like one percent, but at least it's in the right direction." I laugh.

"Sync your phone to the vehicle's Bluetooth. This is going to be a fun drive, Amelia."

Three episodes later, and I think Teddy is my new best friend.

We made a pit stop an hour into the trip because I have a tiny bladder and drank too much water in the car. When I returned to the vehicle, I opted to sit in the front seat next to him.

This turned out to be a great idea, because we get to discuss our suspect theories. But before we find out who the killer is, he lets me know that we're about five minutes away from the cabin. I was so enraptured by our conversation about serial killers, I didn't even realize we were no longer on the highway.

We're now on a dirt road that is canopied by large willowing trees. The ground is coated by a soft layer of snow, no more than an inch high.

It feels like I've stepped into a snow globe with all the faint snowflakes dancing in the sky, as if they're in no rush to make their descent onto the ground. I'm fixated on each one that lands on the windshield, and before I can fully take in the winter wonderland we have just driven into, Teddy brings my attention to the front of the vehicle by letting me know we've arrived at our destination. But this can't be right.

"Um, Teddy. Are you sure you got the right address?" I ask.

"Of course, Amelia. Welcome to your humble abode for the weekend." He laughs as he exits the vehicle and makes his way to the trunk of the SUV to retrieve my luggage. I slowly open my vehicle door and hang off the side of it as I stare at what I can only describe as a wooden mansion. The only way anyone could even fathom to pass this house off as a cabin, is because it is made out of log. Hell, this house alone might be responsible for cutting down a whole forest.

How expensive was this damn Airbnb?? Did Evan foot the bill? I wouldn't be surprised if he did, but even this seems a little ostentatious. Calling this a cabin is an absolute joke. This seems more like a compound. From the driveway I can already see that this two story monstrosity has floor to ceiling windows that look to be at least fifty feet high, maybe more? The stone detailing around the front door is breathtaking, and I can only imagine what the inside looks like.

"This way Amelia," Teddy calls after me, and I quickly follow after him, careful to not slip on the fresh snow.

"Ok, so double checking that this kajillion dollar home is the place where I'm spending Thanksgiving with my family? There's no shame in double checking the address on the GPS, no judgment, we all make mistakes!" I stammer.

Teddy smiles and shakes his head as he drops the luggage at the front door.

He looks up at a very fancy state of the art security camera and waves. The front door clicks open and Teddy nods at me to enter. "Positive this is the right place Amelia. Besides, I've been here before." He drops my luggage off in the foyer of the cabin and begins to say his goodbyes.

"Wait, hold up a second. You can't just leave me here alone. We just listened to three hours of a true crime podcast! We all know what happens to city girls in secluded cabins in the woods!" I shriek. "Besides, where is the owner or property manager? Don't I have to check in for everyone since I'm a day early? And why are you laughing at me Teddy, I thought we were friends now!" I yell.

"I'm sorry, I really don't mean to laugh, but your fears are completely unfounded dear. Besides, the owner of the property is already here." He gives me a confused look. "Although I'm sure you won't have to 'check-in' if that's what you're concerned about."

Huh.

"Ok, I might sound frantic right now, probably because I've never been in a mega mansion before, or maybe because I don't want to be murdered in my sleep, but do you think you could meet the owner with me before you leav—"

"Hello there Amelia," says the smooth velvety voice of a man that should not be in this house a day early.

I slowly turn around, and as suspected, I see Evan looking just as devastatingly handsome as I remember him on the night when he showed up at the club to pick me up. Wearing a charcoal gray three-piece suit, expensive looking watch and a pair of expertly polished black shoes.

"Thanks, Teddy. I'll take it from here. Happy Thanksgiving." Evan waves at him.

"Happy Thanksgiving guys. You two have fun!" Teddy croons as he shuts the door behind him.

"So, how was the drive up? Hope you didn't hit too much traff—"

"What are you doing here?" I shout, only to startle myself at how far my voice has traveled within this mega home.

"Well now Amelia, that's no way to treat your host." He tsks and starts to walk away from me. "Should I give you the tour now or do you want a bite to eat? There's a freshly made charcuterie board on the kitchen island if you're interested," he offers.

"What do you mean host? I thought Vanessa and Abby were hosting this! Or at the very least organizing the Airbnb side of things. What, you offered to pay for some stuff and now you're the Thanksgiving host all of a sudden?"

"Amelia." Evan smiles.

"That doesn't make any sense. Plus, I was supposed to get here a day early and have the place to myself, not have you lurking around every corner," I complain.

"Well..."

"Today was supposed to be a day where I got some peaceful

'me time' away from the city and everyone that stresses me out. Which by the way, you're at the top of that list now, thank you very much." I cross my arms over my chest.

"What did I—" Evan starts.

"I'll just call Abby to confirm the details and prove that you are intruding on my one day vacay and I'm sure you can find yourself a Four Seasons somewhere nearby—"

"Amelia," Evan groans while rubbing his eyes.

"What!" I yell as I rummage through my purse, looking for my phone to call Abby.

"Are you done? May I speak?" Evan asks, his patience clearly slipping.

I take a deep breath and give him my full attention. "Fine."

He takes a moment, then unfurls a massive grin. "Amelia, from what I gather, I'm assuming that Abby, along with everyone else for that matter, happened to leave out the little detail that this very home you are standing in, belongs to me." He smiles widely.

NO FUCKING WAY.

Realization hits me like a rogue wave, and I think back to my dad's birthday party when Nikki barely let Abby speak when going over the Thanksgiving plans.

She knew.

"I'm going to kill her," I whisper to myself as I stare off into the abyss.

"Amelia, babe. Who are you planning on killing?"

"Nikki. I'm going to kill her. She set me up," I say as Evan gently starts to steer me deeper into his home.

"Yeah, I had a feeling I liked her." He eyes me with an amused gaze. "Oh come on, it is a little funny." He nudges me towards a kitchen island stool as I absentmindedly hop onto it.

I put my elbows on the counter and dig the heels of my palms into my eyes. "Ugh noooooooo. This wasn't supposed to be the plan," I moan.

Evan opens one of the massive refrigerator doors and nudges

me on the shoulder with a water bottle he just retrieved. I look up at the water bottle and give him a death glare.

"Stronger Evan. I'm gonna need something much stronger," I demand.

"It's eleven thirty in the morning Amelia, and you should probably eat something," he starts.

"So help me God Evan if you don't want to feel the wrath of a raging Latina while we're in the middle of nowhere, I highly suggest that you produce some hard liquor. Top shelf preferably," I threaten.

Evan blinks a few times, probably gauging how much danger he is actually in. "How about this? One shot of chilled tequila, followed by a glass of Sauvignon Blanc?" He grimaces while he waits for my response.

I nod and he lets out an exaggerated sigh.

He pours me a shot of Clase Azul Reposado and I down it before he even has a chance to slice the lime in his other hand. Damn that was smooth, what kind of garbage tequila have I been drinking this whole time?

"Okay ... You mind telling me what's got you bent all out of sorts?" Evan asks as he reaches for two wine glasses.

I snort. "You've got to be kidding me, right?" I point back and forth between us. "You. Me. In this house. ALONE. This is going to be a disaster!" I take my glass of white wine as soon as he's done pouring it and gulp down half of the contents in one swig. "Wait. Is this your doing? Were you trying to get me up here all alone? What are your motives here Evan?" I ask as I point a finger at him.

Evan takes a respectable sip of his wine and sets the glass down on the counter. "Ok, let's sift through all your crazy now and get it out of the way." He starts. "I let Abby and Vanessa know that I would happily offer up my vacation home to everyone since all of your parents were going away for the weekend. How that information got dispersed is none of my doing. At least that much you figured out on your own. Remind me to send

Nikki a gift basket or something. That reaction of yours was priceless."

"Rude." I take another sip of wine.

"Anyways, as I was saying, I suggested the typical Thanksgiving schedule of Thursday to Sunday. But someone ..." He looks at me, and I innocently point at myself. "Decided that they wanted to be here a day early. So I moved a few meetings around and took the jet so I could land here in time to welcome you into my home." He takes another sip of wine, this one much larger. "You know, some people would say something like 'thank you' but I'll settle on you not murdering me in my sleep." He smiles.

"No promises here," I say into my glass, then tip the rest of my wine into my mouth.

21

AMELIA

"OK, SO NOW FOR THE GRAND TOUR," EVAN SAYS AS HE guides me out of the stool and gestures towards the open concept living space. I was so caught off guard by Evan being here that I completely neglected to take in this beautiful home in all its glory.

The kitchen is the perfect mix of sleek, modern appliances and traditional wooden accents with a splash of emerald green here and there.

The living room space is a real jaw dropper. Multiple deep sitting cozy couches arranged in a U-formation facing the massive TV screen that hangs above a large fireplace. The back wall of the home is one massive piece of floor to ceiling glass, with an incredible view of the back patio and what seems like acres of uninterrupted land. I'm staring at the backyard when Evan leans down towards me. "There's a pond in the backyard that's currently not visible due to the snow, but during the summer months I'm told it's a perfect place to cool off while staring out at rolling hills and trees."

"Wait, what do you mean you've been told? Don't you own this place?" I ask.

"Yes Amelia, I own this home." He chuckles. "I bought it a few months ago, but just came to see it in person last week."

"Hold on a minute. So you just bought a vacation home without even stepping foot inside and seeing it for yourself?" I gasp.

"It's a very competitive market. I've been wanting a vacation home away from the city and my realtor told me about this one before it officially went up for sale. I had my assistant walk the premises for me and take videos. He also FaceTimed me while he was here. He knows me well enough to know what I like. And as you can imagine, this place photographs well. So I jumped on the opportunity." He shrugs.

"Wow, just like that. Must be nice." I nudged his shoulder.

"Yeah well, I'm no longer in the business of letting a good opportunity slip through my fingers," he says barely above a whisper while looking out into the distance.

Okay. Did it somehow just get exponentially warmer in here? Must be the fireplace's doing.

Nope, it's off.

Oh well, moving on.

"Okay, so we cook over there, hang out here, and have meals in the dining room over there. Got it," I say as I move away from Evan and back towards my untouched, newly refreshed glass of wine.

"I'll show you the sleeping arrangements. This way." He gestures towards the hallway on the left side of the house and we walk side by side.

"How many bedrooms does this place have?" I ask as I mentally start tallying the doors we pass.

"Eight bedrooms and ten bathrooms," he says casually.

I stop in my tracks and smack my free hand across his chest. Jeez his chest is way harder than I expected.

"Ten bathrooms?! Are you insane? Do you know how much

toilet paper you will need to keep this place fully stocked?" I screech.

Amusement dances all over his features when he grabs the hand I forgot to remove from his chest. He leans down to match our height and eye level, leaving mere inches between our faces.

"Amelia, you're standing in a twenty five million dollar home, with millions more in upgrades and renovations, and you're concerned about my toilet paper budget. Adorable." He kisses my knuckles then gently lowers my hand, keeping it in his while he tugs me further along the hallway.

At this point I can hear my heartbeat pounding in my ears. My hand feels like it's been set ablaze, and he seems totally unfazed about the fact that he just called me adorable and kissed my hand.

HELLO! Panic with me!

I can barely pay attention to all the details he's pointing out, so I just nod and hum every so often, and hope I'm landing on cue. I think there was something about a steam room, gym, and a hot tub. But I could be remembering old episodes of MTV Cribs at this point.

His phone starts ringing when we make it back to the main living room. "Sorry, I've got to take this. Should only be a few minutes," he says as he releases my hand and walks toward the side of the house I have yet to see.

Once he is out of sight, I make a beeline for the kitchen and pour myself another generous glass of wine. Now that I am left to wander on my own, I take a moment to settle my nerves.

Get it together girl, he's either just being polite or trying to get a rise out of you. Don't let him see how affected you are by his presence. And if my nether regions could stop betraying me and remember why we dislike this man, it will make this night go by faster. Please and thank you.

Evan comes back into view and eyes my glass of wine as I end my pathetic silent prayer. He preemptively puts his hands up as if he means no harm and says, "Listen, you're on vacation, so have at it. But I would personally prefer it if we didn't have a repeat of vomitgate," he teases.

"It was a bad street dog!" I huff. "Besides, it's Thanksgiving weekend so I intend on eating and drinking my body weight in carbs thank you very much." I raise the glass towards him in a cheers even though his hands are in his pockets.

"Very well then, how about I show you to your room?" He gestures to the right side of the house. He grabs my suitcase and carries it down the hallway, not bothering to use the wheels to drag it. Show off. "So this wing only has two bedrooms. The master bedroom and your room," he says casually.

"Hold on a second. So, everyone else is on the other side of the house, and I'm left to fend for myself by sleeping in your lair?" I question as bewilderment overcasts my features. "Why isn't Antonio getting this room? He's the only other single guy on this trip!"

"I've shown the house to Tony already via FaceTime, and he called dibs on the bedroom by the gym and gaming room."

"Wait, there's a gaming room in this house?" I ask, perplexed.

"Amelia, I literally just showed it to you five minutes ago. Are you okay? Do you need some water?"

"No, I'm fine. What I need is to swap rooms with someone else. Why aren't Vanessa and Abby taking this room, huh? Or Priscilla, or—"

"Ok, I'm gonna save you the hassle of going down the list, so here you go. Vanessa and Abby need the second master room to accommodate their toddlers, while also being close to the other kids bedroom. Lucy and Bill, along with the twins specifically requested rooms furthest away from the older kids, so that puts them the two separate rooms with balconies upstairs. Danielle and Luis are newly married so I gave them the third and final master, which just leaves you and Priscilla."

"Perfect! Great, I'll swap with Priscilla then!" I clap my hands.

"Sorry that doesn't work for me, because as we all know,

Priscilla has been trying to sleep with me since high school. And let's just say that my current shift in tax brackets has made those advances a bit more ... forward. So out of an abundance of caution, and for the safety of my penis, I have placed her in the room furthest from mine. So, there you have it. Your room has nothing to do with the proximity of my bedroom." He nods.

"Uh-huh." I pause. "So what you're saying is that I am in this room to protect your penis?" I say matter of factly as I cross my arms over my chest.

"Shit, right. That came out wrong." He squeezes the back of his neck with his free hand and shifts uncomfortably on his feet.

"It's fine, let's get this over with so I can start planning how I'm going to barricade myself in this room tonight," I say as I open the door that Evan has nodded towards.

"That's really uncalled for. Last I checked, you were the one stripped naked in my home. So should history repeat itself, *I'm* the one who should be locking my doors at night, sweetheart." Evan smolders.

"Okay. Ground rules. First, don't call me sweetheart. Second, we're not talking about that night in question, like ever. And third ... Well, I'll think of what else is off-limits, but for now just be aware that I will probably come up with a third. Got it?"

"Ma'am, yes Ma'am," Evan says as he salutes me.

I roll my eyes as I enter my assigned bedroom and am instantly taken aback by the view. The back of the room dons an exquisite pair of French doors that provide an unobstructed view of the backyard.

A quick survey shows that I will be sleeping on a king size bed, with what looks like the fluffiest bedding known to man. I would immediately flop onto it if Evan weren't standing in the doorway. I walk towards what I assume is a closet door, only to be surprised by an ensuite bathroom.

Evan clicks on a remote by the door that causes an automatic blackout curtain to cover the glass doors from left to right. "So is the room to your liking, honey?" Evan teases.

"Okay, there's ground rule number three. No calling me honey," I snap.

"Great. Let's cap the ground rules to just three. Nice, strong number don't you agree?" He raises a playful brow.

Ignoring his taunts, I point out the painfully obvious. "Evan, you do know that this shower is larger than my studio apartment, right?"

Evan laughs. "Unfortunately, I haven't had the pleasure of visiting your apartment. Which reminds me, you've now seen two of my homes and I've yet to visit yours. We should rectify that once we get back to the city." He rubs his jaw while trying to hide the start of a smile.

"Not happening. But since I'm here ..." I giggle. "In honor of tradition, it's time for me to snoop, oops, I mean *see* your room. I mean we are neighbors here, right? Seems like the neighborly thing to do," I say as I sneak past him and speed walk across the hall to open his bedroom door, but he stops me before I can turn the handle.

"Well look who's referencing *the night in question*. Seems like you're so readily able to break your own ground rules, interesting," he murmurs into my ears. "So, here's how this is going to go. You're free to snoop, as long as you understand that there is no kicking me out of my bed this time. If you feel the urge to sleep in my bed, it is with the understanding that it is with me in it. Got it?" he says sternly.

"Pfft. Don't flatter yourself," I say as I start to push the door open, but he stops me again.

"Amelia, I'm serious. Do you understand?" His eyes were more serious than playful this time. Where is this coming from?

"Jeez yeah, okay I understand. Big guy shall not be kicked out of his bed. No worries, I have no intention of having a sleepover with you anyways. Capeesh?" I roll my eyes.

Evan nods, then waves dramatically. His playful side coming back to the forefront.

Moody much?

I take a step inside and marvel at the impeccably-decorated bedroom. His bed, which seems even bigger than a California king, is settled between a moss-colored four poster canopy bed frame. The wall behind his bed is covered with wallpaper with intricate black and gold lines. The walls have a sleek wood paneling that definitely gives off more of a cabin vibe. There is also a reading nook by the bay windows that overlook what seems like endless miles of snow.

There are also two black night stands with gold lamps on each of them, which reminds me of my past mischief.

"This room is beautiful Evan," I say as I make my way towards his bed. He raises an eyebrow, but I ignore him and take a seat on his bed, right by his night stand. "Oh wow, and your bed is so comfortable too, would you look at that," I say.

"Amelia, do we need to go over the no swapping bed rules again?" he asks with a slight annoyance in his tone.

"Nope, just being thorough, per usual." I wink at him, then lean over and open his nightstand drawer. I jump to my feet when I see what is inside. "What the hell?! Evan Cooper you have a box of condoms in your nightstand! I thought you said you've just moved in!" I yell.

Evan smirks and slowly makes his way towards me. Walking like a predator stalking its prey. "Yes Amelia. That is a box of condoms. Unopened, might I add." He takes the box from my hands and puts it back in the nightstand drawer. "Since the last time you went through my personal belongings, I learned a valuable lesson. To always be prepared. For either sex or a nosey Amelia Nuñez, never quite sure which one these days," he mocks.

"Just to be clear, I don't care that you have condoms. Good for you! What I'm confused about is the fact that this is a family friendly vacation. With children carajo!" I exclaim.

"Relax Amelia, like I said, just taking your advice of always being prepared. No families will be harmed in my safe sex readiness." He deadpans.

"Cool. Right. Good to know." I clear my throat and put some much needed distance between us. "Just taking your penis protection duties seriously I guess." I nod.

What the fuck did I just say???

"Anywho." I fake yawn. "Wow, that midday wine is really hitting me now. Plus, that was a really long drive, so I'm just going to lie down for a bit and take a cat nap. Cool? Ok cool. See you later," I say as I hook my thumb over my shoulder, then quickly book it to my room.

I don't even give Evan a second glance, but I can feel his gaze boring a hole into the back of my head.

Once inside my room I quickly close the door and release a big sigh as I lean against the door. What the hell was that all about? I'm pretty sure the Berkshires aren't in the mountains, so I can't blame our weird interactions on the altitude.

I fling myself on the bed and release a soft moan when I feel how comfortable this bed is. I don't really need a nap, just time to figure out if Evan is flirting with me. Flirting? No. Making sexually suggestive innuendos, for sure. He must be playing some kind of game. He knew I would snoop and made sure to have condoms in his nightstand this time.

OH MY GOD, DID HE BUY THOSE CONDOMS TO USE WITH ME?! Wait, no. Of course not, calm your tits woman. Keep it together!

It must be payback for purposely giving the man blue balls. We're just having your regular run of the mill banter. Yeah, that's it. The kind that includes me stripping down to my underwear and him providing condoms while we're home alone in his kajillion dollar mansion. Totes normal.

Yeah okay, maybe not.

But what's with the pet names? Sweetheart? Honey? And the whole kissing my hand bit? What's he getting at?

I let my mind spin endlessly with the possibilities of what is going on between Evan and me. Without realizing it, I doze off into a deep slumber with thoughts of *what if* swirling around in my mind. And just like I've done hundreds of times before, I fall asleep dreaming of Evan Cooper.

22

EVAN

I DON'T THINK I'M GOING TO SURVIVE THE NIGHT.

Amelia's been locked up in her room for the past two hours, and I'm sure if she had it her way, she would stay there until everyone arrives tomorrow.

I had a perfectly composed plan. One where I would be nice and welcoming and provide a clean slate for us to clear the air and start anew. That plan went flying out the window the second I spotted her standing in the foyer of my home. Something about having her in my space spikes my senses into high gear. The moment I see her, I want to push her buttons and get a rise out of her, since it's only fair that she feels as unsettled as I do around her, no?

God that makes me sound like an asshole.

I just can't help it. After all these years of secretly pining for her, I can never let an opportunity pass where I can hold her hand or touch the small of her back. Fuck, I even kissed her hand today. I'm such a goner.

I've tried to keep myself busy by working out in the gym, but it only seemed to make me antsier about not knowing what Amelia was up to. Sure, she could be napping, or maybe trying to sneak out of her room and hitch hiking back to New York. The possibilities are endless in my mind.

I realize that Amelia will probably be hungry when she wakes up, so I decide to whip up a late lunch for us. I decided to keep it simple with a chicken carbonara, her favorite, according to an old Instagram post.

Don't judge me.

And if I know anything about Amelia, it's how much she loves her carbs.

It takes me about half an hour to cook the chicken in the oven and sauté the pancetta. I don't want to overcook the pasta, so I'll have to wait for her to actually leave her room to proceed.

When my patience finally wears out, I decide to head to her room to check in on her.

I knock softly on her door.

Nothing.

I knock a little louder. "Amelia. You okay in there?"

Nothing.

I start to get a little nervous and knock one more time before slightly opening the door. "Are you decent? I'm coming in, my eyes are closed just in case!" I whisper.

After no response, I peek my eyes open and barely spot a sprawled-out Amelia on the bed. Shit, I forgot I left the blackout curtains down. I know how coma-inducing it can be in these rooms when it's pitch black.

Against my better judgment, I decide to click on the button that will sway the curtains open about half way. I don't want to completely blind her when she wakes up.

Now that I see her in this light, I can't help but marvel at her. She seems so peaceful and angelic. The exact opposite description of what I have elicited from her as of late. I'm tempted to stroke her arm and slowly wake her up, but instead I step away and leave since I already feel like I'm intruding on her personal space.

I close the door behind me and get back to the kitchen.

Now I feel as though I'm the one who needs a bit of liquid courage after seeing Amelia, so I gather the items I need to make myself a margarita. Right as I'm about to close the cocktail shaker I hear faint mumblings. I'm pretty sure I hear *where the hell am I?*

I smile like a fool and start shaking up my drink. As I'm pouring the contents into my glass, I spot a squinty-eyed Amelia slowly walking towards the kitchen island.

"Hey there, sleepy head. For a minute I thought I wouldn't see you until morning," I say as I slowly raise my glass to my lips.

Amelia grunts and rummages through her purse until she finds her pair of sunglasses and puts them on. She then stretches her arms high above her head, releasing a loud moan in the process.

"There, much better." She sighs and saddles up onto a bar stool while trying to wrangle her hair back into a ponytail. "You know, you could've warned a girl about the dangers of sleeping in rich people's homes. I didn't even know what day or year it was until a couple of moments ago," she jokes.

"Yeah, those black out curtains are no joke. Did you sleep well?" I ask, but she's eyeing the stove behind me.

"It smells good in here. Did you cook?" Her question is immediately followed by a loud grumble from her stomach. "You didn't hear that," she declares.

My lips quirk and I turn around to start boiling the pasta water. "I made some chicken carbonara for us, thought you'd like it," I say over my shoulders.

"Really?" she asks excitedly, but immediately tries to tone it down. "Oh yeah that's cool, whatever, I'll take a couple of bites of it. Not my fave or anything, but I could eat."

Liar.

I turn back around and see her fidgeting with the cuff of her sweater. "Do you want me to make you one?" I ask as I shake the margarita glass in my hand.

"No thanks. Think it's best for me to pace myself." She shrugs.

I head to the fridge and take out a water bottle, then hand it to her.

"Besides, I still have to survive the rest of the night in this house with you. I might get the upper hand if you drink more than I do for a change." She winks and sips her water.

So, we're back to teasing. Good.

I set my glass down on the kitchen island separating us. "And what is it exactly that you need the upper hand on, Amelia? Last I checked you're the one who stole my bed from me, gave me an excruciating case of blue balls, and showed up to my vacation home a day early. If I were to go off history alone, I would think that you were actually preying on me tonight," I goad.

Amelia blinks a few times, then grabs my margarita and takes a deep sip.

"I thought you said you didn't want a margarita, babe."

"I don't, just needed a sip of yours, *babe*." She snickers.

I turn back around to focus on the stove, but just like my pasta water I can feel Amelia boiling behind me. She didn't think I would call her out on her antics, and now that it's out there in the open for us to discuss, I bet she feels exposed. Before I can think of another way to taunt her, she begins.

"You know, it's not really my fault." She starts swiveling side to side on the stool. "I mean, for all the supermodel tail you get, I just assumed that little ol' me would be safe from any attention from the big bad wolf. Who was I to be the wiser that your pecker could be set off so easily?" She pouts innocently.

Ok. Time to play.

"You're a smart girl ... I mean woman, Amelia. It doesn't take a rocket scientist to know why I was really there at the club to pick you up. Or are we going to play the dumb, innocent, damsel in distress card again?" I mock.

Amelia stops moving instantly, and shoots me a death stare.

Uh oh. I hit a nerve.

"Dumb. Innocent. Damsel. In. Distress? Are you kidding me?!" she shouts.

Oh hell.

"First of all, I'm the woman who managed to kick my cheating fiancé in the balls after I walked in on him cheating on me with one of my coworkers. Oh! And mind you Nikki and Antonio were both at the scene of the crime and I managed to wrangle them in so they wouldn't end up with felonies on their record."

She's fuming now. I may have fucked up, but there's no stopping her now.

"Let's see what else Evan ... oh yeah, I immediately had to move into an overpriced studio apartment, after spending a good chunk of my money on a wedding that didn't happen, put in extra hours at work so I could potentially score a promotion that would get me the hell out of the city, and manage to be there for my dad and brother while we all grieved for my mom."

Fuck.

"But please tell me Evan, how your reasoning for busting into a club and practically kidnapping me is something I should be well aware of?" she yells sarcastically.

"I'm sorry. I overstepped," I say, trying to back pedal.

"No, no. Now's as good a time as any. Please enlighten me, why were you at the club to see someone you barely give two shits about?" she hisses.

Wait, what?

"Wait, *barely gives two shits about*, are you serious right now Amelia? Look, I get it, I fucked up a bit there, but you can't possibly think that I don't care about you," I say as my knuckles turn white from clenching the edge of the kitchen island.

"Oh come on Evan, no need to keep up the façade. Aside from this past weekend and my mother's funeral, you have never given me the time of day. I wouldn't say you hate me, because hate would require some level of attention. No, you're indifferent towards me, barely pay me any mind. For all I know you only see me as Antonio's annoying little sister. I get it. It's fine. But you don't get to ignore me for most of my life, then come barreling in insisting on being the main attraction!" she roars.

I take a deep breath to steady my breathing. "Yes, you're right. I have no right, but I can explain. And your thoughts on my feelings for you couldn't be farther from the tru—"

"No! I'm done with this little game. You tell me. Right now. Why did you go to the club? Why do you keep showing up and taunting me? Why, after all these years of knowing each other, are we playing this little game now Evan?" she demands.

This is going downhill fast.

"Amelia, this is not how I wanted to have this conversation, I'm sorry. I think we should take a minute to cool down, maybe eat something, then we can talk ..." Before I can even finish my sentence, Amelia is hopping off the bar stool and grabbing her purse. "Amelia, please just let me explain!" I yell.

She stops walking for a moment. "Don't bother Evan. If you haven't noticed, I've met my quota of listening to men bullshit me this year. Maybe I'll indulge this conversation in a year or two." She turns and starts to walk towards her bedroom.

Before I realize what I am doing, I lift my now empty glass and throw it into the kitchen sink, sending shards of glass all over the counter, stove and floors. Amelia stops dead in her tracks and turns to stare at me with her jaw dropped.

"I'm sorry, I shouldn't have done that," I quickly said. "Just losing my goddamn mind here. It's fine, I got it. Just go." I crouch down and start to pick up the pieces of glass while trying to figure out how the hell this conversation took such a left turn. I don't even notice that my hand is bleeding until I feel Amelia softly pull on my forearm. I look up at her and I can't read her mind, but at this moment it feels as though our fight has been put on pause.

"Where is your first aid kit, Evan?" she asks quietly.

I sigh. "I'm not sure, probably one of the bathrooms."

She tugs on my arm again to prompt me to stand, and then

keeps her arm there as she guides me to one of the guest bathrooms. She searches around a few bathroom drawers until she finds the first aid kit. I wash my hand in the sink making sure I have no more glass poking around, then reach my good hand out for her to give me a band aid.

"Sit." She nods her head towards the toilet. I do as I'm told and keep my mouth shut for once as she cleans up my hand.

"Well, that was dumb," she says as she's rubbing an alcohol swab on my hand. There were other disinfectants in that kit, but I probably deserve the extra sting.

"It was. I'm sorry if I scared you. I—"

"I wasn't scared. I know you would never hurt me … physically." The pause was momentary, but I caught it. I can feel her walls going up again. It's now or never.

"Amelia." I sigh.

"And would you look at that, they even have a Paw Patrol band aid in here for yo—"

"I have feelings for you," I blurt out.

She stares blankly at my hand for a couple of seconds, then proceeds to put on the band aid.

"Amelia, did you hear me? I said I have feelings for you," I say again, a little louder.

She closes her eyes and takes a deep breath, then removes her hand from mine. "Yeah, I heard you, but … you don't have to say that. We can just ignore that whole argument and go back to ignoring each other for the next decade," she says while avoiding eye contact with me.

"What do you mean? I'm trying to tell you how I feel, why I've been acting like a lunatic whenever I'm around you. I can't hold it in any longer Amelia. I … I …"

"I don't believe you, Evan." She finally meets my eyes, her shoulders sagging before she continues. "Not in the sense that I'm calling you a liar, but rather I don't think you truly mean it. You can't." She turns around to start walking out of the bathroom.

"Let me prove it to you," I say while standing up, taking full advantage of my height. Her eyes take me in, clearly wary of my words.

"And how exactly would you do that?" she says as she crosses her arms over her chest.

I slowly make my way towards her, never breaking eye contact. I cup her face in my hands and her eyes go wide. "Evan, what are you doing?" she croaks.

"Proving it to you." I lower my head so that our lips are almost touching, then I start to let her in on all the moments that have replayed in my heart for years. "Miami. When I came to visit you after you had broken up with your high school sweetheart. I wasn't there because I was on a business trip. I flew down because I knew it was your birthday, and I wanted to celebrate with you. I didn't know it at the time, but I was about to have the best night of my life with the girl who's always had my heart."

Her breath hitches and she drops her arms to her side. "W-what did you just say?" She stares at my lips momentarily, then her eyes meet mine.

"Once I got to Miami, I thought that I could play it cool and just go out for dinner or drinks with you and your friends, but once you spotted me in your dorm room, you lit up in a way I've never seen before. You jumped into my arms and introduced me to everyone, then insisted I join you on your quest to sneak into a party on Miami Beach. That whole night you shared stories of your adventures with your friends, and told everybody about our holiday celebrations in New York. You were in the spotlight and everyone, including myself, was completely enamored by you."

Her eyes are as wide as saucers, and I start to rub her cheek with my thumb.

"Once you successfully snuck us in, we danced the night away. The feeling of having you in my arms, smiling and laughing. Hell, it's a feeling I've never been able to replicate, no matter how hard I've tried. After Miami, I heard from your brother that you'd gotten back together with your ex, and I was completely gutted. I decided the safest way to keep myself from being destroyed by you, while still being able to be in your company was to keep you at arm's length. I was always too little or too late when it came to fighting for your heart. That's why I've never been in a serious relationship after Miami, and that's why I've been secretly holding a torch for you for the better part of a decade."

Amelia is barely able to string together a sentence but makes her best attempt. "Evan, I had no idea. I, um. Oh my God, are you serious? We were, ah, only back together for a week or something. It was dumb. But Evan, why. Why did you never tell me, or make a move?" Her brows furrowed together.

"I did Amelia. But like I said, I was always too late. There was always someone waiting on the sidelines for you, and I was never quick enough. After your mother died, I vowed to be there for you, but I knew you needed time to heal. So I gave you space, and the next time I saw you, you were engaged." I rub her cheek again, while shrugging one shoulder.

Amelia's mouth forms a perfect O as she blinks repeatedly, realization overcoming her. She's probably thinking about our throwdown at the pub over the summer.

"When I saw you going out with Nikki, I wasn't thinking. I just saw your face and bolted to wherever you were. I had assumed you were still engaged, but I didn't care. I just needed to see you, make sure you were safe. At least that's what I told myself. Once I saw your left hand bare of a ring, something clicked inside me. It was time to come out of the shadows and be front and center in your life, even if it meant I kinda had to kidnap you. Also, I'm pretty sure Nikki's boyfriend's brother didn't get arrested that night, another reason I need to send her a gift." I smirk, but her facial expressions grow serious.

"All this time. You felt something for me," she says as a statement more than a question.

I close my eyes and lean my forehead against hers and sigh. "All this time, babe."

I feel her breathing fall in sync next to mine. "So. Does this mean that you're going to kiss me now?" she asks with a touch of attitude.

I open my eyes and straighten up, raising back to my full height as I grab her hands. "No."

"No? What do you mean no? You literally just declared your undying feelings for me! I know you've been out of the game for a while, but this is typically the part when you kiss the girl, you schmuck!" She frowns.

The breath I didn't know I'd been holding gets released with the deep laugh that erupts from my core. "Listen, there's nothing more that I would love than to kiss you right now, but I've gone about this the wrong way. I never imagined revealing my feelings for you while wearing multiple paw patrol band aids. So I'm going to try to redeem myself and give us a proper first kiss. When the time is right." I smile softly.

"Okayyyy. Well, ahem. The moment is just fine now, but as you wish." She shrugs comically.

"Amelia, we've already fought about this before. You deserve better than fine. You deserve the very best, and I'm going to give it to you. Just you wait and see."

23

AMELIA

AFTER THE BOMBSHELL WAS DROPPED, EVAN AND I carefully cleaned up the glass in the kitchen. We'll have cute little toddler feet running around here tomorrow and we wanted to make sure no one gets hurt. The food was also covered with glass, so I threw a freezer pizza in the oven while Evan made a pitcher of margaritas.

I'm clearly going to need that drink now.

We worked mostly in silence, but every now and then I would find Evan looking at me, and I would offer a shy smile.

He looks different now. I know that sounds absurd, but it's true. A curtain has dropped and now I see most of our interactions much differently, especially our night in Miami.

He was right, I was absolutely thrilled to see him there for my birthday. Evan has always secretly been one of my favorite people, but also someone who I wasn't allowed to get too close to. If we were with the cousin crew, he would be expected to hang out with the older kids, and if he was over at my house, he and Antonio would hole up together for hours playing video games. There was never an organic environment for us to hang out alone, until I was away at college.

I remember us drinking and dancing the night away. I remember how I felt so lucky that I was finally able to get a piece of Evan for myself.

The person he met that night was the real Amelia. The one who isn't carrying the reputation of being the youngest of the cousin crew, who should be coddled or excluded from adult activities. In Miami, I was in control and calling the shots and surrounded by people who only knew me as me.

Funny how I am able to be one person with friends yet revert back to being a little kid as soon as I step into a room with my family and the crew. It's as if they'll forever see me as if I'm frozen in time. It's how Evan probably always saw me, until he flew down to visit me. The real me.

I probably should have pulled a Miley Cyrus when I could. Blast that good girl image with a wrecking ball.

But what does that mean for us now? Do we start dating? Do I tell him how I've felt about him throughout the years too?

What is a girl to do when her first crush/current wet dream declares that he has feelings for her?

God, what am I even thinking?!

I literally broke off an engagement three months ago. An ENGAGEMENT for fuck's sake.

I have no business thinking about being in another relationship so soon, especially with someone like Evan. You don't half ass date someone your entire family knows!

Nope. I just have to stay the course. Stay single for at least a year, and work hard to get that promotion in Miami.

Yes, Miami.

If anything, this just proves that I'm meant to live there and continue living my best life without the constant projections of my family.

Ok, good. Glad that's settled.

But what about Evan? Do I ignore that he just poured his heart out to me? Literally made my stomach burst with butterflies and be weak at the knees when he got so close to kissing me. I know I'm nowhere near ready for a relationship, but one kiss wouldn't have killed me! I mean a girls got needs too.

Oh my God did I actually ask if he was going to kiss me?

"Yes, you did," Evan says from behind me.

"Wait, did I just say that out loud?" I cringe.

"Yeah, you did. And I can see your mind going a mile a minute. Please feel free to share the rest of that inner monologue, I'm dying to see how that brain of yours works," he taunts.

My phone alarm goes off.

"Pizza's ready!" I yelp as I shoot off towards the kitchen, only to be stopped by two massive hands grabbing ahold of my waist.

"Easy there. Last thing we need now is you burning yourself grabbing the pizza pan with your bare hands," he says as he nods to the two oven mitts I left behind on the couch when I bolted to the kitchen. "Let's try not to get any more use of that first aid kit. I spotted some Hello Kitty bandaids I'd like to keep for myself." He winks as he hands me the pitcher of margarita instead. "Oh and for the record, when I went full hulk smash back there, I was trying to aim for the recycle bin that's a solid three feet away from the sink." He blushes and scratches the back of his neck nervously. "Sorry, but I don't have those Dominican baseball player genes." He smiles and walks towards the oven chuckling to himself. I smile and try to force myself to relax a bit.

We decide to eat on the couch while watching TV since we clearly need some background noise to flush out all of our lingering thoughts.

Once I'm done eating, I lean back on the arm of the couch with my margarita in hand and stretch my legs out. I'm facing the floor to ceiling glass windows and it's breathtakingly beautiful. The soft snowflakes continue to cascade from the sky and blanket the patio and backyard beautifully. The days are starting to get shorter, which usually makes me grumpy. But for right now it means that I am being treated to a beautiful late afternoon sunset.

I'm pretty sure artists would beg for my spot on the couch to paint this masterpiece.

Also in my line of view is Evan on the opposite couch sipping his tequila neat, looking at me from above his glass.

I'm not quite ready to talk about our earlier conversation, so I try to think of safe conversation starters.

"So. Why did you buy this place?" I ask.

"It was a good investment." He shrugs.

Okayyyy thanks a lot, chatty Kathy.

I give him a look that lets him know I'm going to need a little bit more than that, and he chuckles into his drink.

"I knew I was moving back to the city, but wasn't sure exactly where I wanted to buy. During that process, my realtor heard about this place possibly hitting the market. He knew I was interested in a private vacation property as well so—"

"No Evan. I'm not asking for the logical reasons. I'm sure you could buy any home on the planet and call it a good investment with your kind of money. You could have bought a vacation home in the Dominican Republic. I'm asking why here? Why now? Do you have any ideas for how you want to live in this kind of space?"

"Well if you'd let me finish, I was about to tell you that I am also buying a vacation home in the Dominican Republic, but..."

"Stop deflecting."

"Nothing gets past you huh." He shakes his head while mumbling something under his breath. It kinda sounded like "now or never," but I could be wrong. "I was lonely in California. I missed my mom, my friends, my surrogate Dominican family... you." He locks eyes with me, and my stomach takes a deep dive. "So, I let my company know that I was moving back to the east coast. All of our meetings are mostly remote nowadays, so it doesn't really matter where my homebase is workwise. I decided to come back home and try to plant roots again. When I saw this house, truthfully I thought it was way too big for me. But when I thought of Vanessa and her five kids running around outside,

Antonio and I spending hours in the game room trash talking each other, my mom and all the doctors drinking and cooking up a storm in the kitchen... The family is growing, and as much as I love celebrating in small apartments, I knew that eventually the gang would break up and start doing their own, smaller celebrations with their new families. I figured if I bought a large property that was close enough for everyone to get to by car, we could continue the tradition."

And just like that, my stomach dive makes a U-turn and shoots right up into my heart, performing what I am pretty sure is an impressive fireworks show.

This man ...

"Oh. Wow. Evan, that is so sweet of you. Obnoxiously sweet. Teetering on me never being able to be an asshole to you again, sweet."

"Teetering, huh?" He grins. "Don't worry, I fully intend on earning that heart of yours." He winks.

GULP. Earn?! Not win but earn. How does that sound a million times more romantic?!

"Evan," I warn.

"Amelia," he mock-warns back.

"Evan, there is no full heart to earn here, just scraps. I am not currently in the market for a man, so feel free to turn off your charm any minute now, thanks."

"Ha. You're cute." He takes a sip of his drink. "If you think I'm going to let another opportunity to date you pass me by, you've clearly underestimated me. I've waited ten years, Amelia. Ten years. And that's on me. I was too chicken shit to tell you about my feelings before, but now it's out there. So, if we don't end up together, it'll be because that was the choice you made, and I'll respect it. But don't you think for a second that I'm going to be deterred because you need time to heal. You'll have all the time you need, but in the meantime I'm making sure you know I'm here. And that I'll always be here regardless." He leans back draping one arm over the back of the couch. "Besides, I've got a secret weapon." He raises his eyebrow. Clearly feeling confident with himself.

Holy moly. I'm failing miserably at containing my smirk. "Secret weapon you say? Can you please enlighten me?" I indulge.

Evan looks down at the drink in his hand and swirls the tequila gracefully. "A drunk little birdie recently told me that I was your first crush. And according to *first crush rules*, that means that there will always be a teeny tiny special place in your heart for me. So I fully intend on figuring out what it was about me that made you fall, for the very first time in your life may I add, and remind you of all the reasons why you should take a chance on me."

I grab a decorative pillow and push it against my face while groaning. "Me and my big stupid mouth. Why did I tell you that? You weren't supposed to remember. Weren't you too busy staring at my ass or something?" I lament.

Within a second, Evan is moving the pillow off my face and leaning in close. "I'm a multitasker babe. Another reason to love me." He gives me a chaste kiss on the forehead and stands up quickly to move to the kitchen. "I'm heating up some brownies, any preference on ice cream?" he asks as he reaches for the freezer door.

"Now you're just playing plain dirty, Evan Cooper," I say as I throw the decorative pillow towards the kitchen, but it meekly lands a few feet away from the couch.

He comes back and hands me a deep bowl with a warm brownie and two massive scoops of ice cream, one dulce de leche and the other cookies and cream. He nailed it.

"I've been meaning to ask, why do you call me by my full name sometimes?" he says as he takes a seat next to me.

I smile and make him wait for my response by taking the perfect spoonful of ice cream and brownie. "Uhhhh oh my God this is so good," I moaned.

"Amelia, please answer the question. And for the love of God never make that noise again unless trying to send me to an early grave," he says lightheartedly.

I playfully roll my eyes. "Truthfully, I think it has a little something to do with you being my first crush. It's almost like being a celebrity in the sense that you call them by their whole name, and they're unattainable to you." I risk a glance in his direction and see that he's about to say something, so I continue before he can. "Besides, I guess I've just always liked how your name sounded like you're a made up character. And maybe you are. You do seem too good to be true." I elbow his side. "No but seriously, I usually say your full name if I'm teasing you or if I'm pissed at you. There is no better way to gauge how mad a Dominican mother is at you than by hearing her yell your entire government name. You're just Evan Cooper, so sometimes I call you Evan Fucking Cooper to give you some extra pizazz," I say with jazz hands.

Evan erupts with laughter, then leans in to give me a soft kiss on the side of my head. "You're insane, babe."

I shrug and take another huge spoonful of ice cream. "Yeah, I know. Maybe that's why I'm almost thirty and still single," I say as a joke, one that clearly doesn't land for Evan.

"Or maybe you just weren't with the right person," he says seriously.

"Well, duh! I would hope my person wouldn't be someone who cheats on me. Unfortunately, the cheating ex-boyfriend list runs long." I wave my spoon in the air.

"So you mean to tell me there's another idiot besides Sebastián that messed up the best damn thing to ever happen to them?" he asks.

"Oh yeah. Maybe one or two relationships I was in just 'ran its course' and ended mutually. But everyone else, big fat cheaters."

"You're being serious right now?" he asks, stunned by my confession.

"Evan. I even got cheated on by a college boyfriend who was a devout Jehovah's Witness. He ruined Puerto Rican men for me. Spare me the jokes, I've heard them all." I grimace.

Evan's mouth turns into a frown and his eyebrows furrowed together.

"Listen, I'm not asking for sympathy, so you can stop looking at me like that. I can honestly look back at those relationships and laugh about it now. Although a broken engagement... Sebastián... yeah that might take me a minute to bounce back from." I half smiled. "Oh, and the kicker is I even have the most perfect wedding dress. Glad I didn't waste it on him."

"You should burn it," he says dryly.

"No! I can't!" I shout. I see Evan's confused reaction, so I continue. "My mom and I went wedding dress shopping before she passed. Before Sebastián. So that dress has more sentimental value than any other dress I could buy at a store tomorrow. So yeah, never burning it. Even if I never get married, I guess they'll just have to bury me in it," I say as I stab a piece of brownie with my spoon.

Evan's eyes warm to the mention of my mother, and nods in understanding.

"What was different about him? Why was he the person you decided to say yes to, to marry?" Evan asks gruffly.

When did this conversation turn into a therapy session?

"Sebastián and I just fit. Everything seemed easy at first. Our families loved each other, he was Dominican, very attentive to me and my feelings. There was that bond of being with someone in the medical field too, I guess. I knew all the struggles my mom went through as a physician's wife and knew all the stories about sticking it out throughout the hard times when he's busy doing his residency or fellowship." I bow my head because I can't muster the courage to look at Evan while talking about Sebastián. "I mean, hindsight is 20/20. Now I know that those struggles we went through towards the end had nothing to do about me being a supportive partner, and more about the fact that he was sleeping with my coworker." I wince. Guess it still stings. "He also happened to be ... my first."

"First?" Evan ventures.

"You know, my first. Deflowered me, popped my cherry, took my v card. Whatever you wanna call it. It happened years before we ever started dating while I was a freshman in college. It was stupid, but I just didn't want to be a virgin anymore, and he seemed like a safe first. We reconnected through a family friend a few years ago and he awkwardly asked me out. At the time my idiot brain saw it as a cute full circle moment that he could potentially be the man who was my first and last. But that was before our merry go round of breakups and makeups."

I continue, "I now know that I should never have called him when my mother passed and picked up where we left off. I was using him as a crutch. I really wish I would have never gone back and made such a mess of everything," I say as I rub my hand back and forth on my forehead, as if I could in that moment magically erase the memories of Sebastián. "He was the last person I dated before my mom died. She wavered in her feelings about him every time we broke up, but she always made a point to say that he was a good man, but just had a little bit of growing up to do. I have memories of them together, of them laughing and dancing. I think I clung onto him at the end because I wanted to marry someone my mother knew, someone she approved of. Now that she's gone, I'm left without her seal of approval. I feel like I'll always be second guessing if I'm picking the right person to be with now, because I've always had my mom guide me through life. My mother will never know my husband and that is a gut-wrenching feeling." I take a couple of calming breaths. "But enough about my mom and Sebastián, please. I'll spill my guts about anything else, but I really don't want to go down that rabbit hole. That's what I pay my therapist Kelly for." I smile tightly.

I stare into my melted bowl of ice cream and soggy brownie as the silence between us starts to get awkward. I'm frantically thinking of how I can pivot this conversation into happier territory when Evan finally speaks up.

"Amelia."

"Mmm."

"Amelia, look at me," he says hoarsely. I slowly raise my gaze to him, and am immediately taken aback by how troubled his eyes seem at this moment.

"Why didn't you call?" he says as he maintains his eyes locked on mine.

I gulp loudly. "What do you mean?"

"At your mother's funeral. I held you. I told you to call me whenever you needed someone. For dinner, a hug, whatever you wanted. I let you know I would be there for you in a heartbeat if you needed someone, but you never called." He takes a deep breath, steading his shaky voice. "But you called Sebastián. I know he was an ex, and a familiar comfort. But you could have called me too. Ever since the day you announced your engagement, I've always wondered why you never called me, too." He leans his head back on the couch, defeated.

"Evan," I say softly as I take both of our bowls and place them on the coffee table, then turn my body in his direction while placing his hand in mine. Almost instinctively he interlaces our fingers and faces me. "I wanted to call you. I thought about it countless times."

"What stopped you?" he asks while his thumb sweetly brushes against mine.

"The truth?" I pause.

"Always. Please."

"I obviously wasn't in a good place, and the thought of calling you and having you fly out just to see me space out during dinner, or see me crying while doing the dishes... I just couldn't do it. I've pathetically spent most of my life trying to present myself to you in the most flattering light possible. And while mourning my mother,

I didn't have the energy to do that, but I also wasn't willing to be vulnerable and be hurt by you."

"Why would you think I'd hurt you?" Evan asks.

"Everyone hurts me Evan," I say the words before my brain can stop them. I don't even realize I'm crying until I feel Evan use his free hand to wipe a tear from my face.

"Baby, please don't cry," Evan begs.

I take a few shallow breaths. "Please don't call me baby. My heart can't handle you in peak Evan Cooper form." I faintly smile as I will the tears away.

He squeezes my hand. "I want to tell you so many things. How I'd never hurt you, how I would always be honest and loyal to you, but I know you probably don't have a lot of faith in men right now. So I'll save my speech for another time." He kisses my hand that is intertwined with his.

"Well, you kinda just gave me the cliff notes, so it's good enough for now I guess." I laugh. "Can we please get out of this funk and salvage the rest of the night?" I plead.

"What can I do to make you feel better? Name it." He lifts an eyebrow.

There he is. Playful Evan, my favorite. "Hmmm decisions, decisions," I say as I tap my chin repeatedly. "Oh there's this new true crime series on Netflix that I've been dying to see. Nothing like serial killers and small town detectives to cheer me right up!" I glee.

"So basically you want to Netflix and chill... all you had to do was ask," he teases as he begins to tower over me on the couch and smother my cheeks with sloppy kisses.

"Uhh get off of me, you're a slobbery Saint Bernard!" I say in a fit of laughter.

He finally concludes his mauling of my face and stands up. He reaches both hands out, a silent invitation to stand with him. I put my hands in his and he lifts me into a much-needed embrace. Our height difference makes me feel tiny in his arms, but then he rests his chin on my head and we create the perfect mold.

How can something so confusing feel so right?

I squeeze further into his hold and feel him release a big sigh.

"You ok up there, big guy?" I ask as I tip my head up and back to look him in the eyes. What I didn't intend was for our lips to be mere inches apart.

"Yeah. I'm good, Amelia. And you will be too," he says as he moves his hands to the back of my neck, letting his thumbs rub my jawline and cheek.

Oh my God. This is it. It's happening! Evan Cooper is about to kiss me!

I close my eyes in anticipation as I feel him lean down towards me. I feel like it's taking a million years for those lips to travel down to mine. And when they finally touch me, I realize they haven't traveled far enough.

He kisses me on the forehead. Again.

What the hell?!

Before I can wrap my head around that major let down, Evan is out of my arms and headed towards the couch furthest from us and grabs the tv remote.

He presses a button and speaks into the remote, "Play some creepy murder crime thingy for my girl." He throws a teasing wink my way.

My girl. If only.

TV speakers announce, "Now playing, Don't Fuck With Cats, on Netflix."

He offers a devious smirk, "Is this murder-y enough to lighten the mood babycakes?"

Babycakes?

I'm so mind fucked I just shake my head and laugh. "No, I already watched this one. Hand over the remote ... Sweetcheeks."

After deciding that we're better off not trying to come up with pet names for each other, *for my sake*, we decide on a three part serial killer documentary and settle into the couch across from the fireplace and TV.

I lie out on the end of the couch and stretch out my legs sideways so I can guarantee physical space from Evan. My poor brain feels like it's going to short circuit every time he's close to me. What I didn't expect was Evan interpreting my accommodations as an invitation to take my fuzzy socked feet and place them on his lap. I give him a stern look at first but don't protest further. Whenever the show gets too scary, he distracts me by rubbing my feet.

I know. Poor me.

We complete the show and move to clear out the dishes and glasses we've accumulated throughout the night. We clean up the kitchen quickly in silence, and somehow the ease of the night has turned into tension.

Evan literally had so many moments that could have been considered "perfect" to kiss me, and yet...NADA.

Have I hallucinated the whole day? I really must have. Because how the hell has this man had me all to himself all day, declared his feelings for me, and not made a single move?

I'm in uncharted territory. I have made it crystal clear that I am not looking for a relationship, yet I want to kiss this man as if my life depends on it.

This is where being a hopeless romantic is really biting me in the ass. I wish I could just be *casual* with Evan. *Pfft yeah right.*

I don't think Evan is the kind of man you walk away from unscathed.

But look at me. I've played it safe all my life, and look where it's gotten me, no closer to my happy ever after and a couple thousand dollars in debt with wedding vendors.

"Knock knock," Evan says while gently tapping his index finger on my temple. "I think I see steam coming out of your ears. What are you mulling over now woman?"

I clear my throat. "Nothing. Just tired. I'm going to head to bed. Big day tomorrow and all." I start to turn when he grabs my hand and intertwines his fingers with mine.

"I'll walk you to your place," he says with a cheeky smile.

"Are you making dad jokes now, Evan? I know this is a mansion and all, but I'm sure I could manage the sixty second walk," I say, without making any effort to release my hand from his.

"Yeah, you're right. Maybe I just want to make sure you don't steal my bed again," he says with a raised brow.

"Ah I see. Poor little Evan wants to make sure that big bad Amelia doesn't make another appearance," I say while pouting and batting my lashes.

"I mean—actually ..." he stutters.

"Well, this is me," I say as I jerk my thumb over my shoulder to point at my bedroom door behind me.

Evan takes a deep breath and chuckles. "I had a great time tonight—"

"Wait, isn't that supposed to be my line?" I interrupt.

Evan laughs. "Goodnight Amelia. Glad we had tonight to ourselves. Get some rest," he says as he leans in and gives me a kiss on the forehead.

I hate my fucking forehead now.

He leans back and is about to release my hand when I squeeze it tighter. He looks down at where we are joined and then looks back up to me.

"Ok. So I was thinking. This whole kiss situation from earlier—"

"Amelia," Evan interrupts.

"No, wait. Hear me out. I get it. You're looking for the perfect moment to maybe sorta sweep me off my feet, and I'm all like, 'boo love, woe is me' while also wanting to kiss you. So I get it, confusing as hell, right?"

"Amelia."

I'm completely ignoring him at this point and keep going. "So anyways, I got to thinking, and by that, I mean like a full ten seconds ago. And I came up with the conclusion that no matter how I spin it, I still want to kiss you, repercussions be damned!" I point an enthusiastic finger in the air.

"Amelia, let's—"

"Like we're consenting adults, no one's the boss of us, right? We're home alone and quite frankly we could be doing far worse damage, and no one would be the wiser. And it's just one kiss—"

"Amelia, please stop talking," Evan groans loudly.

I blink and forcefully shut my mouth while looking down in embarrassment.

"Amelia." Evan lifts my chin with his index finger and thumb slowly, until our lips are almost touching. "I need you to stop talking so I can kiss you senseless."

Before I can catch my breath, Evan's lips meet mine and an electric shock pummels through my body. He inches back for a brief moment, breaking the kiss to meet my eyes, as if he felt it too. A wild expression on his face. I reach my hands around the back of his neck and pull him back down again and it's as if a rubber band has snapped within us. The second time our lips touch is not gentle or measured. Evan kisses me like a man who has waited a decade to do so.

Because he has.

His hands roam to my waist and lower back, pressing me into him so there is no space left between our bodies. My hands venture up into his hair as our kiss deepens. I've never kissed like this before. As if we're melting into each other. A soft moan escapes his throat and my legs almost give out from how light-headed I'm getting. But before my knees buckle, he leans down further and grabs the back of my thighs and in one effortless swoop has my legs crossed behind his waist, pinning me to the wall, never breaking our kiss.

I hang on to him like my life depends on it, our mouths fused together, never coming up for air.

Just as I come to terms with the fact that I will happily die from lack of oxygen, he breaks our kiss and leans his forehead on mine, panting. "Amelia."

"Wait, don't stop." I pull him back in, these kisses much gentler, almost like caresses.

"Baby, we need to stop," he says as he peppers soft kisses on my lips, cheek and neck.

"Why?" I ask breathlessly.

He grabs my ass with both hands and lowers me a few inches and I feel his—*why*. Hello there, we meet again, erection.

"Amelia, I need you to be a good girl and go to your room and close the door within the next ten seconds," He says, his voice gone husky.

"Are we playing 'daddy' again Evan?" I ask with a chuckle and eyeroll.

Evan rests his forehead on the wall he's holding me against and lets out a hearty laugh. "You're gonna be the death of me woman, and I don't even mind one bit," he says as he slowly lowers my feet to the ground.

"That was one hell of a kiss, Evan," I say as my heart tries to regulate itself to a normal beat.

"First kiss." He corrects as he lays one more kiss on me. He turns me towards my door and gives me a gentle pat on my ass. "Now please go inside before I lose all resolve and turn into a cave man."

I do as he says and head into my room. Before I close the door, I say one final goodnight. "Oh, Evan. I'm locking this door, so don't get any ideas," I tease.

Evan groans as he walks backwards towards his door. "Woman, we already regret this decision. Don't make it harder for us." His face distorts in pain as he points to the bulge in his pants. "Good-night Amelia. My door won't be locked. Just in case you're afraid of the dark or something, of course." He waves a sad little wave my way and we both close our doors at the same time. I hear a *thunk* right after, and I'm pretty sure it's Evan banging his head against his door. The visual in my head makes me chuckle as I touch my swollen lips.

Who am I right now? I don't even recognize myself, and yet that makes me feel happy?

I really wish I could call my mom right now. I wish she could tell me I was being an idiot or to just go for it with Evan.

I often chat to my mom. Quiet conversational mumbles or questions shoot up to her, trying to guess how she would respond. Tonight, I find myself doing this.

"Ay, Mami. What have I gotten myself into?. What am I to do about Evan Cooper?" I giggle as I rub my face in my hands.

I kissed Evan *Fucking* Cooper.

It's all I can think about as I lie awake in bed for hours before finally drifting off to sleep.

With my bedroom door unlocked.

24

EVAN

Amelia is going to freak.

Completely lose her mind. I can already see it. And not because of our mind-blowing kiss.

That, I will make sure she wants to do over and over again.

Nope, the reason my darling Amelia is going to go ape shit is because of Anna, and I'm not talking about her late mother.

I've just gotten off the phone working logistics with my assistant Hayden when Amelia pads into the kitchen, her hair swooshing from side to side, freshly showered wearing black cropped leggings and a light blue sweater. She's walking toward the coffee machine when she spots me by the kitchen island. "Good morning." She shyly smiles.

I get up and round the island until I'm standing next to her. "Good morning." I drop a kiss on her head. "How did you sleep?" I say as I take over and make her a cup of coffee.

She eyes me suspiciously. "Fine. Surprised I didn't find an intruder in my room."

"Oh yeah? The locks in this house work pretty well, so you didn't need to worry about an intruder." I play along. Handing over her coffee.

Without breaking eye contact, she lightly blows into the cup, then takes a small sip. "My door wasn't locked, Evan." She pats my chest twice as she breezes past me to sit on a bar stool by the kitchen island.

With my hands leaning on the counter, I bow my head down. "Jesus Christ Amelia. We should talk about—"

"Holy crap that's a lot of snow!" Amelia says as she hops off the bar stool with her coffee and walks toward the windows. "You never get to see the snow get this high in the city. The kids are gonna love it. I can only imagine the amount of ugly snowmen that we'll have to build today." She smiles broadly.

"About that ..." I unmute the tv and let the weatherman be the bearer of bad news.

"I tell you Joanne, this is unprecedented," the poor weather man says as he's being whipped by nasty looking winds. *"This is the first snowstorm of the season here in Massachusetts and it seems like we're going to be breaking records this weekend. So far here in Boston we've gotten over 24 inches of snow and there seems to be no indication that this storm is slowing down, causing major changes in everyone's holiday travel plans. Seems like storm Anna is definitely a force to be reckoned with. Back to you in the studio."*

I walk towards Amelia so I can try and calm her down before she inevitably spirals, but before I get to her, I'm taken aback by the sound ceramic crashing against the wooden floors.

"Ow! Shit!" Amelia yelps and jumps around as her bare feet are splashed by hot coffee and shards of sharp ceramic edges.

Before she can cause anymore damage to herself, I swoop her into my arms, cradling her while I walk us over to the kitchen island sink. I set her on the center of the island and guide her feet into the deep sink where I immediately turn on the cold water. "Don't move, I'm getting the first aid kit," I say quickly.

I'm gone before she has time to protest and by the time I get back, she literally hasn't moved a muscle. Staring off into the abyss as if she's seen a ghost.

Truthfully, the fact that the storm is named after her mother is a little trippy. I mean sure, Anna is a common name, and the storm was named after that character from the movie Frozen, but it still feels a bit eerie. Even to me.

When I'm back by her side she almost seems catatonic until I start tending to her blotchy burn marks on her feet and ankles.

"Evan, stop. I'm ok, just a little hot coffee. Gimme that." She reaches for the burn gel, but I hold it out of her reach.

"I got this Amelia. I'll be quick." I turn off the water and gently start rubbing a generous amount of the burn gel in the affected areas. I spot a small cut on her ankle and place a Hello Kitty band aid on it. "See, told ya these Hello Kitty band aids would come in handy." I look up to her and her eyes look panicked.

"Evan. Tell me that this storm is not named after my mother please," she pleads as her eyes start to glisten with tears.

"Amelia, I know it's weird, but Anna is a very common—"

"Wait! W-what about everyone? They're still coming right, I mean they must be on their way now, right?" Her breathing becomes more labored.

I hold her face in my hands and force her to focus on me. "Baby, I'm gonna need you to take a couple of deep breaths for me."

She swats at my hands. "Evan, I don't have time for this *baby* talk. We need to call the drivers and make sure they're safe and—"

"They're not coming Amelia," I say in a stern voice that I usually reserve for the boardroom, so that the message gets across clearly.

Amelia's stills, then blinks repeatedly. "They're not coming," she says as a statement instead of a question.

"No, they're not coming. The storm started sometime last night and started to pick up speed before dawn. I've been on the phone all morning with my assistant while he made sure that no drivers were sent out to pick up anyone. There's now a state of emergency and only essential employees and emergency vehicles are allowed on the roads here in Massachusetts.

"Last night. The storm started last night?" she whispers. I'm not sure if she's talking to me or herself at this point.

"Amelia, are you going to be okay? Do you need to lie down?"

Amelia's phone starts ringing and I see Abby's name flash on the screen. Amelia immediately dives for it and answers the call.

"Hello? Abby?!" she screeches as Abby's face fills up the screen.

"Amelia, are you ok? This storm is pretty tame in the city, but definitely a lot worse where you are. Is there a way to get you back to the city safely? We're sick to our stomachs here thinking about you being alone in that house! Do you have enough food? I'm going to call Evan and see if that fancy jet of his can fly you out. Do you know if he's in the city or—"

"Hi Abby, I'm right here," I say.

Abby's mouth just about hits the ground when she sees me standing by Amelia. Vanessa must have heard my voice too because within seconds I see her running down the hall and yank the phone from Abby's hands.

"You guys are stuck in that house TOGETHER?!" she says as her eyes bug out of her face. "Ay Dios mío se van a matar." I'm pretty sure she just said we're going to kill each other. I don't think now is the time to catch her up on current events.

I speak for the both of us. "Yes, we're stuck here. Together. We have enough food, and more importantly, enough alcohol for poor Amelia to put up with me for the weekend. We just need all of you guys to keep yourselves safe until this storm blows over."

"Oh no. This is too good. Hold on a sec," Vanessa says as her screen is paused. Within a few seconds she's back, as well as a few other squares with familiar faces.

"Amelia! Oh my God are you okay?" says Lucy.

"Wait, Evan is also at the cabin with Amelia?" Priscilla says in an annoyed tone.

"Guys, get this. Amelia and Evan are snowed in at the cabin. TO-GE-THER!" Vanessa broadcasts.

Gasps and laughter erupt simultaneously.

"They're gonna kill each other!" Xioana exclaims.

"Amelia please don't end up on Dateline! Doesn't matter how much you love Keith Morrison, killing Evan isn't the way to go out!" Roselyn yells.

"Wait, what do you mean Evan's alone with my sister?" Antonio snarls.

Oh shit.

"We got snowed in, man. Wasn't exactly a part of the plan," I say diplomatically.

"Amelia, are you sitting on a kitchen island? What the hell is going on over there?" Antonio is fuming. He may be my best friend, but he also knows I'm a man alone in a house with his sister. I wouldn't trust me either right now.

Amelia finally speaks up. "Look guys, we're fine. I dropped my coffee mug and got a tiny burn and cut after I heard the news that they've given the storm the name *Anna*, like Mami."

Facial expressions soften.

"And Antonio, I would appreciate it if you didn't talk about me as if I'm not on the call. Last I checked I'm someone who's perfectly capable of looking after myself. So if you can all give me a bit more credit and stop treating me like I'm some wilting fucking flower, that would be fantastic," Amelia snaps.

Silence.

"Oh. And while we're at it, Evan and I made nice last night. No need to keep Keith on speed dial." She rolls her eyes.

A couple of eyebrows are raised, but no one decides to ask for any follow up details.

"Sorry Amelia. I'm your big brother, it's my job to worry. This storm just came out of nowhere, so I'm just a bit out of sorts.

Kinda makes me think it is Mom playing a sick joke on all of us. She always did love Thanksgiving." Antonio's tone softens significantly.

"Thanks Tony. It's fine, because I'm purposely going to spend an hour in the game room just to spite you." Amelia playfully glares at Antonio on the screen.

"The fucking game room! C'mon Evan, can't money like yours buy a blizzard-proof plane or something? I've been looking forward to getting in there ever since you bought the place." Antonio groans.

"Sorry man. Don't have 'evil genius' level of money." I smirk.

"Don't worry, big bro. I'll take a selfie in there and send you a pic." Amelia winks and the whole call erupts into laughter.

"Ok Evan. You now have my blessing to kill my sister." Antonio deadpans.

"Alright everyone, we gotta get back to wrangling our circus of kiddos. Text us all updates on how you're doing. Happy Thanksgiving!" cheers Vanessa.

"Happy Thanksgiving!" we all say right as Amelia ends the call.

I hand Amelia some paper towels and she pats her feet dry, then eases off of the kitchen island.

"So," she says.

"So ..." I repeat.

"We're snowed in." She eyes me nervously.

"Yes, we're snowed in," I confirm.

"Alone. Together. After last night." Her eyes widened.

"Correct." I smile.

"How much alcohol did you say we have?"

25

AMELIA

Ask and you shall receive.

Thing is, I didn't ask for a freaking snowstorm, Mami!

All I did was ask for a sign, you know, something small. Maybe spotting a bird that lingers too long. Or finding something in my luggage that reminds me of my mom to somehow help me figure out what to do.

But no. Anna Nuñez has never been accused of being subtle, and now I am convinced that she orchestrated this whole set up. That, or I'm simply becoming unhinged.

Both plausible scenarios at this point.

"Amelia, you're doing that thing again where you look like you're gonna give yourself a brain aneurysm. Stop spiraling," Evan says as he wraps up cleaning up the mess made by my shattered coffee mug.

He tugs me away from the window and down to the couch, snug next to him. Why did the man have to wear a tight black t-shirt that shows off his broad chest and ripped biceps AND gray sweatpants?

GRAY FUCKING SWEATPANTS!

"I'm not spiraling. Anymore. I'm just trying to figure this all out," I say.

"There's nothing to figure out. We have to stay put for a couple of days until the storm dies down and the roads are cleared." He puts his arm over the couch, next to me.

"Evan, we kissed last night. And it was a *really* good kiss."

"Thank you." Evan smirks.

"Shut up."

"Sorry, carry on." He feigns seriousness.

"And now, we're stuck in this house with all this ... this ..."

"Tension?" Evan supplies.

"Sexual tension Evan!" I throw my hands in the air.

"Welcome to my world Amelia, nice of you to finally catch up." He chuckles.

"No Evan. This is a new normal for us now. We know how to bicker extremely well. I know how to sexually tease you from the safety of knowing that you would never actually touch me—"

"Boy were you off on that one," he mumbles.

I nudged his arm. "I'm being serious here! We don't know how to be around each other after last night."

"You don't, but I do," Evan offers. "Nothing really changes. You know where I stand, and I know where you stand. I want you and you need time. And while I wait for you, I'm more than happy to supply as many earth shattering kisses as you require." He leans in and places a chaste kiss on my lips.

God his lips are intoxicating. Maybe that's why an idea pops in my head instantly.

"Actually, I think I have a better idea," I say, biting my bottom lip.

"I'm listening." Evan uses his thumb to pull my bottom lip out from under my teeth, and I almost lose my train of thought.

Here goes nothing.

"So, I've been thinking." I take a deep breath. "I still don't want to be in a relationship."

"Geez, that was anticlimactic." Evan snickers, so I cover his mouth with my hand, and I can feel his smile growing underneath.

"Like I was saying. I don't want to be in a relationship because I'm still too weak to handle the judgment that comes along with dating."

Evan tries to mumble something under my hand, but I continue.

"My family always has an opinion on everything. They talk about me if I'm in a committed relationship, and they talk even more if I'm single. There's no winning. And to add the cherry on top, with Sebastián, I realized that I was the type of girlfriend who just morphed into her partner. Emulating their personality." I take a deep breath. "But I will no longer be that person. Ever. I'm not going to be the girlfriend who fakes being into your hobbies just so I seem more compatible. I'm not going to morph myself into looking the part and changing my sense of style just to compliment my new partner. And ... I'm not faking orgasms anymore."

That gets me an eyebrow arch from Evan. He doesn't have to say what I know he's thinking. Men love to promise that they're the best you'll ever have in bed.

"So even though I know all these things that I need to change about who I am in a relationship, it's still too soon for us to start dating. Because I know myself, and I'm still too sensitive to let the world in on my relationships or how I'm feeling."

Evan pushes my hand down gently. "Amelia, I—" I move my hand back up to cover his mouth and he rolls his eyes dramatically.

"There's a 'but' to this spiel Evan." That seems to perk him up again, so I lower my hand away from his mouth and let it settle on my thigh.

I take a deep breath. Here goes nothing.

"*But* I also know that things have changed between us this weekend. And I'm no longer in the business of holding back my *wants* for my *shoulds*. So, I'm prepared to make you a one-time offer."

"Evan crosses his arms over his chest and eyes me suspiciously. "Go on."

"For the remainder of this weekend, you and I can date."

"But you just said—"

"Not fake date like that rom com I was telling you about earlier. More like 'trial run' date, no strings attached kinda thing."

"You can't be serious." Evan gets up and walks towards the kitchen.

"Look, the way I see it, we can both benefit from this arrangement," I say as I hang over the back of the couch, facing Evan.

"And how exactly is that?" he asks as he opens the refrigerator to grab a water bottle.

"Bubbles please, two glasses." I offer an innocent smile with a tilt of my head.

Evan puts the water bottle back in the refrigerator and grabs a bottle of *very* nice champagne and two champagne glasses. I think I have him hooked.

"Continue," he says as he walks back over to me, trying to seem unenthused with my idea.

"Well, you yourself said that you've had feelings for me for a very long time, almost a decade! Which I'm still not over that, but we can discuss that at a later time. Anyways, in the last year alone I feel like I've changed so much. I can't imagine that the person you fell for is still the person I am today."

Evan opens his mouth, but then closes it. I'm reeling him in, I can feel it.

"So, since we've been given this opportunity to spend a weekend together, away from our nosey friends and family, you can see me for who I really am. Unfiltered Amelia. We skip the weird first date convos and go straight into the living together part of the relationship."

"I don't know, I could just wait until you're ready." He rubs the delicious scruff on his jawline.

Focus, Amelia!

"Do you know how messy it would be if we started dating, and then after a few months decided to call it quits? It would make holidays weird, Antonio would want to kill you, and nothing would ever be the same. But here, you can figure out if what you feel for me is just physical or if you really do want to pursue me in the future, when I'm ready. If not, no harm no foul. We can leave this weekend behind us as our little secret." I nod towards the bottle of champagne, already tasting victory on the horizon. "Look, Evan. It's one weekend. We get to be ourselves, away from the rest of the world. We get to leave our responsibilities and familial obligations behind. Once we get back to the city, we'll go back to non-dating. Depending on how this weekend goes, you'll decide if you're able or even want to wait for me to be fully ready for a relationship, and I'll know if you live up to all of my first crush dreams." I playfully nudge him, then switch into my serious tone. "I want to do this with you, but I'm not ready for the judgment that will no doubt come from us dating, especially so soon after my disastrous breakup." I pout for extra effect.

Evan releases a deep breath as he pops open the bottle of champagne and pours us each a glass. I grab my glass and tilt it towards his. "So do we have a deal?" I flash him a mischievous smile.

"Amelia, this could all go down in flames. Me and you have a good thing going now. We're finally having open and honest conversations, so we both know where we stand." He sighs as he leans back on the couch. "Although you do make some valid points ..."

Ok Amelia. Now or never.

"Well." I take a generous sip of my champagne, then set it on the coffee table. "We would be able to spend all weekend doing things like this." I put my hands on his shoulders and slowly swing my left leg across to the other side of his thigh until I'm straddling him. "Does it seem like such a bad idea now?"

Evan's eyes go wide, and I take the opportunity to grab his

champagne glass and take a small sip. His hands grab a hold of my waist and dig in softly.

"So, do we have a deal Mr. Cooper?" I say as I slide both arms around his neck until I'm leaning just a breath away from him.

Evan lifts his right hand to the back of my neck and whispers. "It's Evan *Fucking* Cooper. And yes, we have a deal."

And it's sealed with a kiss.

We spent the rest of the morning attached at the hip. Literally.

Once I pulled that straddle move on Evan, it was as if he put a ban on me sitting on any other surface in the house.

We put together a cute brunch spread, made out some more on the couch like a couple of horny teenagers and cuddled up to watch a thriller in front of the fireplace all before noon.

Living the dream.

"How many more serial killer movies are you gonna make me watch on the floor babe?" Evan mumbles into my ear while cuddled up behind me.

I've created a poorly formed pillow fort in front of the fireplace with cozy throw blankets and oversized accent pillows. Evan has been big spooning me the whole movie.

"Oh, come on. That was a classic." I scoff as I walk to the kitchen to get us some water.

Evan stands and starts stretching his back. "Ok. Next movie is happening on one of these massive couches. My back is already a wreck from laying on a pom pom for over an hour." He picks up a tiny pillow and throws it back on the couch.

I come back to the living room and hand him a water bottle. "Sorry, old man. Blame Pinterest for setting unrealistic expectations of watching movies in front of a fireplace."

"Old man, huh?" He quips.

"Yeah, maybe you should head to the gym and loosen up those muscles."

"Hmm, I can think of another way I can achieve that." He pulls me in for a kiss.

"Easy there Romeo, this isn't an all access pass." I move out of his reach.

"Alright alright. You should come with me to the gym. We can work up a sweat together in a not-so-fun way then." He jokes.

"Oh, ok sure."

I pause.

"Actually, no."

"Okayyyy." Evan looks unsure of my answer.

"Yeah, I don't want to work out. Old Amelia would have just tagged along with whatever you were doing and ignored what she really wanted to do. Which is cuddling up with a good book and some hot chocolate in your breakfast nook that overlooks the backyard."

Evan smiles. "Thank you for telling me what you really want to do." He places a quick kiss on my forehead.

Huh, guess I don't hate that so much anymore.

"And you don't mind?" I ask.

"Not at all. Like you said, I want to get to know the real you while we're here. Although, I'm sure you'll be leaving this cabin with my heart regardless." He winks as he heads towards his room to change into gym clothes.

Half an hour later, I'm fully hooked on a psychological thriller paperback I picked up specifically as my vacation read. I inhale my bougie hot cocoa and now I'm taking a moment to fully let the last twenty-four hours sink in.

Evan has feelings for me.

We've kissed.

We're fake-ish dating?

That definitely wasn't in my bingo cards for Thanksgiving weekend.

Just as I'm processing these wild events, a prickly sensation starts to build in the back of my neck. I start to feel like I'm being watched.

Geez Amelia, put the book down and stick to your chick flicks.

I look out into the backyard in hopes that the view will provide the sense of serenity that it usually does, but it ends up doing the opposite.

In the horizon, I can't make out what I see exactly, but I notice a few flickers. There is something glaring back at me, like a tiny mirror making purposeful movements in the distance.

No one is supposed to be here. We're on acres of private land. We're snowed in. Panic starts to build, and I scream.

"Evan!"

I'm already bolting from the kitchen nook, barely saving another coffee mug from being shattered, when Evan rounds the corner, dripping in sweat towards me.

"What happened? Are you okay? Did you hurt yourself?" Evan pants as he scans my body quickly. He must have jumped off a speeding treadmill by the way he's breathing.

I struggle to string words together while pointing at the window. "I saw—I think I saw. Something. A reflection. Shiny glare. Out back." I point to the backyard.

"Amelia, slow down. You think you saw something out back?" he asks as he holds on to my shoulders, trying to steady me, while looking out the window.

"I was reading, then I felt this overwhelming feeling of being watched. I am reading a thriller, but it's about a husband who killed his wife. Ya know, *it's always the husband.* Anyways, I saw something flickering, almost shining in my direction. I didn't see a person, but there's so much snow and I just. I don't know. We're in a goddamn cabin. This is why city girls shouldn't head into the countryside, this shit can turn creepy real quick!" I pant.

"Amelia, take a deep breath." Evan pulls me in for a hug. I'm still panicking, but Evan is sweaty and shirtless, so my senses are struggling with which matter to take up first. *Who even has a six pack nowadays?* "Come with me."

He grabs my hand, and we head to a room I haven't seen since he gave me the house tour that I mostly ignored. There is a large desk with three massive monitors. He takes a seat at the desk and pulls me down to sit on his lap. After a few keystrokes, he opens up his security system app and all three screens fill up with what seem like dozens of different camera angles of the property.

"I didn't go into the security features of the house, because it didn't seem necessary, but we're safe here Amelia, look." He points to the screens.

He walks me through the system, and how every inch within a hundred yards of the house is fully under security monitoring. There are motion detectors, motion activated cameras, shatter-proof windows, and all entryways are custom designed to keep out even the most skilled burglar. As well as a security firm that is in contact with his own personal security team to make sure this home is safer than the White House.

"Wow. Do you even need all of this? I've never seen you with a security guard before," I say in awe.

"Exactly. It's designed that way. Plus, I don't like being crowded with dudes that are more ripped than I am." He smirks. "I know we don't need to beat a dead horse, but I'm worth a lot of money now, which means I can easily be a target for just about anything. Blackmailing, kidnapping, extortion, influencers trying to make me their next baby daddy. Real scary stuff," he says light-heartedly.

"Wow. I had no idea, Evan," I say as I scan through all the camera angles.

He still senses my unease and reaches for his phone to make a call. "Hey Rocco. I need you to do a full sweep of my security system up at the cabin. My girlfriend thinks she might have spotted something out by the backyard." I pinch him at the mention of *girlfriend* and he dramatically winces. "Ok, great. Give me a call when you're done. Happy Thanksgiving." He ends the call.

"Girlfriend, really?" I mock.

"Hey, this weekend is to test things out. I haven't had a girlfriend in a very long time. I had to practice and see how calling you my girlfriend feels."

"Verdict?" I raise my eyebrows.

"Rolls off the tongue." He pulls me in for a kiss and I slowly start to relax.

Goddamn authors and their silly antics to stress out their readers.

26

EVAN

Amelia was properly freaked out.

I thought about teasing her a bit about overreacting to nature outside of the concrete jungle, but thought better of it once I saw how rattled she was.

Luckily, her anxiety subsided with a luxurious jet tub with bath bombs in her bathroom. Not so luckily for me, she took this bath alone.

I don't know how I ended up in a trial relationship with Amelia, but I selfishly try not to second guess it since it allows me to be closer to her than I've ever been before. And to be honest, she made some pretty valid points.

But now, I worry if she's using this phantom spotting as a way to pull out of our ill-fated arrangement. I'm just about to get up from the breakfast nook and head to her room when she strolls into the kitchen in a bathrobe.

"Evan, I get it now. All ten bathrooms are very much worth the investment. And these robes?! Do you think these are appropriate work attire?" She sighs as plays with the waist ties.

"Only if you're working from home. Or this cabin," I challenge.

"Oh yeah, sure sure. I'll take all my calls from the middle of nowhere." She laughs.

"You do know that there's a New York housewife around here who owns an estate. You may run into some Bravo-lebrities if we ever decide to come back up here in the future."

Amelia stills. "Evan, don't you dare talk about *Housewives* unless you're one hundred percent sure you want forever with me," she playfully threatens.

"Sorry, didn't mean to bring up Bravo, I know that's your sweet spot, honey."

"One of these days, these pet names are gonna get you in trouble Evan," she says as she tips my chin up with her right hand.

"Is it now?" I pull her into my lap.

"Yes, but today's not that day." She plants a sweet kiss on my lips, and I'm reminded to come up with a plan to keep this woman in my life, forever.

∾

We're prepping a low-key Thanksgiving dinner when I get an incoming call from Rocco.

"I gotta take this, keep an eye on the oven babe," I say as I place a quick kiss on Amelia's cheek while I head towards my office. Once I close the door, I answer the call.

"Hey Rocco, what you got?"

"Hey boss," he says in a tone that has me straightening in my office chair. "So, we checked your cameras, and surveillance from surrounding areas and we didn't spot anyone."

"Okay. Why am I sensing a but?"

"Because there is boss." I stiffen. "One of the cameras pointed to the east of your backyard seems to have been put on a loop. It was hard to catch since it's been snowing nonstop, but we noticed."

"So, someone's tampered with my security system?" I raise my voice.

"It looks like it, but remember, kids nowadays are more talented with cyber security, so it might have been a neighbor bored with his holiday plans. We already fixed it, but we're still sending someone up there in a day or two once the roads open up so we can manually go over the system."

"What good is a day or two when I'm here with my girlfriend now, Rocco?" I scold.

"Listen boss, you basically have a Fort Knox setup on your hands. As long as you don't leave any windows or doors open, you're safe from everything including a zombie apocalypse. So stay put, and I'll personally be there to handle any loose ends."

I huff out a deep breath. "Okay, so what else have you found?"

"Well, it seems like your girlfriend has a good eye, because we also spotted the reflective glare on the security cameras. It's most likely someone with a camera, so we're suspecting paparazzi. Didn't think the vultures would be working during a snowstorm and the holiday, but I guess Hollywood has no soul."

I take a deep breath and feel a sense of relief that the danger looming is more due to personal interest than personal injury.

"Ok Rocco. Thanks for the update. Just make sure someone fixes my camera and we review my security options. I can't have my girl in the line of fire when it comes to these issues, got it?"

"For sure boss, will do. And if I may, it sounds nice to hear you worry about a lady friend. About damn time," he jokes.

"Eat your stupid turkey and fix my system Rocco." I laugh. "Wish your wife a Happy Thanksgiving for me even though I know she's probably cursing me six ways till Sunday."

We spent Thanksgiving dinner eating side by side and chatting into Amelia's phone that was propped up against a flower vase. We were able to get everyone on video chat so we could all cheers and give an update on how we're all doing. Once the doctors got added to the call, all hell broke loose.

Amelia was mortified at the sight of her father in a bright pink Speedo. Apparently, everyone in Punta Cana got drunk, and began daring each other to do embarrassing things. Possibly because I upgraded them all to the multiroom Presidential Suite that comes with an unlimited drink package, but Amelia doesn't need to know that right now.

The wives all wore those hideous oversized t-shirts with sexy bikini bodies airbrushed over them, Dr. Ricardo Ortega danced during the poolside aerobics class and Dr. Manuel Astacio, the hairiest man on the planet, shaved his chest. All things none of us should have borne witness to.

After we cut them off the call to sober up, we chatted up the cousin crew who were all pleasantly surprised that Amelia and I had made up after our infamous pub fight and were able to coexist alone in the same house. Antonio's facial expressions let me know he still wasn't happy about the set up, but I asked him to join me for a few rounds of online gaming tomorrow, and that seemed to do the trick for now.

We say our goodbyes and as soon as I press that red *end call* button, Amelia is on my lap showering me with kisses, arms draped around my neck.

"God, that call took forever!" she complains.

Never in my wildest dreams would I imagine myself to be so lucky as to have Amelia jumping into my arms and being affectionate. It's barely been twelve hours since we made our little arrangement, but it is painfully clear that I belong to her.

Always have, always will.

Guilt consumes me as I think about a future with Amelia, when she has no clue about the secrets I keep. I don't deserve her, but for the time being I'll lie to myself and say I'm just going along with her deal, because I'm a selfish bastard.

"Ohhh is this what you mean when you say you can see the wheels turning in my head? I totally get it now" she says, pulling me from my thoughts.

"Sorry about that." I lean in and give her a soft peck on the lips.

"What were you thinking about? Is everything okay with the security system? I saw Rocco calling you earlier."

"Slight glitch in the system, but all good. He'll be up here as soon as he can to double check everything, no need to worry." I kiss her cheek.

"Oh, so it wasn't Michael Myers's knife glistening in the distance?" She jokes.

"Afraid not, the only man you need to worry about chasing after you is me." I grin.

"Really?" she says as she plays with the top button of my Henley shirt. "So, what's the reason for this?" She taps at the deep set wrinkle between my brows.

I let out a breath. "Just thinking about how I don't deserve you, that's all." I shrug. At least it's a half truth.

"Woah, where did that come from?" She leans back to study me.

"Sorry, just got a lot going on in my head, not trying to kill the holiday mood."

"Hmm. Self-sabotage. Another toxic trait I'm far too acquainted with myself." She nods and looks at me as though she's analyzing me.

Suddenly, mischief is written all over her face. "You know. You never asked me what I'm thankful for this Thanksgiving." She pouts.

I'll bite. "Alright then, what are you thankful for this year, Amelia?"

She smiles, "Well as you know, I've had a shit year. But even so, I'm thankful for my dad and brother, even though they drive me insane for different reasons—"

"Pink Speedo?" I Interrupt.

"Never speak of the pink Speedo again! I'll have to double my therapist's hourly rate!" She laughs. "I'm thankful for Nikki, the cousin crew, this crazy storm called Anna, and ..."

"And ..." I smirk.

She starts shifting her weight off of me, and I think she's going to straddle me again, but just ends up hovering over me, causing me to lean on the back legs of my chair. "And I'm thankful to be spending the weekend with my first crush, who if I'm not mistaken, promised to be the only man I should be worried about chasing after me ..."

She shoots up and gives my chair a hard nudge, sending me flying back towards the ground while I hear her laughing maniacally, running towards the living room.

She's going to pay for this.

I'm on my feet immediately, wondering how she got the jump on me. Clearly, I need to watch myself more carefully around Amelia. I never know what to expect from her.

As soon as she sees me darting towards the living room she lets out a yelp and books it to the hallway leading to our bedrooms. Now she's in danger.

I quickly make up the distance between us just as she's about to dart into her room. I'm able to hook an arm around her middle, and haul her into my bedroom as she has trouble catching her breath due to her incessant laughter.

"Put me down! It was a complete accident, I swear!" She kicks the air as she struggles to get loose from my tight hold on her.

"Sorry sweetheart, you're in the lion's den now," I whisper into her ear.

And with that, she stops struggling.

27

AMELIA

I'M STILL CATCHING MY BREATH AS I TAKE INVENTORY of the situation.

I'm in Evan's bedroom

He has me pinned to his body.

We've been teasing each other all day, to the point where I'm glad you can't see lady boners.

It's finally happening.

"It's not happening, Amelia. So you can relax," Evan says as he gently places me on the ground.

"Umm, what are you talking about?" I say as I right all my clothing.

"I know how your mind works. Next you were probably going to offer me a sex pact. I have to draw the line somewhere." He places his hands on his hips, making him look like a sexually frustrated Superman.

I hesitate, then start making my way deeper into the room. I sit on the edge of the bed, facing Evan. "Ok then. If you know what I'm going to offer, why don't you go ahead and have the whole conversation for me. What's your rebuttal? Some kind of moral high ground? Feels like you're taking advantage of me? Blah blah

blah." I wave the words away. "Why can't we just have sex like two consenting adults?" I ask as I cross my arms in front of my chest like a petulant child.

Evan walks towards me with an unreadable face. He cradles my cheeks in his hands and tilts his head close to me. After a long pause, he says, "Because I'm in love with you, Amelia."

My breath hitches in my throat and my eyes go wide.

IN LOVE WITH ME?!

Not just the ominous *has feelings for me*, but actual naming said feelings as LOVE?

His words crash into me and I replay every interaction I've ever had with Evan in an instant. From the holiday parties with family, to our fight in the pub. The stolen glances we've shared to our unforgettable night in Miami.

All this time. It's always been Evan.

But. It's still too soon.

He continues, saving me from having to use my words. "You don't have to say anything back. Actually, I forbid you to."

Well, that gets me going.

"*Forbid*?" My eyebrows shoot up.

"Yes. While we're in this little weekend arrangement, I don't want you saying anything that can be misconstrued. Don't want you to say anything in the heat of the moment, then regret it when we're back in the city."

I stand up, moving his hands from my face to my waist. "I don't regret anything I've said or done here, Evan. And I won't." I rest my hands on the back of his neck, pulling him in for a soft kiss.

Evan rests his forehead on mine, his will visibly slipping by the length I feel growing between his legs. "Amelia, we can't."

I know I may need more time to heal. Have more of a grace period before my very loud and very opinionated Dominican family are given free rein to comment on my relationship with Evan.

But I'm also not a dumb bitch.

C'mon. I've seen this hang up dozens of times in rom coms. This is the part where everyone yells at the girl for not realizing what's right in front of her.

I get it.

I might be terrified to fall in love again. And I very well know that I may not survive Evan. But I also know that I would regret it for the rest of my life if I didn't give this a chance. Give us a chance. So, in true Amelia form, I'm willing to negotiate.

"Evan we are going to have sex. And I am going to tell you why," I say matter-of-factly.

Evan's hold on my waist tightens. "Amelia, I'm not making another deal—"

"It's you," I declare.

"What?"

"I know I'm not ready to jump into a relationship right now..."

Evan's shoulders slump and he drops his gaze to the floor. I hold my hands on his cheeks and lift them up, so he's looking at me when I make my confession.

"But when I'm ready, it's you. If you're willing to wait a while until I'm ready, you're the person I want to be with, have dreamt of—"

Before the words can fully leave my lips, my back is crashing against the mattress and Evan's body is pinning me to the bed.

"Say it again," he growls.

"It's you, Evan. It's always been you," I say breathlessly.

He presses a hard and all-consuming kiss on my lips. Stealing any bit of air that I apparently don't need, because I have his lips.

As soon as he rolls his hips into me my brain goes into overdrive.

I'M ABOUT TO HAVE SEX WITH EVAN FUCKING COOPER.

I reach around to pull his shirt over his head when he breaks our kiss.

"Ok Amelia. Time for my ground rules," he says with a panty dropping smile.

"Wait, you're negotiating with me?!" I point at myself. "At a time like this?!" I point to his bulge.

"Take it or leave it." He runs his fingers over my collarbone and I'm almost a goner.

"Take it, take it!" I say pleadingly.

Real smooth Amelia.

Evan grows serious and gently grabs me by the back of my neck.

"Rule number one. Within these cabin walls, you are mine. You belong to me."

Oh God.

I nod slowly, absorbing his words.

"Rule number two. I am yours, and I belong to you."

"Within these cabin walls?" I try to finish from his previous rule.

"No. Everywhere Amelia. I love you, so that means that I am yours, and I belong to you. When we have sex, I will be making love to you. Understood?"

I nod again weakly. What in the sex Gods have I gotten myself into?

"Ok then, ground rules established," he says as he starts to lean into me for what I assume is the sex initiation kiss, so I interrupt him.

"Rule number three!" I yell.

Evan raises an amused brow, as if he knew I just had to get the final word in.

"Yes, love?" he whispers against my lips.

Squeal.

"Um. Uh. No blindfolding or tying me up. Okay mister?" I pitifully narrowed my eyes at him.

Evan releases a deep laugh. "You run a hard bargain Amelia, but I think I can agree to your terms." He humors me.

"Sorry, it just seems appropriate to have three ground rules. Easier to remember, ya know? They say good things come in thre—"

"Amelia, I need you to shut up so I can fuck you now," he says brushing his lips lightly like feathers against mine.

"Oh. Wow. Ok, proceed," I relent.

Evan smiles as he kisses me. "My Amelia."

The last words on his lips before he makes good on his promise and makes love to me.

Ok and he also fucked me.

There was a clear distinction between the two, and we alternated between love making and soul crushing sex.

I'm waking up in his arms with the overwhelming feeling of satisfaction ... and soreness. Such a simple price to pay for five mind blowing orgasms.

"Good morning, you sexual deviant," he moans into my hair.

I laugh and roll over to face Evan.

That's right, I'm not too shabby between the sheets either. After orgasm number two, I decided it was time for me to show Evan that *Little Miss Amelia* wasn't so innocent after all.

"Good morning Mr. Cooper. How are we feeling this morning?" I smile bashfully.

"Duped. Bamboozled. Hoodwinked. You name it. You could have warned a guy that he was about to have the best sex of his life. Multiple times in one night! You totally stole my thunder there for a bit. Thank God I have a huge cock." He smirks as he pulls me close to him and kisses my forehead.

"Amen." I sigh, and we both fall into a fit of laughter.

I head into the kitchen after bickering with Evan about not having shower sex. Apart from the fact that my ladybits desperately need a break, I also was not in the mood to have my blowout turn into a frizzy mess. Lessons to learn about dating a Latina with naturally curly hair.

After my solo shower, I find myself smiling like a fool making coffee and putting some frozen pastries in the oven.

Evan comes into view and my smile turns up even higher. He saunters into the kitchen still wet from his shower, with his towel riding low around his waist. "Come here often?" He winks.

"Five times last night, but who's counting." I stand on my tip toes as he pulls me in for a kiss.

"God Amelia. We're such idiots. We could have been doing this for years." He sighs into the crook of my neck.

"I somehow have a feeling we'll be just fine making up for lost time." I scrape my fingers along his scruff.

"Ugh I don't want to game with Antonio now. I want to get back in that bed with you and not come back up for air. I'll tell him you poisoned me last night. Kind of true since you seem to have put some kind of spell on me." He grins.

"No. We can't let Antonio get suspicious. If you thought he was bad before, he's worse since mom died. He's now overprotective big bro and super strict Dominican Mom all rolled into one package. Go spend some quality bestie time with him. Besides, I'm pretty sure I'm going to need the day to recover from last night."

Evan rolls his eyes as he makes his way towards the freezer. He digs around for a minute until he's found what he's looking for. "Here you go," he says as he hands me a bag of frozen peas.

"Why are you giving me peas at nine AM?" I lift a quizzical brow.

"It's not for you, it's for her." His eyes drop to my nether regions with a grin. "Ice my baby up. You have the morning to recover before I go full caveman again. See you in a few hours." He plants a quick kiss on my lips and starts running backwards, as if he doesn't trust me to not chuck the frozen bag at him.

He shouldn't.

I almost roll my eyes out of my head while I laugh by myself.

I pull the pastries out of the oven and head towards the breakfast nook. Then grab my phone to call Nikki. I haven't updated her on anything since I've been up here, and I'm sure I will have my best friend card revoked if I wait any minute longer.

Nikki's face pops up on my screen on the second ring. "Ahhhhh Amelia! How are you? How is it up there at Evan's luxury cabin," she sings. Of course, the little sneak knew and kept this information from me. Typical Nikki.

She's standing by herself in an old building. She must be bored out of her mind in middle-of-nowhere Florida.

"Well, I have this." I lift the frozen peas next to my face.

Confusion riddled all over Nikki's face. "Um, I thought that Evan would have some fancy catering, not frozen peas."

"They're not for eating Nikki." I bite my lower lip to try to stretch out this moment for as long as possible, but I'm failing miserably. "They're meant for my vagina. I'm trying to ice her back to health after the pounding Evan gave her last night."

Nikki goes wide eyed and silent. After a few moments I hear another woman's voice. "Nikki, do you mind taking that call outside. We'll continue the tour of the church while you're out there, dear."

I slap a hand over my mouth and my eyes bulge out of my face. I give Nikki a look that should translate "Why didn't you warn me you were around people" but all I can see is her speed walking until she opens a door and is out in the sunshine.

"Oh my fucking God Amelia!!! I'm not even going to touch on the fact that Justin's mom was standing right in front of me as she gave us a tour of the church her and Justin's dad got married at, that's been under renovations. We're going to go ahead and jump to the part where you and Evan had sex?!" she screeches.

"Yup." I nod like a goof.

"Ok. Start from the beginning and don't you dare skip any details. This church parking lot is about to hear a lot of unholy chatter. Go!"

I spend the next hour having breakfast with Nikki on the phone, going over the last two days. She cried when I told her Evan said he loved me. And that is just one of the many reasons I love Nikki. She puts up a hard shell sometimes, but is pure mush for the lucky few she loves.

"Ok Amelia, but you guys have to cut the crap with the fake/trial dating bullshit. You are full blown dating now. I'm sure it's probably great for a weekend sexcapade, and must make things feel a bit more naughty, but you're not gonna pull that crap once you're back in the city. I won't let you," she scolds.

"Easy there, tiger. I know things have changed, but I can't go from being engaged three months ago, to dating a man my entire family knows. Plus, even if my family weren't *chisme* piranhas, Evan also comes with his own slew of complications. The man's photo is on Page Six whenever he walks within six feet of another woman." I groan.

Nikki grows serious. "Amelia. He said he loved you. This isn't something that family gossip or tabloids are going to detour. You might be the last one to figure it out, but you and Evan are going to be together after this."

"She's right," Evan says from behind me, sending me jumping six inches off the chair. "Hi Nikki, hope you had a good Thanksgiving," he says while leaning down and planting a sensual kiss on me.

Sweet baby jesus.

"Easy there, mom and dad. Leave some steam for the rest of us mere mortals. Oh and by the way, Evan. Amelia mentioned something about you sending me a fruit basket? But you see, I'm not an elderly lady who knits so that fruit basket better be a massage gift card, or booze, or—"

"One week vacation. Any place in the world. You name it. All expenses paid. For you and Justin. How's that sound?" He smiles.

Nikki and I drop our jaws in unison.

Nikki has a coughing attack, but quickly recovers. "Okay, yeah.

That will do. Thank you very much, Evan. I will be available for engagement ring shopping whenever you need me."

"Nikki!" I yell.

"Thanks Nikki. I'll keep you posted." He winks at me.

"Ok lovebirds. I gotta go and google bougie vacation spots. Bye!" Nikki hangs up.

"Really Evan. A week-long vacation anywhere in the world?" I ask as I stand to hug him.

He smiles. "She was able to get you up to this cabin. Even if it was by omitting important details. I will forever be indebted to Nikki, because I now get to do this." He lifts my chin and places a gentle kiss on my lips.

"Well, I'm pretty sure you can do much more than that now." I lift the bag of half melted peas. "I'm sure it did the trick." I wink.

Without hesitation Evan throws me over his shoulders and starts jogging us back to his bedroom as I giggle like a little school girl.

I make a mental note to invest in some industrial grade ice packs from now on.

28

EVAN

WE SPEND THE NEXT TWO DAYS IN BED. WE ONLY GET UP to make food and shower. We have earth shattering sex and watch girly rom coms. I'm living in such bliss and contemplate locking us in this cabin forever.

Our mornings have consisted of me walking in on Amelia making us coffee while having a full dance party to the likes of Taylor Swift, Bad Bunny, and Juan Luis Guerra. Her taste in music is as eclectic as her cultural influences.

The snowstorm weakened yesterday, and by today the roads are clear and safe to drive on again.

While Amelia napped, I met with Rocco and he went over my security system. All seems to be functioning fine. Rocco and his team will be working on searching nearby surveillance cameras just to be safe.

Once Amelia is done packing, it's time to head back into the city. As much as I'm dreading it, I know that things will move in the right direction with us. I will make sure of it. I will gladly respect her wishes and give her time to process how we will move forward with telling her family.

We've temporarily agreed to wait until after the holidays before we're seen out in public together. I need to man up and have a chat with Antonio, but Amelia wants me to wait until after Christmas. Once it's the new year, we won't be expected to hang out as often with the cousin crew and doctors, so it will give us time to date away from the nosey Tías.

"I'm all packed babe," Amelia says from the front door.

Babe. My heart swells.

"Great. Our car will be here shortly and taking us to the airport."

"Wait, airport? Isn't Teddy picking us up?"

"Nope. My baby gets to ride on the jet today." I lean down and kiss her on the nose.

She rolls her eyes. "Okay big shot. Let's hope your plane is as big as your... other assets. I hate small planes and I will make you pay if there's turbulence." She points her index finger at me.

I grin like a mad man.

God, this woman has me by the balls. And I wouldn't have it any other way.

29

AMELIA

Evan's jet is huge, just like him.

I'm back in my apartment unpacking while smiling at how my life has taken a turn for the unimaginable.

Trial dating has turned into undercover real dating, while we try to take things slow.

Ha. Slow. Trial dating lasted all of two minutes before I became a stage five clinger.

Way to hold out Amelia.

But I can't complain. I am so enamored by Evan, and I'm glad he's willing to give me time to figure myself out before we go public.

We plan on having secret dinners at his apartment while we're staying under the radar. Work is going to be busy this week for the both of us, so we're playing it by ear. I also have my company holiday party that I'm dreading going to this Friday. I hope I don't run into Christine, but it's probably inevitable.

My doorbell rings.

I smile. That's probably Evan coming back for another goodbye kiss. I practically had to pry him off of me when he walked me up to my apartment.

I open the door and look down to see a vase with a dozen red roses. I instantly smile.

I pick it up, close my door and bring it to my kitchen. I pull out the note.

Amelia

Love is a beautiful thing.

Sorry if I scared you, the best is yet to come...

Very soon.

Huh. That's weird.

I text Nikki to meet me in my apartment. She got back from Florida last night.

Ten minutes later she's banging down my door.

"Oh hey there sex kitten!" she croons as she pulls me in for a hug.

"Nice to see you too. Looks like you didn't get murdered by a Florida man. So I'm guessing it was a good getaway?" I ask.

"For the love of God Amelia, lay off the Dateline." Nikki laughs. "It was actually an interesting trip."

"Interesting?" I pull out two wine glasses and a cold bottle of Sauvignon Blanc.

"Yeah." She sighs. "At first I thought the family was giving me a tour of their town because they're super sentimental. But it turns out Justin's dad wants to hand over the family business to him."

"Oh wow. That's amazing." I pause when Nikki doesn't react. "Or not. Do we hate this idea? I'm not following."

"The family business is a farm in the middle of nowhere, Amelia." She picks up the bottle of wine and pours us a generous amount. "And the kicker is that Justin wants to take him up on his offer, and wants me to move down there with him. To the farm." She tips her head back and clears half of her glass in one swoop.

Yikes. Trouble in paradise. I'll have to table my weird flowers conversation for a later time.

We spend the rest of the day going over pros and cons of what Justin's decision might mean for Nikki, but it's all in vain. I don't want her to leave New York any more than she wants to. We discuss long distance, remote work and keep coming up short, but unwilling to put into words what we may believe may happen.

"Amelia, this is so weird. I feel like I'm standing on the edge of my life. Like this decision that I make might be the big one that I either regret for the rest of my life, or thank my lucky stars for making. I love Justin. I really do. But is love really enough? Will I really turn into one of those women who has a small town romance and ends up loving small town living, wears cut off shorts and cowboy boots?"

I slowly take the empty wine bottle from her death grip and put it on the coffee table.

We stare at each other for a few beats, then burst out laughing.

"Look. The way I see it, Justin still hasn't made his decision. Give him some time to think about it before you make any rash decisions. Just like you have to think about the possibility of moving out of state for love, Justin needs to think about the possibility of staying for love. Only fair in my eyes." I take a sip of my wine only to see that my glass is also empty.

We both erupt with laughter again. We are clearly the blind leading the blind.

"Want to order pizza and talk about how Evan Cooper has ruined every other man for me for as long as I live?"

"Do you even have to ask?"

And that is why no matter what happens with Evan, Nikki will always be my soulmate.

❧

It's Friday evening and I am dragging myself to get ready for my company holiday party. I would usually jump at the idea of an open bar and an excuse to dress up, but for obvious reasons I know tonight is going to be a shit show.

I've been able to avoid Christine like the plague ever since I caught her riding Sebastián into oblivion. I used vacation days for the days I knew we would be at the same in-person meetings, and have picked meeting rooms on floors that belong to different departments. I know I have nothing to be ashamed of, and if anything, *she* should be the one trying to avoid *me*. But I never want to give her the satisfaction of seeing me off my game. Or catch me on a bad day when my emotions may be running high.

Tonight is the night that we are all forced to mingle and play nice. I could have easily feigned illness, but Marcos Mirabal will be there tonight, and he is the lead partner on the Miami account I am trying to get on. I'm hoping that if I get on his good side, it will make the possibility of landing the account much easier, and therefore securing my transfer to Miami. Being a Latina woman in corporate America is tough, but it's even tougher when I feel like I'm sometimes only brought onto projects to fill up some 'diversity' quota. New York is obviously one of the most culturally diverse places on the planet, but the Wall Street mentality still bleeds into my finance world, meaning it's usually the older white guy leading all the important accounts.

In Miami, I remember interning at a company where the Partner ordered Cuban 'cortadito' coffees for all staff meetings, along with an eclectic variety of Hispanic baked goods. Everyone would greet each other with a "Buenos Dias" and cheek kisses. If I ever said "Good Morning" to someone on the elevator here in New York, I would be ignored or looked at as if I'd grown an extra head. And the cheek kiss would guarantee an HR nightmare.

I'm still trying to figure out if Miami will be the solution to my cultural identity crisis. You know, the one where I constantly feel like I'm not Latina enough, because I was born in the states instead of the island. While also not being gringa enough because one look at me, and you can see the lineage of my ancestors in my eyes, hair and hips.

I've gone through this plan a million times in my head, but tonight a flash of guilt shoots right through me.

What about Evan?

I had this plan in motion well before my mother got sick. I put it off after we got her diagnosis, and while in the depths of my grief, started the process up again after her death. When Sebastián and I got back together, it was off again, only to be promptly started back up a few months ago when we broke up again. I know I need to stick to the plan and stop having my relationships interfere with my career goals.

Plus, Evan literally has a jet. The man can fly down to see me whenever he pleases.

Although I have yet to see him this week. Since dropping me off at my apartment, we have both been busy with sixteen hour days. I was supposed to have dinner at his apartment last night, but fell asleep in my towel, sitting on my bed after my shower.

Evan is working at least until midnight tonight since he does business with people around the world. Meaning his nine to five is really a twenty four seven. We have promised to make Saturday work. I will meet him at his apartment in the morning and we will spend a full day and night wrapped in each other's arms.

It's insane how badly I miss him. I didn't know you could actually ache for a person. Physically ache! I never had that with anyone before, and it's blowing my mind. Thank God he video calls me about ten times a day. I'm pretty sure he does it in front of his board members too which is quite cringe, but I take whatever I can get.

I give myself one final glance in the mirror. Typical corporate holiday party attire, red cocktail dress that hits me right below the knee. It was supposed to look a bit more conservative, but I got my period earlier in the week and my boobs look like they're about to pop out of the v neckline and my hips are stretching the material a bit more than I would like, but there's no turning back now. I put on my trusty old black pumps, the ones I know won't give me blisters by the end of the night, and make my way to my front door. I grab my wool peacoat and purse and take a deep breath.

Let's get this shit over with.

30

EVAN

One more night, and I'll be reunited with Amelia.

I repeat this thought in my head numerous times while sitting through my torturous meetings today.

Sometimes I consider what would happen if I stepped down. Walked away from it all. No more CEO, just founder and silent partner. I think of the freedoms that it could provide Amelia and me. I clearly have more money that I could ever spend, but it has never been about the money for me.

I know exactly why I'm here, sitting in a conference room on a Friday night. It's because I need to prove to everyone that I belong here. That I've earned this seat at the table. I need to make sure everyone knows that I didn't cheat my way up to the top.

Because I did.

In reality, I just stay because I'm trying to convince myself. No one here knows my secret and I have no intention of ever telling anyone. Except Amelia.

I dread the thought, but I know that in order for us to move forward, I need her to know exactly who the man she is spending her life with is. I just can't bring myself to tell her any time soon.

Maybe I'll tell her after the holidays if I can grow massive *cojones* by then.

My phone buzzes on my conference table.

I glance down and see a text message from an unsaved number. I grab my phone and open the text from under the table.

Nikki: Hi Evan, this is Nikki. Amelia's friend. I swiped your number from her phone the other night when we were drinking in case I ever needed it for emergencies.

My blood turns cold. Amelia has an emergency?! Before I can react to what I've just read, she texts me again.

Nikki: Amelia is fine!!! Sorry, I just realized that sounded bad. Just wanted to give you a heads up on something!

I sigh deeply. Jesus Christ I'm going to have to have a conversation with Nikki about appropriate text lingo. I reply.

Evan: Hi Nikki. Thanks for saving my number. What's going on?

She instantly replies back.

Nikki: Oh thank God you answered. So ... don't judge me, but I have a finsta account. You know, "fake Instagram" account that I use to stalk certain people. Anyways, Amelia is out at her company holiday party, so I looked at Christine's stories.

She's rambling. No wonder she's Amelia's friend. I reply, annoyed that she's taking me down the rabbit hole with her.

Evan: Christine? I'm in a meeting Nikki, can you get to the point? :)

I added the smiley face so that I don't get accused of being an asshole to Amelia's friend.

Nikki: Ahh yes sorry. Super busy rich man haha. Anyways, Christine is the skank who was sleeping with *He Who Shall Not Be Named.* She is also her coworker and will be at this party. Ten minutes ago she posted a photo of her holding hands with a guy with the caption "date night." The guy was wearing a watch that I helped Amelia buy a few Christmases ago. It's him! Skank and Ex-fiancé douchebag are going to the holiday party and are totally going to ambush our poor little Amelia! I was supposed to go with her but I've been puking all day due to bad sushi. Sorry if that's TMI. Anyways, I've been trying to call her and give her a heads up, but haven't been able to reach her. The woman is incapable of letting her phone battery charge above 10%!

Fuck. I can see it now. Amelia face to face with Sebastián. She told me she hasn't seen him since the breakup, but he's tried reaching out to her.

A work event isn't the appropriate time for them to meet. Actually, if I had it my way, he would never lay eyes on her again.

My Amelia.

Without hesitation I text Nikki back.

Evan: Over my dead body. I'm getting our girl out of there. Text me the location.

I stand, and my chair makes a loud noise as it scrapes across the floor. "My apologies everyone, it seems I have a family emergency I need to tend to." I stand and button my suit jacket. "Hayden, please have the meeting minutes emailed to me once the meeting is over. Text Teddy now and let him know to pull the car around, please." I nod to my assistant.

I walk out of the conference room, and smirk once I read the last text I received from Nikki.

Nikki: Evan fucking Cooper. Our hero. Give him Hell!

Oh yes, I will.

31

AMELIA

I'm standing by the bar in the massive ballroom where the holiday party is being hosted. I'm tempted to take advantage of the open bar, but I can't. I need to have this chat with Marcos Mirabal, then I can dive into my Trader Joe's wine at home.

I scan the room looking for him, but there are too many bodies in here. Clearly free food and booze got everyone in the holiday spirit tonight.

I'm actually thankful that there are so many people here. That makes the chances of running into Christine little to none.

But just as if I have summoned her with my thoughts, I hear a woman clearing her throat. "Ahem, hi there Amelia. Haven't seen you in forever."

I slowly turn, and am brought face to face with Christine. The woman who slept with my fiancé, all while pretending to be my work friend. The audacity of her to even speak to me as if she didn't play a part in my world crashing down.

"Christine. Nice to see you ... clothed," I snark.

Atta girl. Keep your shoulders back and chin up. This *puta* has nothing on you. Hold your ground.

"Oh, I see we're making jokes now. See, I told Sebastián that we would all look back at this one day and laugh. It's all really silly when you think about it." She bats her eyelashes.

Wait, what? They're still together? What the fuck.

It never really occurred to me what happened after I caught them together. I guess I just assumed that it was no longer fun for them to fuck when they weren't sneaking around behind my back.

Before I can come up with another snarky remark, a familiar scent consumes me and the hairs at the back of my neck lift in dread.

"Amelia?"

It's him.

He's here.

My body is unable to respond. In a time of fight or flight, I just freeze. My legs feel weighted to the ground by boulders and I forget to breathe.

A few moments pass and then finally, Sebastián makes his way next to Christine, and they both stand in front of me. My eyes locked with his.

I know for a fact that I don't belong to Sebastián, and that we would never have made it in the long run. But seeing him for the first time is causing a pain in my heart that I didn't know still existed. The sensation alone is sending me into a tailspin.

After an uncomfortable amount of time, Sebastián breaks his eye contact and stares at Christine in contempt. "You said Amelia wouldn't be here. You promised," he spits. I've never seen this side of Sebastián before, but I guess there's been a lot I've never seen.

"Oh, my bad. I just assumed that since I never saw her at the office, she must have quit or something, honest mistake," she says innocently as she grabs his hand.

He pulls his hand out of hers as if it's burned him, and her eyes grow angry.

His focus turns back to me.

"Amelia, I'm so sorry. I wouldn't have come if I knew you were here. I've been trying to reach out and talk to you. But this obviously isn't the right time or place. Can we grab lunch together or something? Does tomorrow work for you?" He holds his hands out and slowly starts to move forward as if he's testing the waters for a hug.

This whole time I've been quiet and in a haze, but I know I need to say something. I need to stop him from moving forward and touching me.

This bastard does not deserve a fucking hug from me.

I open my mouth to respond, but then all of a sudden, I feel a large hand holding the back of my neck possessively. Before I can react to the invasion, I feel a warm breath on my ear as I hear a husky, familiar voice. "Hey there, baby."

Evan pulls me sideways and arches my neck up to him, giving me a very hard and passionate kiss.

Woah.

For the second time tonight, I am frozen in place. What the fuck is happening to me?!

Evan speaks first when we separate. "Sorry for taking so long, the bathroom line took forever." He winks at me, then leans back down to whisper in my ear. "Wake the fuck up baby, don't let him see you sweat."

Oh my God. This man!

I smile widely and pull him back in for a soft peck.

"Excuse me, Amelia! What is this?" Sebastián exclaims.

"Oh my apologies, I didn't realize you had company, love," Evan croons.

"Love?!" Sebastián snarls while staring at me.

"Yes, love. Boyfriend, love of her life, orgasm dispenser, you name it, that's me." Evan grins widely.

I hear an audible gasp from Christine and can't help smiling like a fool. Evan reaches his hand out to Sebastián. "Hi I'm—"

"Evan Cooper! What a surprise to see you here," says a tall Latino man making his way into our circle.

"Hello, have we met?" Evan says as he looks at me for backup. I would have been able to respond quicker if my brain wasn't total mush at the moment.

The tall gentleman laughs. "No, I have not had the pleasure. My name is Marcos Mirabal, and the company I have been working with has been hounding yours for a meeting for the last six months.

Holy crap, Marcos Mirabal!

Evan and Marcos shake hands, then look at the rest of us.

Completely ignoring the shit show that is Christine and Sebastián, I reach my hand out to Marcos. "Hello, my name is Amelia Nuñez. I'm a senior account manager here and I've been looking forward to seeing you tonight and talking about the new Miami account you're leading."

"Wow, all business and to the point. I like it." Marcos smiles.

Evan pulls me closer to him. "That's my girlfriend, nothing keeps her down." He throws a telling look over to Sebastián, whose head looks like it's about to explode.

"Girlfriend you say?" Marcos wiggles his eyebrows. "That's quite impressive, Amelia. I'm going to have to hear the story of how you snagged the CEO and Founder of PassportMed."

"That's where I know you from! I've seen your photos online!" Christine yells, only to realize that she probably should have kept those thoughts to herself.

Marcos completely ignores her and focuses back on us.

"Well actually Marcos, I've been pining for this woman for almost a decade. I'm just the lucky bastard who finally wore her down." He winks down at me. "And she's also the boss of me, so if you ever need to get to me or my company, I suggest you keep her close by." He raises a knowing brow.

Marcos laughs in agreement and shakes our hands again. "Lovely to meet you both. Amelia, my office and I will be in contact with you. Enjoy the rest of your evening, it's been a pleasure." With one final wave, Marcos disappears into the crowd.

"Wait a minute. Evan Cooper? You're Antonio's friend," Sebastián says as relief seems to wash over him. "I see what this is." He points back and forth between Evan and me.

"And what exactly is it that you see?" Evan drops a kiss on top of my head.

"I get it. You're doing your friend a favor by being Amelia's date. You see me and up the production value. Kudos. A little overkill and unnecessary if you ask me. I know Amelia would never move on so fast from a serious relationship. That's not her style." He takes a sip of his drink, clearly pleased with himself.

I roll my eyes and finally get ready to let Sebastián have it, when Evan beats me to it. "Well, it seems as though you don't know Amelia very well." Evan gives me a mischievous smile. "I happen to know her very intimately. So intimately, I get to enjoy that small heart shaped birthmark on her left breast every night."

OH FUCK ME.

Sebastián turns beet red. There's no way for Evan to know about that birthmark if he hasn't seen me naked, and Sebastián gets the message loud and clear.

"Amelia! A word. Now," Sebastián hisses.

Evan hugs me from behind. His right arm possessively wrapped over my stomach and the left up around my shoulders. He leans into my left ear. "Your call, boss."

I love that even in this pissing match, Evan is able to put his ego aside and give me the space to check in and allow me to figure out how I want to approach this situation. His stance allows me to face Sebastián head on, while also leaning me onto him, letting me know that he literally has my back.

Feeling his heartbeat vibrate through me helps regulate my breath, and brings in a sense of peace I've been missing since I last saw him Sunday.

This is my man.

"Sorry Sebastián, but as you can see, I'm good right where I am." I smile smugly.

This infuriates Sebastián, and I'm not gonna lie, I'm enjoying this now. "Amelia, we have unfinished business. We have things to talk about," he practically spits out.

I feel Evan stiffen behind me, so I put my arm over his right that is holding my center, and brush his hand reassuringly.

"Okay then. Talk. I have no interest in ever being alone with you again," I say with a little more heat. Time to remind this man that I nearly took away his chances of having kids when I kneed him in the balls.

"Amelia, look. I know I don't have a leg to stand on, but we need to discuss things. Like the wedding vendors. I wanted you to know that I paid them off, so you don't have to worry about that anymore." He lifts his hands as if to say *I come in peace*. "And there are other things that have been happening since we last saw each other." He momentarily looks at Christine who's too busy ogling Evan.

I fucking dare you bitch.

"At the very least Amelia, we need closure for God's sake. We can meet tomorrow or next weekend if that works for—"

"Closure?" I laugh. The nerve of this man. "I don't think a man who imploded his engagement by being balls deep in another woman has the right to request *closure*," I say that last word with air quotes.

"She's got a point there," Evan mutters.

I continue. "The very least you could do is pay for the wedding that you clearly had no intention of honoring with your philandering ways." I huff. "And just so we're crystal clear, I have no need to ever see or speak to you again. So don't call, don't text or send me weird flowers. You can assume this conversation is the last conversation we'll ever have. So, you and your closure can go fuck yourselves." I force a fake smile.

Sebastián's mouth is wide open and looking at me as if I'm currently experiencing an exorcism.

"So, what do you want for dinner, babe?" Evan chuckles behind me.

I turned to him. "I'm in the mood for some ramen and lychee martins."

"Perfect, I know just the place." He grabs both of my cheeks in his hands and plants a soft kiss on my lips, and lingers there for a moment, before finally standing to his full height. "Sebastián, Christine. It has not been a pleasure. You're actually absolute shit people, and I hope to never make your acquaintance again. Especially you." He nods to Sebastián.

With that, he takes my hand, and we head out of the party, grinning ear to ear. I have a feeling I'm going to have a lot more than a bowl of noodles in my mouth by the end of tonight.

"Oh God, Evan, this tastes amazing!" I say as I take another bite of my pork buns. We've agreed to not be seen alone in public until after the holidays, but there is no scenario in which I turn down food.

We're at Momofuku, sitting on the counter stools that face the bustling kitchen. Evan asked the chef for a tasting menu, and I'm sure I'm going to pop out of this dress any second now. I'm on my second lychee martini, but I think my buzz is all because of Evan.

"I can't believe Nikki texted you. God I love her." I chuckle into my drink.

"Yeah, at this rate, I should just give her a credit card and let her use it every time she comes through for you." Evan smirks.

I put my drink down and hold his hand on the counter. "I missed you so much, Evan." I dreamily sigh.

He offers me a small smile, then brings my hand up to his lips, laying a soft kiss on my knuckles. "Amelia, you have no idea how incredible it is for me to hear those words come out of your mouth. I've dreamed of moments like this." He leans in and kisses my lips.

Swoon.

"So, I know that I was supposed to come over tomorrow, but since we're already together, I was thinking—"

"Baby, if you think you're going anywhere besides my bed tonight, you need to get your head checked." He chuckles into his drink.

I playfully roll my eyes, then lean in to kiss his neck. God Evan has so many kissable places, and I can't wait to get back to his place.

We continue to work our way through the delectable dishes, to the point where I think Evan's going to have to roll me out of this place if I don't stop.

Then Evan's phone rings on the counter between us. The letters **LC** pop up on the screen.

Evan stiffens and grabs the phone instantly. "Sorry, I have to take this, be back in a minute." He takes off before I can even respond.

That's odd. Evan took countless calls in front of me when we were at the cabin, and never seemed this rattled.

Within thirty seconds he's back. What kind of phone call ends that quickly?

"Hey babe, so bad news. Something came up at work. An emergency, and I'm going to have to take off," he says.

My shoulders slump and unease begins to build in my stomach. "Oh okay. Is everything alright?"

"Nothing to worry about," he says as he looks over his shoulder. "But I've got to get going, so I'll pay the bill and leave you with Teddy, he can drive you to my place. I should be home in a few hours."

Something's not right. Evan's acting weird and I don't know how to call him out on it, but I guess there's nothing I can do about it now.

"No, that's fine. I'd rather Teddy drop me off at my place," I say flatly. Evan's face bunches up, but I continue. "We were supposed to meet tomorrow anyways. Besides, I need to pack a bag. I need a shower and my nighttime routine stuff. It actually works out better this way," I lie.

Evan eyes me for a few moments, but seems to be distracted enough to not call me on my lie. This isn't great. He's great at calling me on my bullshit, something must really be off.

"Okay, let's go babe. I'll walk you to the car." Evan sighs.

We make our way out of the restaurant and cross the sideway to the waiting car. He opens my door for me, and I climb in.

"You sure you don't want to stay the night? Teddy can drive you to your place to pack, then bring you back to mine? Or I can come to your place once I'm done?" he asks eagerly.

I put my hand on his cheek. "I had a great time tonight. I'll see you tomorrow." I lean over and place a small peck on his lips. When I try to pull back, he holds me in place, deepening our kiss.

That's my Evan.

"Text me when you're going to bed. I wanna wish you goodnight." He places one more kiss on my lips, then leans back to give me one final look before closing the door.

He looks distressed. Something is worrying Evan.

My mind immediately makes me think that LC is another woman, but I can't let my situation with Sebastián taint my new relationship with Evan. I won't let it.

I need to remind myself that Evan now lives in a different world than me. He probably has stressors that I can't even imagine. I need to trust him.

These are the thoughts running through my mind as the car pulls out into the street, pulling me further away from Evan.

32

EVAN

It's nine AM and I'm knocking on Amelia's apartment door.

Leaving her last night was the last thing I wanted to do, but I guess that's what I get for letting my past creep up on me.

I knew the second she got in the car her mind was spinning, and I need to make sure she doesn't get the wrong idea.

Finally, a groggy Amelia opens the front door. "Hi," she croaks.

My heart swells in my chest at the sight of her. She's wearing my t-shirt as a nightgown. The same t-shirt I gave her the first time she came to my apartment and stole my bed from me.

She yawns as she wipes sleep from her eyes. "What are you doing here?" She frowns. "I thought I was meeting you at your place."

"I couldn't wait another second to see you. And I brought breakfast." I lift a brown paper bag and a rectangular donut box with my right hand. "And of course, coffee." I push the coffee tray in my left hand towards her.

She offers me a half smile and takes the coffees as I enter her apartment and close the door behind me.

Fuck, she seems off.

We sit at her tiny high top table for two that's pushed off to the wall.

"Hey." I grab her hand over the table. She keeps her eyes on her coffee. "I'm sorry about last night. I hate that I had to leave you like that."

"Hmm." She nods and avoids my eyes.

I stand and walk over to her chair and pull it towards me. With my index finger and thumb, I tilt her chin up. Her eyes eventually meet mine.

"I'm sorry Amelia. It won't happen again. I promise." I place a soft kiss on her lips, and I can feel her melt into me.

There she is.

"It's okay. Work comes first." She shrugs. "I just missed you last night, that's all." She smiles weakly. "I swear I'm not that needy." She nudges my arm.

I shake my head and smile. "No Amelia. You come first." I wink.

That earns me a slap on the arm and an infectious giggle from Amelia. "You idiot." She pulls me in for another kiss.

"I'm serious babe. I've put in my time. My company has been my top priority for years. But that changes now. I'm not giving you a reason to spook and run out on me. I'm here to stay." I rub my hands up and down her arms as I watch her smile slowly widen. "Now hurry up and eat, I've got a surprise for you today." I grin.

"Surprise? Oh God. In your world I have no idea what that could be. Hmm, is it an invitation to dinner, or a small island?" She taps her chin dramatically.

"Stop being a smart ass and hurry up. We've gotta leave here in an hour."

She opens the brown paper bag and frowns. "There's only one bagel sandwich here. What about your breakfast?"

I hover over her closely. "Don't worry babe, I fully intend to eat before we leave."

We're in the car driving down fifth avenue.

My morning with Amelia already has me feeling like I'm on cloud nine, but we're just getting started.

She leans over and whispers in my ear. "Last I recall, we're not supposed to be seen together in public until after the holidays," she mockingly scolds.

"We won't." I interlace our fingers. "Don't worry, I've thought of everything." I bump her shoulder with mine.

We pull up to Bergdorf Goodman's exclusive VIP underground parking garage.

"You've got to be kidding me," Amelia mumbles. "Please tell me you're not going to pull a *Pretty Woman* on me, Evan."

"Let me guess, another Julia Roberts movie?" I chuckle.

Amelia grabs my forearm with superhuman strength. "Please tell me that you're joking, and that you actually *have* watched Pretty Woman?!" She sneers.

"Yes, Amelia. I've watched Pretty Woman. You can retract your claws from my arm now, thank you very much." I pull out of her grasp.

Teddy parks us in front of the service elevators, and I get out and open the door for her. We make our way up to the personal shopping floor, and she keeps chuckling and smiling to herself. To be able to get free access to her inner monologue right now...

We are greeted by a group of personal shoppers. At the very front of the line is my personal savior, Maribel.

I met her years ago when she was working the perfume counter downstairs, and I was trying to figure out how new money was supposed to smell. I assumed that my axe body spray needed to go at that point and she was kind and knowledgeable about all things fashion.

Maribel is a Spanish woman in her early sixties who had to

enter the workforce later in life due to the untimely death of her husband.

She was new to being a working mom, and I was new to not wearing sweatpants every day, so together we forged a bond. She became my personal shopper, therefore receiving all of the hefty commissions that came from my purchases. The store offered to place me with a more experienced personal stylist, but I refused, and have exclusively worked with Maribel for the last decade. Something that Maribel constantly reminds me that she is grateful for, even though I'm the one who feels lucky to have her.

"Hola, mi Evan." She kisses both of my cheeks. "I see you have brought company today." She smiles as she eyes Amelia.

"Yes, I have. Maribel. Meet Amelia, my girlfriend." I beam.

Amelia seems to have choked on a bit of air, but miserably tries to cover it up with a cough. She sends me a knowing look, then reaches her hand out to Maribel. "Hi, pleased to meet you." Amelia smiles shyly.

"The pleasure is all mine! I can't believe I see the day I get to dress the infamous Amelia Nuñez!" Maribel grins. "I've already picked the samples you've requested. I'll bring out the champagne and you two can make yourselves comfortable before Amelia is ready to start trying on gowns." She pats my arm. And with that, the team of personal shoppers disappear behind her.

"Umm, infamous Amelia? Trying on gowns? Evan Cooper, start explaining yourself. Now!"

Uh oh. She said my full name.

"Well, infamous because she's known about you for about ..." I pause to count in my head. "... Seven years. She's badgered me for that long as well to bring you in and meet her."

Amelia's jaw is practically on the ground. I use my index finger to close her mouth, then lean down into her eye level. "I told you I've been crazy about you for years. You're just the last person to find out about it apparently." I shrug.

Amelia's at a loss for words. A first, given how easily my

woman rambles. So, I continue. "And then there's the matter of the gowns..."

"Uh, yeah. Explain the gown part," Amelia says, her voice sounding hoarse.

"Well, if I recall correctly, last night I attended your company holiday party. Actually, I rescued you from an excruciatingly painful interaction." That earns me another playful slap on the arm from Amelia. "So, I thought it was only fair for you to return the favor." I lick my lips.

She crosses her arms over her chest. "Isn't that what breakfast was, Evan? Returning the favor." She raises a telling eyebrow. God, I've met my match with her.

I tap her temple twice. "Get your mind out of the gutter. I'm talking about you being my date for a holiday charity event that my company is hosting. Being the Founder and CEO, it is near impossible for me to finagle my way out of it, and therefore I need a date."

Amelia opens her mouth to protest, but I raise my hand to interrupt her before she does. "And if I don't guarantee a date now, I will be hounded by every socialite in the city, asking to be on my arm that night. If not for my company, then for exposure."

Amelia ponders my words.

I pull Amelia into my arms and speak into her hair. "And since I don't want to be murdered in my sleep by my beautiful Latina girlfriend, I thought it best that you come with me, even under the pretense of friendship, rather than have another woman on my arm for meaningless PR," I finish.

I feel Amelia take a deep breath. "I take it you've watched your fair share of Dateline?" I can hear the playfulness in her voice.

"Come on. It won't be that bad. We'll be there for two hours. Three tops. Then back at my place in time to watch Bravo."

She leans back to look at me. "Wow. Pulling out the big guns, huh." She smirks.

"Come on, Maribel is waiting for us, and I'm sure she's dying to get you alone and ask you a million questions." I grab her hand to walk her to the dressing rooms. But she pulls me back.

She narrows her eyes at me. "You're getting real comfortable, throwing around that boyfriend/girlfriend title, huh."

I smile. "Quite the contrary. I only plan on keeping the title temporarily."

Amelia frowns in confusion.

I lean over and whisper in her ear. "I plan on moving us up in the ranks, when the time permits. That is, of course, whenever you're ready." I meet her lips to mine, and allow my words to marinate during our kiss.

Amelia shakes her head while smiling but doesn't say a word. Although her expression is clear with what she would have said.

Evan *Fucking* Cooper.

After spending a full thirty minutes complaining about the dress prices, Maribel steps in and playfully bickers with Amelia in Spanish. After another hour of dress up, Amelia finally settles on a dress that she likes.

She picked my favorite, but I didn't say a word because I didn't want to influence her decision. I want her to feel confident and secure when she's on my arm at this party, and I'm just glad that she actually agreed to join me.

The party is a Winter Wonderland theme. So all the dresses picked are various shades of silvers, golds, and blues. Along with the typical red and greens for holiday parties.

Amelia picks a subdued, long sleeve golden gown that hugs her curves beautifully, while also leaving enough to the imagination. I knew she would pick it because she is probably going for comfort versus glam for our first outing together. I can't imagine her wearing something that will make her even more self-conscious while at an event with an absurd amount of media coverage.

nights at Evan's apartment. We're both insanely busy, but when we finally turn in for the night, it's nice to end the day in each other's arms.

And in true Evan fashion, he surprised me on Wednesday with a whole new wardrobe so that I don't have to carry an overnight bag to his place. He had Maribel pick the items for me with the measurements she took when I went gown shopping last week.

Now the *hers* side of his closet is lined with brand name clothes all in my size. I'm talking sweaters, jeans, leggings, work clothes, and even lingerie.

At first, I thought it was Evan's sneaky way of trying to get me to move in with him, but then I remembered that in his world, money buys convenience, so I tried not to read too much into it.

But not everything is perfect. Although he tries to hide it, Evan has seemed more stressed than usual. It's hard for me to gauge what his normal stress levels are, since we just started dating, but I can feel that something is keeping him up at night, other than me.

Tonight, Evan is cooking me a pre-birthday dinner, since we still can't be seen out in public alone. Dress code is cozy attire since I plan on eating dinner on the couch while cuddled up with Evan. I'm hoping we can have some wine, and enjoy this alone time before my family inevitably does something embarrassing for my actual birthday tomorrow.

I walk out of my building and the December chill convinces me that I should probably take a cab to Evan's place tonight. The days of leisure walks in the city are officially over.

It's six PM on a Friday night, meaning hailing a cab is going to be a nightmare, so I decide to walk a block towards a less busy avenue to up my chances of catching one before freezing to death. I'm walking with my head down, since the wind has started to pick up, when I get the sinking feeling in my gut that I'm being watched. I immediately take in my surroundings, but don't see anyone out of the ordinary. I start to pick up speed and turn the corner on the block I intend to hail a cab from.

I stand there with my arm in the air, and chance a glance behind me, and that's when I see him.

The same familiar man I saw last weekend when I came back from Evan's. He's wearing a beanie, sunglasses and a puffy coat. The sun sets at four PM at this point so there is clearly no need for sunglasses in the middle of the evening during winter. I can now tell that he is definitely Caucasian and is trying to not be seen by me by the way he falters in his stride under my gaze.

I'm officially creeped out.

I'm luckily saved by a cab that pulls up to the curb and I immediately jump into it. When we tear away, I look back to get another glimpse of the man, but he's gone. I slump in my seat and take a deep breath.

Why do I live in a city full of weirdos?

Evan's apartment door opens before I make it half way up the hallway.

"There's my birthday girl." He smiles widely, looking as edible as ever in an emerald green Henley and gray sweatpants.

I barely make it inside before he scoops me into a hug, lifting my feet off the floor.

"How did you know I was already here," I say as I eagerly accept all of the kisses and affection coming my way.

Evan closes the door behind us, and I hear a beeping noise. "New security system." He points to a fancy touch screen by his front door. "I can see who's on the street, lobby and hallway. It also has a new anti-hacking system which can't be overridden unless it's done manually with my thumb print."

"Oh wow. That seems like a bit much, no?" I ask as Evan guides me into the kitchen. A bottle of red already decanted with two wine glasses waiting to be filled.

"I take every precaution possible. Especially now that you're staying here more often. Which can I say, I'm enjoying very much." He leans in to kiss me. I smile and watch him pour the wine into our glasses, then he hands me mine. "Happy birthday baby. To your best year yet. Welcome to your thirties." He clinks his glass with mine and we end our cheers with another kiss.

Evan leads me out of the kitchen and that's when I notice that the dining table is overflowing with gifts, cake and floral arrangements.

"Evan, you can't be serious!" My eyes threaten to pop out of my eye sockets.

"Come on, let me show you what I got before you judge me as a rich prick." He chuckles.

Once I get closer, I can tell that these gifts are more heartfelt than pretentious.

"So, in the center you can see that I had a Dominican cake ordered for you. Please don't tell Tía Lourdes I didn't order from her, she'd kill me." We both laugh because this is very true. "Then I got your favorite fuzzy socks from TJ Maxx. These remind me of the ones you wore when we were at the cabin."

"You went shopping at TJ Maxx for me?!" I can stupidly feel my heart swell at the sentiment that he took time out of his day to buy the same brand of fuzzy socks for me when he could have easily asked Maribel to send over a fancy brand.

"Of course I did babe. Besides, I picked up some extra underwear for myself. They've got the good stuff." He winks at me. "I picked up some of your favorite Dominican candy. The kind that's almost impossible to find. I hunted it down at a bodega near eighty sixth street. I need to take you there sometime." He grabs my hand and kisses the back of it. "The rest are just a couple of things that would make you feel more comfortable here. Like your own throw blanket, since you don't like to share. Full size bottles of your shampoo and conditioner, along with some other stuff I was roped into buying. Apparently it's the hottest thing on the market to keep curly hair healthy and shiny, or at least that's what I was told by the sales clerk."

I'm now a full koala, clinging onto Evan's side as he continues to talk through the rest of the gifts. I feel a tear escape and quickly dissolve into Evan's shirt, but I don't dare move or interrupt him.

"And then, I got these flowers arranged for you. I wasn't sure what your favorite flower is, so I asked for an array of everything. But these flowers in the center are yellow tulips." He points to the understated flowers in a beautiful clear vase, and I hold my breath. No, it can't be. There's no way he would know, could he?

"I remember your mom loved yellow tulips. She always found a sneaky way to integrate them into the typical holiday decor, and all the Tías would be up in arms because apparently it clashed with the tablescape. But I always loved how she stuck to her guns and had them at every family function."

Before I know it, I am overcome by emotion and am a blubbering mess. Tears pour out of my eyes faster than I can wipe them away.

"Shit. I'm sorry baby, I didn't mean to upset you." Evan pulls me in for a tight hug. "Shhh, it's okay, let it out baby." He rubs my back as the waterworks slowly start to subside.

It takes me a few minutes to regulate my breathing, but once I do, I know what is coming next.

Evan hands me a couple of tissues and I wipe my eyes and blow my nose.

Way to keep it classy Amelia.

I take a couple of deep breaths, and look up at Evan's worried face. He's reading the situation completely wrong.

"I'm sorry for bringing up your mom babe, I know it's still too soon. I just wanted to incorporate her in a small way for your birthday."

I hold both his hands in mine, and take one more deep breath before my eyes settle on his. "Evan, this is the sweetest thing anyone has ever done for me. The fact that you would even know that yellow tulips are my mother's favorite flower just blows my mind." My thumb caresses his hand as he stares into my eyes, still worried about whatever I'm going to say. "I am very much at a loss for words, except for five." Evan's face bunches up in confusion.

"I love you, Evan Cooper." I smile softly.

I hear an audible release of air from Evan's chest as his shoulders slump. A few moments pass in silence. "Say it again." He squeezes my hands with his eyes closed, causing me to smile like a fool.

"I love you Evan, I am so in love with you, it's ridiculous," I whisper close to his chest.

He gently grabs my face with both of his hands and places the world's gentlest kiss on my lips. "Are you sure? I don't want to pressure you. I know I'm coming off strong, and I just want you to be sure." He desperately searches my eyes for the confirmation he's looking for.

"Evan, I don't think I've ever stopped loving you since the day you became my first crush. So if you really think about it, I've been in love with you longer than you've been in love with me." I smirk into his lips.

"You always have to one-up me, don't you?" He says in a fun-loving tone. He proceeds to lift me in the air, and I take advantage and wrap my legs around his waist. We kiss while he walks us into his bedroom.

"Hey! Wait! You still have to wine and dine me before we get to this part!" I giggle as he throws us onto his bed.

"I promise I will." He laughs. "But first I want to feel what it's like to make love to you, knowing that you love me, too." He kisses my nose and I chuckle. "What, too cheesy?" He winces.

"Yes, but that's not what I find funny." I grin.

"Care to enlighten me?" He sits up by the headboard, and I settle into his lap.

"All this time, I've never stopped playing by the cabin rules. I've always belonged to you, regardless of whether or not we were within the cabin walls. And it's a joke to believe that I would never admit to being madly in love with you, because I'm yours and you're mine." I wrap my arms around his neck.

Evan rests his forehead on mine, and releases a deep breath. "You're killing me here, Amelia." He pauses, then pleadingly looks into my eyes. "Okay, now that we got that out of the way, how long are you going to make me wait until I can propose to you?" He grunts.

I throw my head back in laughter. "Let's just eat some Dominican cake first and take it from there." I pat his chest playfully.

When Evan doesn't mimic my reaction, I start to believe that he's being serious. Before I can say anything else, he crashes his lips into mine. "Let's just get to this love making part and I'll handle the rest Little Miss Amelia," he finally teases back.

I think I'm going to love my thirties.

34

EVAN

We've just finished having dinner and I feel like the luckiest man alive.

Amelia loves me.

After a couple of rounds in my bed, we finally showered and ventured into the kitchen. I cooked while Amelia stayed close by, drinking her favorite wine. I'm surprised I was able to cook anything edible given the fact that I wanted to keep her tucked into my side the whole time I hovered over the stove.

After dinner, I pick up a folder off my entrance table and walk over to the couch to drop it on Amelia's lap.

"What's this?" she asks.

"My realtor and I have narrowed down my options for my new place to three homes. I wanted to get your input." I shrug nonchalantly.

Amelia eyes me suspiciously. "Evan, this isn't you buying me a new place to live, is it?"

I laugh. "No babe, it really is for me. Although, it may as well be for us given how things are going." I place a kiss on her head.

"Evan, we are still hiding out at your place, I think it's a little early for me to be moving in with you." She deadpans.

"Quit your whining and just give me your opinion. It never seems to be a problem with anything else I do," I tease.

"Fine." She rolls her eyes. Then ten seconds later, she replies, "This one." She points at the brownstone.

"Wait, what? That fast? You made a decision between the three of them that quickly? There's no way."

"Well, to be fair, I couldn't pick based on prices since you did a hack job at sharpie-ing off the prices." She levels a glare at me. "So, then I was just going off the three options, the apartment in Soho, the loft in Brooklyn, or the brownstone in the Upper West side, it was a no brainer."

"The brownstone, huh?"

"Well yeah. It's in a location you already consider home, there are multiple levels so you can have your own space when you have guests, and you have your own private patio space and attached indoor garage. That's unheard of in the city. These other fancy apartments just look cold and industrial. The brownstone gives off cozy vibes."

"Cozy vibes, huh. Guess I should have just had you work with my realtor and I could have closed on this home months ago." I kiss her forehead.

"Yeah, but it seems you only started making smart decisions about your life the second you told me you had feelings for me." She scrunches her nose in delight.

"Yeah, well I'm not gonna argue with you on that one." I give her a kiss, then stand to walk towards the dining table. "You want some cake, babe? I could also move some of the flowers around so you can see them everywhere."

"Yes, to cake and flowers please!"

I bring them to the coffee table, then head to the kitchen to open another bottle of wine.

Amelia's now rearranging the flowers when she says, "Nice to see that you upgraded your flower guy."

"What do you mean?" I ask, perplexed.

"I'm just teasing! They were all lovely, I swear. I just think these flowers look much more glamorous than the other bouquets you've sent me."

Huh?

"What do you mean the other bouquet's I've sent?" I feel my muscles tense. "I've never sent you flowers before Amelia."

Her face drops and her eyes go wide. "Oh."

I put the wine bottle on the coffee table and sit by Amelia. "Is someone sending you flowers and signing my name? Is it Sebastián?" I feel my blood pressure start to rise.

"No. I mean. I don't know." Amelia starts to stammer. "I've just gotten two bouquets of flowers sent to me, one sent to my dad's place on his birthday, and one sent to my apartment, but it was never signed. At first, I thought it was Sebastián, but then the second bouquet arrived after our weekend in the cabin, so I just assumed it was from you. The messages were a bit weird and cryptic now that I think about it." She frowns.

After the cabin? Fuck.

"What did the cards say Amelia?" I ask, harsher than I intend to.

"Um, I'm not sure. I threw out the first one, but it basically just wished my dad a happy birthday, and that they hoped to *see me soon*. The second one I still have because I thought it was from you. It said something like, *love is beautiful, don't be scared, you'll see me very soon* or something like that?"

It's him.

I need to call Rocco. I shoot up from my spot on the couch and head to the kitchen counter to grab my cell phone.

"What is it, Evan? Do you think it's something bad? It might just be Sebastián. I could call him and ask if he's been sending me flowers." She wrings her hands nervously. "Or maybe it's that guy ..." she whispers to herself.

"What guy?" I ask as my finger hovers over Rocco's name on my phone. Amelia looks like she's about to cry, so I sit back down next to her and try to reel in my rage. I hold her hands in mine. "Go on sweetheart, what guy?"

Amelia bites her lip and eyes me nervously before she starts. "Okay, so it's probably nothing, but last Sunday when I was walking to my apartment, I spotted a man who looked a little off, like suspicious."

"Suspicious how."

"I don't know how to explain it. I just got a weird feeling that I was being watched, and when I looked up this guy was looking at me, but then turned around and walked in the opposite direction once I spotted him."

There are plenty of bizarre people roaming the streets of the city, so this could be nothing.

"But then today ..." she continues, and I feel my shoulders tense up again. "I saw the same man while waiting for a cab. And I know for a fact he was trying to not be seen by me because I acted like I didn't see him, and then turned around suddenly and he looked like a deer in headlights. As soon as I got in the cab, he vanished."

I feel the blood drain from my face. Amelia is being tailed, and it's all my fault.

Twenty minutes later, Rocco is at my door with his security team.

"Evan, this could be nothing. Don't you think this is a bit much," Amelia says while biting her thumb nail.

"No. I don't. Stay here. I'll just be outside the door in the hallway discussing this with the team. Have a glass of wine and try to relax." I give her a peck on the cheek.

"Oh sure, super relaxing night in with the Navy Seals at your front door," she mumbles under her breath.

I close the front door and move down the hall so Amelia can't hear us.

"Status update. Now," I bark.

"We've kept eyes on him, sir. Mr. Valentine has been out of

town for the past week. He's been in Puerto Rico attending his mother's funeral. He is due to fly back today, so there is no way he could have been the one tailing Amelia," Rocco explains.

"Fine, but we know he doesn't do his own dirty work, he could have sent someone in his place." I rub my neck roughly.

"True, but Mr. Valentine's team is exclusively Puerto Rican. I have yet to hear of an associate of his to be white. Is Amelia sure about the description?"

"The only thing she's sure about is that she's annoyed and scared on her birthday," I sneer.

"We're looking at all of the florists nearby Amelia's apartments and will follow any leads to figure out who has been delivering the flowers."

"That's gonna be a waste of time. It'll take you forever to track down all the florists, especially since he didn't sign for the card. And if it really is him, we know that he hand delivers the flowers to his targets, himself. That sick fuck." I say, fuming.

Rocco places a heavy hand on my shoulder. "We got this, Evan. We'll have two guys stationed downstairs for the night, plus two in your hallway. Set the alarm when you get back inside and try to focus on her tonight. We'll take it from here and reconvene tomorrow morning with updates. Okay?"

I nod hesitantly. "Text me with any updates. I'm serious. Keep me in the know." I point at the team.

"We will. Goodnight, Evan," Rocco says.

I enter the apartment and immediately activate the alarm system.

I look over at Amelia on the couch. She's pulling her knees to her chest and looking at me nervously. "Hi."

I walk over to sit on the couch, then pull her legs onto my lap. "Hey baby. It's gonna be fine." I tuck a piece of hair behind her ear.

"Are you some kind of CIA operative? Is being a CEO a front

for some kind of international sting operation?" she asks with a weak smile.

I start rubbing her feet. "Sorry to disappoint, just a regular old CEO I'm afraid." I lightly tease.

"Seriously Evan, what the fuck is going on? Are you in danger or something? You can talk to me, I can handle it."

I sigh. "I'm not in danger sweetheart, but just for peace of mind the security team is surveilling the building overnight. Tomorrow we'll be back to normal," I lie. I know Amelia will stay up all night if I show her a hint of distress.

Amelia let's out a heavy sigh. "Sheesh, overprotective boyfriend alert. Really had me losing my mind there for a second."

"Come on, let's have some more wine and watch a Julia Roberts movie." I smile.

Amelia pulls her feet from my hands and inches herself closer to me until she is sitting sideways on my lap. "Hmm, great idea. I knew I loved you for a reason." She kisses me.

We spent the next two hours watching a movie and drinking wine. I couldn't listen to a single word said because my mind was too preoccupied with more pressing matters.

Like how I'm going to keep Amelia alive.

35

AMELIA

I LOVE EVAN COOPER.

Besides last night's security fiasco, it was one of the best nights of my life. I told Evan I loved him, and we spent the coziest night together, watching movies and drinking wine.

For the first time in a long time, I'm following my heart. I'm not following a timeline or acting based on what I assume are the expectations others have of me, and it feels so liberating. Evan isn't a checkmark on my list, he's what my heart yearns for, and I'm finally going to live my life in a way that makes me happy.

I had brunch scheduled with my dad and Antonio this morning, so Evan had one of his security guards drop me off. It seemed a bit excessive, but I wasn't gonna turn down a cushy, warm ride in this weather.

After brunch, Nikki and I got our hair and nails done. I know that there is probably going to be a surprise get together tonight, because everyone in my life is terrible at keeping secrets, just like me. Plus, they've been quite heavy with dropping hints.

Nikki and I are heading out for "dinner" when I spot Teddy leaning on the familiar black SUV. "Good evening birthday girl. Your chariot awaits," he says as he opens the back passenger doors.

I laugh to myself and don't even question it. I've never seen a crew be so bad at keeping a surprise party a secret. "Thanks Teddy, nice to see you again. This is my friend Nikki." I gesture to her.

"So, are you gonna make me wait until everyone jumps out and says 'SURPRISE' before you tell me where we're going?" I ask Nikki sarcastically.

"I have no idea what you're talking about, we are going out for a fancy dinner, just you and I." Nikki bites her lip, probably to keep herself from spilling the beans.

I roll my eyes and play along.

We pull up to *The Avenue*. The pub where Evan and I had our infamous fight. I smile foolishly at the memory.

"Just thought we'd grab a quick drink here first," Nikki says in a high pitched voice. Jesus, the woman is coming apart at the seams holding in this surprise.

Nikki pushes me into the dimly lit bar first, then I see the lights flash on brighter, followed by a motley crew of familiar faces.

"SURPRISE!" Everyone in the room yells and I produce a mock surprised face.

"Oh wow! A surprise party? I had no idea!" I sing-song as I make my way to hug my loved ones.

"Nikki told you, didn't she," Antonio huffs.

"I did not! How dare you question my surprise party duties?!" Nikki glares at Antonio.

"Happy birthday Amelia!" Vanessa yells as she pulls me in for a hug. "We can't believe the baby of the group is in her thirties. God we're getting old." She laughs.

One by one, everyone greets me.

My dad and brother are here, along with the doctors and Tías and of course the cousin crew. Including Evan.

How do I go from telling this man I love him, to acting like we barely tolerate each other in a room full of people who know us better than anyone else? A fun light punch to the arm? Yeah no. Simple greeting it is.

As Evan gets closer, he gives me the most seductive look on the planet. Is this man insane?! Is he trying to get us caught, or worse, killed by my brother? I shoot him a glare and he eases up.

"Happy birthday Little Miss Amelia." He pulls me in for a hug. "I'll give you your present later tonight in my bed," he whispers in my ear.

I push him off a little harder than I expect, which causes a few of the onlookers to laugh.

"And just when we thought that these two were finally getting along." Abby chuckles.

Well, at least we're not under suspicion.

I want to stay glued to Evan's side, but I know that's not an option tonight. Unless I want to announce to my entire family that we're in love and watch a bar brawl break out between Antonio and Evan.

Nope, not today.

Although this does make me realize that our days of hiding out in Evan's apartment are numbered. I don't want to have side conversations with other people just because they are standing the furthest from Evan. What's the point of following my heart and living a more authentic life if I only allow myself to have that behind closed doors?

All of a sudden, I feel myself standing a bit taller. A decision firmly made in my mind. Not tonight, but any day now, Evan and I will tell everyone that we're dating. We'll obviously have to tell Antonio first, since he'll be the one to take it the hardest, but who cares. He's not a man child, he can get over his best friend dating his little sister. But maybe I'll tell him when my dad is in the same room, just to be safe.

With this new plan in my mind, I break free from the small crowd and walk towards the small circle of people Evan is talking to. I plan on standing right next to him, maybe just to test the waters to see how it feels. God I'm such a chicken shit.

Just as I'm closing in on Evan, I see him pull his phone out of his jean pockets. The name **LC** lighting up the screen. Before he notices me, he steps away from the group, and walks out of the pub to take the call.

Who the fuck is this LC bitch?

I'm talking to Lucy when a few minutes later, Evan walks back inside. His face already tells me I'm not gonna like what he has to say.

He nods towards the bar, and I make an excuse about needing to ask for a different cocktail, since my current one isn't strong enough. I'm about to test that theory.

We make it to the bar at the same time, and leave some appropriate distance between one another while I order another drink.

Evan runs his hand over his face. "I hate to do this but ..."

"You've got to be kidding me, Evan," I whisper while looking straight ahead.

"I know, I'm sorry. But I need to handle this work thing. It's probably going to take a while, but I'll meet you back at my place. I promise to make this up to you."

I feel my anger reach a boiling point. "A work thing huh? Funny. I've never heard you mention an LC."

I can see him tense up in my peripheral vision. "Are you looking through my phone?" he whisper-shouts, and I feel the crazy Latina in me dying to make an appearance.

His phone beeps with a notification.

"Why Evan, should I be? Seems like we have a pattern of her calling and you running off. Tell me I'm wrong."

"You're wrong."

"Fine. Then who is she? What is the work emergency? If it's not a big deal, why do I feel like you're keeping a secret from me."

He stays silent. Fuck.

"Wow, you're awfully quiet for an innocent man."

His phone beeps with another notification.

"Amelia, it's not what you think ..."

Those words instantly throw me back to the moment when

Sebastián said those same words to me. The moment when I caught him cheating.

I think I'm going to puke.

"I never learn, do I?" I whisper to myself.

Evan steps closer. "Amelia, stop it. You've got it wrong. Let's talk about it tonight. I swear, I can explain."

It's as if his words make him sound guiltier. I'm starting to have a hard time breathing.

"Leave. Now." I stare at him.

"No. I'm not leaving until we fix this. I swear, it's just a misunderstanding Amelia."

"Evan, if you don't leave this very moment, Antonio is going to see me crying next to you. Do you really want me to have to tell you how the rest of that scenario is going to go?"

Evan's phone starts ringing in his pocket. I know it's LC.

"Fuck. Amelia. We're talking about this later. Don't you dare shut me out now. Not when we've come this far."

"Evan, tell me who LC is right now. If you can't do that, you can forget about there ever being an *us*," I spit out.

Evan looks pained, and pauses a few moments. "Amelia, now is not the time. I promise I'll tell you everything, but—"

"Goodbye, Evan." I grab my drink and make my way towards the crowd.

Behind me I hear a loud *thump*, followed by a muffled *fuck*.

I turn around and see Evan storming out of the pub.

"What's gotten into Evan?" Antonio says, eyeing me suspiciously.

"Maybe his company stock went down or something," Priscilla mocks.

Antonio nudges my shoulder. "You good, sis?"

I nod. Realizing that my eyes are probably watery and red, I say, "Yeah, just missing mom today."

Antonio pulls me into his side, and I rest my head on his

shoulder. "Yeah. I miss her, too. But I'm sure she's here. She's always here looking over us."

I sigh and stare at the door Evan walked out of.

Sorry mom, no snowstorm can save us now.

"Another round of shots!" I yell and the crowd cheers me on.

Look, I know that booze doesn't make your problems go away, but it's my birthday and I'll numb my pain if I want to.

My dad and the older crowd left shortly after Evan, so that we could drink without being judged.

Nikki and Antonio are currently in a tug of war over me. Nikki wants to get me drunk, and Antonio wants me to hydrate. Nikki followed me into the bathroom after Evan left and I filled her in. She texted Justin immediately letting him know she would be staying with me tonight.

"Amelia, slow down. At this rate you're staying at my place, I need to make sure you don't die in your sleep," Antonio mutters.

"She's fine Antonio! Plus, she'll have a two day hangover anyways now that she's in her thirties, so let her live a little tonight," Nikki says while pulling him to the bar to order another round of drinks.

Priscilla sees this as an opportunity to saunter over to me with a smug look on her face. "Birthday girl is throwing back the drinks tonight I see. Too bad you'll be going home alone. And here I thought I might have caught a little something brewing between you and Evan." She tsks. "But then again, our sweet little Amelia wouldn't even know what to do with a man like Evan Cooper..."

"What the fuck is your problem, Priscilla. Like seriously? Who dipped a dildo in acid and decided to have it permanently wedged up your ass?" I sneer.

Priscilla's jaw hits the ground while her eyes come dangerously close to popping out of their sockets.

"And while we're on the subject of dildos, why have you always had such a hard on for me? I get it. I was the baby of the group. Big fucking whoop. But why do you take every opportunity to try to knock me down a peg when you see me? Why always pick on me?" I demand.

Priscilla's eyes turn into slits. "Oh please. Spare me the victim card, Amelia. You don't seem to mind being the baby of the group when everyone dotes on you, or when you get special attention from everyone... even Evan."

"Evan? Is this really about Evan? It can't be. You couldn't have been this much of a bitch to me for this long over a guy who has only recently shown me any attention publicly."

She chuckles darkly. "Publicly. Is that a joke? I've seen how Evan has looked at you for years, Amelia. YEARS! And what do you do when a handsome, successful and rich guy can't take his eyes off of you? Oh yeah, you up and date another handsome, successful and soon to be rich guy. It's like you think you're so much better than all of us. As if you could do better than Evan. But clearly with the way he left today, he hopefully saw whatever it is he needed to see to break free from whatever trance you've put him under." She rolls her eyes victoriously.

"You think that I think I'm better than everyone?! Is that a fucking joke?!" I say louder than I intended, garnering us a few stares from the cousin crew. "Living in your shadows has given me a freaking good girl complex! Always making sure my actions seem to please others while holding back what I really want to do. Who I really am! Worrying about the '*qué dirán*', the '*what will people say*' ..." I close my eyes and try to ignore the blatant stares from everyone I know. "But that ends now. From this moment forward, this is the Amelia that you will be confronted with from now on. I'm now in the business of matching people's energy, and doing whatever the hell I want. So you remember that the next time you try to pull one of your stunts on me." I grab my empty glass and turn to leave a seething Priscilla. "Oh, and one last thing. Stay the hell away from Evan. He and his penis want nothing to do with you. He told me himself." I wink at Priscilla as I finally saunter my way back to the bar, imitating Priscilla's signature walk.

Maybe I should have let her know that this new Amelia is also openly petty.

I hear the pub door open, and I'm not sure if this man is walking in slow motion, or if I'm just that drunk, but he makes quite the entrance.

I need to squint to focus. Why does he look familiar?

He's tall, tanned and I can spot tattoos peeking out from under the collar of his dress shirt, and his hands. Do I even know anyone with more than a handful of tattoos?

His dark brown eyes match his well styled wavy hair. Shorter on the sides, but longer on the top.

He locks eyes with me and slowly breaks into a megawatt grin.

Oh my God. Is that...

"Wow. Amelia, is that you?" he says to me.

"Julian? Julian Vasquez?" My mouth drops.

He releases a deep laugh. "The one and only. Damn it's good to see you." He pulls me in for a hug. Gosh he smells good.

"How have you been?" He releases me, but grabs my hand. It sizzles under his touch.

"I'm good. It's actually my birthday today." I shrug shyly.

His eyes glimmer. "Really? Well happy birthday." He smiles, but then grows serious. "I heard about your mother's passing. She was a lovely woman. So sorry about her loss." He pauses. "I also lost my mom to cancer, so I get how painful it can be."

"Oh no. Doña Fela was a sweetheart. I'm so sorry Julian." I squeeze his hand.

Julian smiles, but I start to feel a bit unsettled. I shouldn't be holding another man's hand. Evan just left two hours ago. Guilt consumes me so I drop his hand and hold my drink instead.

Julian looks up and I can tell Antonio is standing behind me. Ever the protective bodyguard.

"Anyways, I was just picking up a to-go order. Heard the wings are great here," he says while looking directly over my shoulder at Antonio.

He grabs a large paper bag filled with food, then turns back to me.

"It was great running into you Amelia, we should catch up sometime." He winks, and I hear Antonio grunt.

"Yeah, nice seeing you too, Julian!" I say as he starts walking away.

He reaches the door and gives me one final wave.

Wow. Julian Vasquez.

The man who gave me my first kiss.

36

EVAN

I'M MISERABLE, AND I ONLY HAVE MYSELF TO BLAME.

It's been a week since Amelia's party, and she still hasn't returned any of my calls.

Nikki took pity on me after she found me sitting by Amelia's apartment door. She let me know that she has been staying at Antonio's. The one place she knows I can't barge into.

She assured me that she didn't think I was cheating on Amelia, and to just give her time to cool off. I always knew I liked Nikki.

I've royally fucked up. And LC isn't helping. I've shut everyone out this week besides Rocco. I've had my assistant Hayden cancel all of my meetings and have given up on even showering. I'm pathetic.

I had it. I finally had my happiness, right in the palm of my hand, and I ruined it.

I wish I had just sat Amelia down and explained everything, but every moment with her always seemed too perfect to ruin.

And now it's too late. At the meeting after Amelia's party, the deal was made. I stay away from Amelia, and her safety is guaranteed. I saw how close Mr. Valentine's people were getting to

Amelia, and I can't risk her getting caught in the crosshairs, no matter how painful it is to stay away from her.

I've lived the last decade of my life knowing what it is like to love Amelia, but now I have to live alone in a world where I know she loved me back.

37

AMELIA

I'M MISERABLE, AND I ONLY HAVE MYSELF TO BLAME.

Did I really think life was going to throw me a bone in the same year that my mom died, and my fiancé cheated on me? Yeah, no.

That's what I get for watching all those stupid rom coms.

It's really quite laughable. To think I would get swooped off my feet and fall in love with my first crush. Stupid me.

Well now my feet are firmly planted on the ground, at Antonio's place. He bought my excuse about having my plumbing being redone in my building. Plus I think he enjoys having company, even though he wouldn't admit it.

But I can't hide out here forever. I need to go back to my place today and gather more clothes, and come up with a plan as to how to act in case I run into Evan. Nikki told me she's seen him a few times sitting on my doorstep. The visual makes my heart wrench, but I can't give in.

He's keeping secrets and lying to me.

I refuse to put myself in that situation. Even if it feels like I'm dying with each passing day that I don't see him.

I even got a call from Marcos Mirabal. *The* call. Congratulating me for landing the Miami account. The cherry on top? They need me in New York for *at least* another year while the new team is formed. So running away to Miami is no longer an option. Guess I have to be a big girl and face my problems head on.

Annoying.

I can't believe I got the promotion I've been pining for, and I can't even muster up enough excitement to even tell anyone about it. This is becoming pathetic.

I'm walking down the street when I hear someone call my name. I turn around and I'm faced with him. Ugh not now.

"Hey, I thought that was you," Sebastián says as he jogs up to me.

"Goodbye Sebastián. We have nothing to talk about." I turn and start walking away, but he follows beside me.

"Look, Amelia. You have every right to hate me. But I just need you to know that I really am sorry for what I did, there is no excuse."

I roll my eyes.

"Hey." He tugs at my arm, so I stop walking. "At one point, we were friends, and we loved each other. I know that I took a massive shit on our future, but I just wanted to properly apologize to you." He grips at the back of his neck. "You deserve so much better than what I was giving you. And the thought that my actions caused you pain keeps me up at night." He sighs. "I'm way beyond asking you for a second chance, I'm not delusional. But I just want you to know that I was selfish. Us not working is on me, and I hope you don't carry an ounce of shame. I know how it works with most of the women in our culture. They try to act as if the woman did or lacked something, and that's why the man strayed. It couldn't be further from the truth, Amelia."

His honesty takes me by surprise. I suddenly feel my eyes watering. He continues.

"I've been going to therapy since we broke up," he confesses. I'm unable to keep the shock off my face. He was always against going to couples therapy with me every time I suggested it whenever we would get back together after a breakup. "I've been working on myself. At first, I went for you." His eyes start to water. "And then I realized there was so much shit I was repressing. I thought therapy would be a band aid for us when you suggested for us to go. But now I realize it's handed me a shovel to start digging up all the shit I've buried." He chuckles.

"Wow, Sebastián. That's incredible. I'm glad." I half smiled.

"Yeah, it is. But anyways, I just wanted to tell you, as someone who used to be your friend. You were the best, and I'm still very much a work in progress. If you and Evan have something good going, please don't let any of the shit I've put you through seep into your new relationship. That's all I ask. You deserve to be happy." He wipes away a tear.

I let out a hard laugh. "Yeah well, no need to worry about Evan anymore."

He gives me a quizzical look but doesn't press further. "It was nice seeing you, Amelia. Good luck in life." He places a quick kiss on my cheek, and turns to walk away in the opposite direction.

Well, looks like we got that closure after all.

I'm almost at my apartment when I realize that I need a coffee after that impromptu conversation with Sebastián.

As I make it to the register to order, I can see the reflection of a familiar face outside of the coffee shop.

It's him. The man who's been following me around.

I order an extra coffee, and ask for it to be scalding hot. Someone is learning a lesson today.

I walk out of the coffee shop looking down, but keeping him in my peripheral vision. I feel the adrenaline pumping through my body. This is probably a stupid idea, but I'm tired of feeling sad all week. Now I just feel anger pulsating off my body.

I turn the corner, and quickly duck into a skinny alley. He's going to have to walk by me if he actually is stalking me.

In the next moment, he passes me, and I creep up behind him.

"TELL ME WHO THE FUCK YOU ARE OR I'M THROWING THIS HOT COFFEE ON YOUR FACE!" I shout loudly, causing people to look our way.

The man takes off his hat and sunglasses, giving me a good look at his face. How the hell do I know this man?

He puts his hands up in surrender, then has the audacity to smile at me.

"You can put the coffee down, Amelia. I'm not here to hurt you," he says calmly.

"Stay back! How do you know my name? Who are you?!"

He shakes his head, then reaches his hand out for me to shake. Does he not see how close I am to giving him third degree burns?!

"My name is Luke. I'm Evan's dad." He grins. "Are you gonna still throw that coffee on me or can I drink it?"

WHAT. THE. FUCK.

38

AMELIA

AFTER LUKE SHOWED ME A PHOTO ON HIS PHONE OF HIM and Evan at a Yankees versus Red Sox game last month, I lowered the coffee and handed it to him.

He guided me into a different nearby coffee shop so he could explain further. We take our seats, but I'm too stunned to speak. Evan looks exactly like his dad. That's why he seemed so familiar. I focus on every little feature, until Luke starts to laugh.

"Anybody ever teach you that it's rude to stare?" He chuckles and I break out of my trance.

"Anybody ever tell you that it's rude to stalk strangers?" I retort.

He smiles and takes a sip of coffee. "I take it you're pretty confused about this whole revelation, huh?"

"You can say that. Evan and his mom said that you walked out of their lives when he was a teenager. Although I guess this wouldn't be the first time Evan has lied to me," I mumble that last part under my breath.

"Well, that is kind of true." He sighs. "Fifteen years ago, I was arrested and sent to prison," he says cautiously.

I stiffen at the confession, but nod for him to go on.

He tears at the coffee cup sleeve for a moment before he proceeds. "Look, I loved my family dearly, but money was tight." His shoulders sag and he takes another sip of coffee as if he needs it before carrying on with the story. "I was offered a job to be a driver for a not so kosher job. I was told we were robbing a pawn shop. In and out in two minutes. All I had to do was drive. But the guys got sloppy, and the shop owner was shot and killed. Even though I didn't pull the trigger or even step foot onto the crime scene, we were all given the same sentence. Twenty years to life."

I swallow hard, but I want to hear the rest of this story, so I try to keep my composure.

He starts again. "I got out in a little under fifteen due to good behavior. While locked up, I got my college degree and once I got out, I got my private investigator license." He smiles tightly.

"So you didn't really leave them on your own accord. You were in prison," I say, making sure I'm getting it right.

"Exactly. Evan and his mom moved out of Boston and here to the city to start over. It was hard for Evan to be the kid whose dad was locked up. It was much easier for them to say that I had gotten up and left than to have to divulge the truth."

I nod in understanding.

"Look. Evan doesn't know I'm here. Actually, he doesn't even know that I've been keeping tabs on you."

"Oh God. I told him someone was following me, and he totally freaked. You need to tell him, so he doesn't keep installing more security systems."

"I tried, but he's been holed up in his apartment ever since you dumped him. Reeks like hell in there. You really did a number on him, woman." He shoots me a stern look.

The *cojones* on this man!

"Look, Luke. I know you're Evan's dad and all, but you don't know everything that's happened, and I don't think it's appropriate for me to be spilling our personal business to you." I cross my arms over my chest.

His facial features soften, and he breaks into a full grin. "Evan did say I would like your spunk." He shakes his head. "And I do think it's my business to talk about your relationship with my son, because you're both being idiots."

My jaw drops. "Oh really, and why is that?"

He leans back in his chair, looking much too pleased with himself. "My name is Luke Cooper. I'll give you a minute to catch up, Amelia." He smirks.

I roll my eyes. "You already told me your nam—"

Luke Cooper.

LC.

Holy crap.

"You're LC?!" I shout.

He releases a full belly laugh. "That one and only."

I feel myself sink into my seat. What the fuck.

LC wasn't another woman, it was his father.

Why the hell didn't he just tell me himself.

This makes no sense.

Luke interrupts my spiraling session. "Look. Evan wanted to be the one to tell you, but you both seem too dumb to pull your heads out of your asses. My son is in love with you and from what I hear, you're in love with him too. So cut the crap and figure this shit out together."

I stare at him blankly. So he carries on.

"Look, there's a lot more going on than Evan hiding me from the world. There's some serious shit that Evan is dealing with, which is why your security is so important."

"What other stuff?"

He puts his hands up defensively. "I've already said too much. Evan needs to be the one to tell you the rest. And I know for a fact that he's dying for an opportunity to tell you himself. Might work if you answered your goddamn phone." He points at my phone on the table.

I stare daggers at him. "You know, for a guy who hasn't been around for a while, you sure know how to nag like an annoying dad." I look up to the ceiling.

He laughs softly. "I've been trying to earn a place back into Evan's life. I thought saving him from losing the love of his life might earn me some brownie points. So if you don't do it for yourself, do it for his old man." He smiles.

I groan. "I've been ignoring him for a week. How do I just walk up to his apartment and say, 'sorry for accusing you of being a lying piece of shit, still love you though!'" I throw my hands in the air.

I can't believe I let this happen.

I let my insecurities from my previous relationships meddle with Evan and I, and now I'm hoping that there's still a relationship left to salvage.

"I'm sure all you have to do is show up, and he'll be happy. Although ..." He raises an eyebrow while taking a sip of his coffee.

"What, although what??"

"I did hear that he's attending a fancy charity event tonight. Might be nice for his date to show up." He replies, mischief written all over his face.

I like this man.

The plan immediately starts coming to life in my mind. If I'm going to ask for my man back, I better look good doing it.

"I need to get to Bergdorfs ASAP! And I need hair, and makeup and ... Teddy!" I shoot out of my chair.

"That's the spirit! I'll get you to your fancy store. I also have the contact of Evan's assistant. This is a full on operation Amelia." He locks his arm with mine.

Operation *Get My Man Back*.

∽

I all but sprint to the personal shopping floor. I'm sure security thought I was stealing, but they let me be once they saw Maribel greet me.

"Amelia, I thought you weren't going to the party anymore. Evan's assistant emailed me saying that I shouldn't worry about getting your dress altered," she says in a tone laced with judgment.

Uh oh, I've upset Evan's second mama bear.

Without catching my breath, I dive into it. "Look Maribel, this week has been a mess. I thought Evan was cheating, but he wasn't. But he left my party after someone called him, so obviously I thought it was a girl. My ex-fiancé cheated on me, did Evan tell you I was engaged before? Anyways, he was hiding a secret from me, but it wasn't that secret, and now he's going to be at this event surrounded by beautiful women. And we haven't talked since my party, and he's going to forget that I love him, and that I didn't mean—"

"Breathe, Amelia." Maribel grabs me by my shoulders. "You love him?"

"Yes, I love him. I love him, holy fuckballs I love him so much and all this time he's been so patient with me and after one fight I just up and leave him. Maribel, please you need to help me," I plead breathlessly.

"Dear, I say this with affection. But you need to learn to shut your trap so I can help you already."

"Yes!!! Thank you, thank you, thank you Maribel." I smother her cheek with kisses.

"Okay, I'll call down to the salon and get you a hair, makeup, and waxing appointment."

"Waxing?" I say in a high pitched voice.

Maribel gives me a once over. "If the downstairs are looking like the rest of you, then a waxing will be necessary. Are you trying to win Evan back or send him on a safari?" Her eyeline drops to my crotch.

"Sheesh, okay fine. But I swear to God if this man doesn't forgive me after I get a bikini wax—"

"Brazilian."

"Ughhhhhhh. The things I do for Evan *Fucking* Cooper!"

Three hours later I am in perfect hair and makeup, and down south I am as bare as the day I was born.

Maribel makes me change into a luxurious robe when I get back to her floor. I'm going to have to go with a sample piece since there is no time for alterations.

"Thanks so much Maribel for all of your help, you have literally been my fairy Godmother today. I don't know how to thank you."

She smiles warmly. "Just make sure to have me style you for all of your pre-wedding festivities," she says with a playful wink.

"Okay, so now the dress. It's winter wonderland, so we're limited on the colors," I say as I walk by all the immaculate dresses lined up on the hangers.

Maribel calls two younger gentlemen over and the three of them start chattering quietly to themselves. One of the men eyes me up and down to the point where I feel exposed, so I pull onto my robe tighter.

The other puts his hand over his forehead and is saying "no" a million times at lightning speed, in a French accent.

Maribel steps forward and the other two men follow suit. "It could work, she does have the body for it," the shorter one says.

"And there will be a lot of press." Maribel continues.

"You've got to be kidding me." The tall French man scoffs, then walks up to me.

"Um, you guys want to let me into your little pow wow anytime soon?" My words falling on deaf ears.

"Maribel, you say there will be plenty of press at this event?" The French man says while moving his fingers in a circle, indicating that he wants me to spin. I'm wearing a chucky robe, what are they even looking at?

"Guys, I hate to break up the fun, but the party already started, so I need to be out of here in ten minutes!" I shriek in a panic.

They all look at one another, then nod in unison.

"I'll grab the Louboutins," says the short man before he disappears.

"I'll grab the shapewear, we're gonna need it," says the French mean one.

"Follow me Amelia, we have your dress. In the room next door," Maribel says over her shoulder.

I scurry behind her, trying not to trip in my oversized fancy slippers.

Maribel stands in front of a closed room with double doors.

"You store more dresses in there?" I point to the room behind her.

Maribel smiles. "Not any dress, but *the* dress." She proceeds to open both doors at once and in the center of the room is one dress fitted on a glossy mannequin on a stage.

Oh. My. God.

It looks like a piece of art. Surely I can't be trusted to wear it.

It's a black, off the shoulder dress with a very full skirt. The top layer of the skirt has a shimmery material that makes it look like the stars in the sky. And there is a slit. A very high slit. I'm talking Angelina Jolie, leg popped out slit. Thank God I just got waxed.

My breath hitches when I glance down in front of the small stage and see the name *Oscar de la Renta*.

Mami, is this you again?

I didn't notice at first glance, but this is a *much* sexier version of my future wedding dress. In a completely different color, material and a few alterations like that high slit, but the similarities are there.

I close my eyes and take a deep breath.

"Spill anything on her, and Evan might lose a zero on the end of his net worth," Maribel teases. "Now let's get you dressed; we have a prince waiting for you at the ball."

So much for showing up to this party while flying under the radar. Guess it's time to make a splash.

"Maribel, any chance I can get some of that yummy champagne from last time? Something tells me I'm going to need it."

39

EVAN

"I'll have another scotch," I say to the bartender.

"Evan, are you sure you don't want to pace yourself? The night is young after all," my assistant Hayden says.

"It's my second drink. What's the big deal?" I scoff.

"Oh nothing. It's just that you usually don't drink at charity events. Plus, you have so many people to meet and mingle with, right?" he asks while nervously eyeing the crowd.

"Is everything okay, Hayden? Is there something you need to tell me?" I ask.

His gaze shoots back to me like a kid whose hand got caught in the cookie jar. "Nope, nothing to say. All good in the hood. Yep." He nods.

"Maybe you need a drink, you seem a bit on edge. Consider yourself off the clock. I don't intend on staying much longer anyways." I pick up my fresh glass of scotch.

"No! You can't leave. I mean, at least not yet." He looks down at his phone and types ferociously. It beeps in his hands, then he looks up at me more relaxed. "Actually, you're right. I probably just need a glass of champagne or something to relax." He smiles as he takes a glass off a tray from a waiter walking past us.

I swear everyone is losing their damn minds this week.

The music goes from low, instrumental strings to a song with words and bass. Is there a performance happening tonight? I look over at Hayden and he looks like he is bursting at the seams, biting on his bottom lip while avoiding all eye contact with me.

This song. It sounds familiar. This sounds like something off of Amelia's playlist when we were up in the cabin.

Or maybe it's just a popular song and I just can't get my mind off of her.

I slowly start to notice people's gazes turning to the front door. There are men cranking their necks trying to get a look at what all the fuss is about. Probably a hot chick. Idiots.

I finish the last of my drink and set the glass on the bar.

"I think I'm going to head out, Hayden. Have a good night."

"Are you sure about that boss?" Hayden smiles widely.

Then I hear the bartender speak. "Fucking hell. Who the fuck is that goddess?"

I follow his gaze until it reaches the woman in question, and I need to lean against the bar to prevent my knees from fully buckling and sending me to the ground.

Amelia is parting the crowd simply by walking with such determination and sex appeal. Her dress ensures that no one can get within three feet of her unless they want to be taken down by her full skirt. Every man she passes seems to have trouble catching their breath.

And then I notice her leg.

From the red-bottomed shoe, all the way up to the top of her thigh, her leg pops through the shimmering black fabric every time steps forward.

Cameras flash all around her as the media photographers try to get a shot of the moving siren.

Her hair bounces with big smooth curls, swaying all the way down her back and her lips look deviant in a luscious red.

I can see her searching the crowd as she smiles, walking past some of New York City's elite in the process. Then she spots me, and her eyes lock onto mine.

"I think she's here for you boss." Hayden straightens me out and nudges me in her direction.

I will my body to regain its composure and manage to help close the distance between us, but not by much.

I'm still stunned as she gets closer to me. I don't want to scare her off. I don't want to say the wrong thing. My brain is scrambled at the moment and all I can think about is *don't fuck this up.*

It might be all in my head, but I feel the music get louder and can feel the bass in my bones as she smiles at me.

Don't fuck this up.

Say you're sorry.

Beg if you have to.

Cling onto her for dear life.

Amelia finally is standing within arm's reach of me, when she stops.

"Amelia …"

She walks into my embrace and wraps her hands behind my neck. I close my eyes and I rest my forehead on hers.

"Amelia…" is all I can manage to say as my brain is in overdrive. I don't even notice the mob of photographers surrounding us.

Amelia leans back an inch. "Evan Cooper, you better look at me when I say this," she smiles as soon as my eyes meet hers.

I pull her closer by the small of her back and keep her flush to me.

"I love you, Evan. I messed up, and I'm sorry. I came here to let you know that I'm ready." She smiles tenderly. "I told you at the cabin that it would always be you. When I was ready, I would be choosing you. Well, that's now baby. I'm ready for us, and everything that comes along with that—"

Before she can carry on, my lips are crashing into hers and I can feel her smiling on my lips.

I can faintly gather that people have now surrounded us and are cheering us on while snapping photos.

"Wait, wait. Say something! Am I forgiven?!" Amelia giggles as she tries to escape from my desperate kiss.

"I love you. I love you so much Amelia, I am so sorry I hurt you. I swear to you it is not what you think. I'll tell you everything tonight, I promise." I brush her cheek with my thumb.

"Oh, I know," she says, eyeing me mischievously.

"You know?" I ask, perplexed.

"I had a nice little chat with LC today. Crazy family resemblance if I do say so myself." She smirks.

My jaw drops and she leans into my ear. "Baby, they're taking lots of pictures of us, can you please not look like I just told you that I'm pregnant or something?" She chuckles.

I suddenly become hyper aware of our surroundings and holy hell has it gotten hectic around us.

I feel someone tap my shoulder and notice that it's Hayden. "Teddy is out front with the car. Now you can leave boss," he says with a wink.

I look back to Amelia. "He knew?! What the hell is happening?" I ask, shocked.

"We can talk about it in the car. Let's go before you owe Maribel a fortune for ruining this dress!"

I grab her hand and I start to lead us out of the venue. Flashes never falter as I stare down at her and she beams at me. We must look like a runaway bride *and* groom.

Which reminds me. My plan to get her to marry me is back on.

We make it to the awaiting SUV, and it takes both Teddy and I to carefully get all of Amelia's dress in the car, and I'm loving every second of it. Once she's finally settled, I run to the other side of the car while waving at the awaiting paparazzi. I don't think I've ever even acknowledged them, and now I'm smiling at them like a lovesick fool with red lipstick smeared on my lips.

We make it to my apartment in record time and we wish Teddy a goodnight. Once Amelia arrived at the charity event, she had the forethought to let Hayden know that I would want us to have security for the night, so I am greeted with my usual team at the entrance of the building, and the rest wait upstairs in my hallway.

"Am I that predictable?" I ask as I open the door to my apartment.

"I wanted everything to be perfect tonight, and I knew you wouldn't relax unless you knew I was fully safe while staying at your place." She kisses the back of my hand.

Once the door is locked and the security system is activated, I pull her into my arms again. "I love you so much Amelia. Please never leave me like that again," I say as I stare into her eyes.

"Well technically, *you're* the one that left, but let's not get lost in the semantics right now." She grins.

"Okay, now get in the shower while I make us some food."

"You're not going to join me?" she asks, dumbfounded.

"No sweet cheeks. We're doing showers, food, and then having the conversation of the century. No distractions. Once it's all on the table, and you decide if we're all in, then and only then, will we get to the love making part."

"Sheesh. Tough crowd. Fine, but I need two favors first."

"Okay." I squint at her.

"First, I need you to help me out of this corseted top."

"Alright, that I can do." I smile as I walk up to her.

"And second, you need to look away once the dress gets loose enough because I'm pretty sure I look like a stuffed sausage under all this." She gestures all over her upper body.

My woman is weird, but I wouldn't have it any other way.

∼

We're now both showered, fed, and in sweats sitting on my couch.

Amelia made us some tea, and I feel like I'm going to need to add whisky to mine by the way my right knee keepings bouncing.

Amelia nestles closer to me and places her hands on my leg to stop me from shaking the couch. "It's okay baby. Whenever you're ready. I'm here to listen, not judge."

I close my eyes and take a deep breath. I'll start with what she already knows. "So, I'm guessing you know by now that my dad was incarcerated. So technically, he didn't walk out on us, he was in prison."

That's the first time I've ever said that sentence out loud.

I feel Amelia take hold of my hands, and instantly feel better, so I continue. "It was tough being the kid at school whose dad was locked up on a murder charge, even if he didn't actually commit the crime. The bullying got really bad. I was in a fist fight at least once a day. I only lasted one month in school after he went to prison, when my mom pulled me out, and moved us to New York. She wanted us to have a fresh start. She also struggled with being the wife of a convicted felon, and she knew she was one shift away from being fired due to the hospital gossip."

"Evan, I'm so sorry. That must have been such a hard time for you and your mom. I had no idea you guys struggled so badly before we met you. But it makes sense," she says.

"Why do you say that?"

"You and your mom are some of the most resilient people I know. I thought it had to do with her being a single mom in the city, and you having to grow up quickly to help support her, but now I see it was all of that and much more. You're a fighter baby." She kisses the back of my hand and my heart sinks with guilt, the story isn't over.

I take another deep breath. "My dad never stopped sending me letters. During my teen years I was angry, so I never took his calls, and after a while, he got the hint, but he never stopped writing to me. Over the summer, he sent me one that said he'd been out of prison for a few months, and had moved to the city. Left his contact details and asked if we could meet. It was the first letter I responded to. After a few awkward phone calls, we agreed to meet in person, and he explained why he got involved in illegal activities."

I look over to Amelia and her eyes are soft with sympathy, so I keep going. "Apparently, money was tight and he had a few neighborhood friends who made easy money by making simple drop offs."

"Drop offs? I'm assuming that's lingo for drugs and not laundry?"

"You would be correct. My dad made a handful of drop offs without a hitch, which helped our financial situation immensely. So when his friend asked him to drive him to a drop off, my dad said yes. Once there, he realized he was actually the getaway driver, and his pals were robbing a pawn shop. He heard a gun go off, and his instinct was to drive off as soon as his friends got in the car. He says that if he had ran off and called an ambulance or the cops, then his sentence would have been reduced. But because of his split second decision, the judge thought he had a hand in a man's death, and therefore they all got the same sentence."

"Wow," is all Amelia can say to that information overload.

"Yeah. The fucked up part is that growing up, I always promised myself that I would never be like him. That I would pave my own way in life, even if that meant I had to struggle a little." I take a sip of tea. "But once he told me his story, I realized that I had done the exact opposite. I was no better than my dad. In fact, we're both guilty of the same crime."

No turning back now.

"Wait, what are you saying? You were a getaway driver in a crime?" Amelia asks, stunned.

I give her a tight smile. "No. Not quite as dramatic as my dad's story, but its consequences are just as bad."

Amelia cups my face in her hands. "Evan, spit it out. No more beating around the bush. I'm not going anywhere. We will figure this out together. And if you question how serious I mean it, you're gonna have a very pissed off Dominican woman—who got waxed in ungodly places might I add—lighting your shit on fire." A small smile escapes her lips as she adorably tries to put the fear of God in me.

She's actually going to stay. It's finally time to let her in.

"As you know, I've loved computers all of my life. My mom worked a lot of shifts, so I would have all the time in the world to build computers, play games on them, and create programs."

Amelia nods.

"So when I was in college, I created the software that is now known as PassportMed. I knew that with the right funding, I could turn it into what it is today, but back then, I was having terrible luck finding investors. Every kid in college believes that they have the million dollar idea, so it was hard to stand out in the crowd. During that time, my mom was clearly burning out. Money was still non-existent, and yet she always managed to send me a couple hundred dollars, even when I told her not to."

Amelia squeezes my hand in solidarity.

"Anyways, I couldn't take seeing her struggle anymore. I knew in my gut that I was sitting on a solid software that could generate millions, so like my dad, I took a detour to get it done. I asked an old friend for money."

I look over at Amelia, and she seems none too impressed with my story. "You asked a friend for a loan? Okay … Am I missing something here? Because Nikki and I used to borrow money off of each other all of the time, Evan."

I smile at her innocence. "Not just any little loan Amelia. A fifty-thousand-dollar loan. Given to me at the age of twenty-two. That's life changing money."

"Wow, okay. I didn't know you had fancy rich childhood friends."

"I don't. This is where the similarities with my dad come into play. The person I borrowed this money from doesn't have a nine to five … He's in the cartel business."

Amelia's reaction is noticeable for a second, before she takes control back, and grips my hand tighter. "Go on babe," she encourages.

"I used to know this kid. He lived near my neighborhood, and we sometimes would play basketball together. I knew even back then what his family did for a living, but he was never involved, he was a solid kid. But then I started spending more time with Antonio and your family, and less with him. During that same time, he started dabbling in the family business. And we drifted apart. Fast forward a couple years later, I ran into him at a bar, and he'd completely transformed himself. He now goes by Mr. Valentine. He wears nice clothes, expensive watches, and seems to have a higher rank than just errand boy." I run my hand over my face, hating that I'm reliving the worst decision of my life.

"Anyways, we got a little drunk reminiscing on old times, and we got to chatting about my software. And just like that, right there and then, he offered to front me the cash, no questions asked. For old time's sake. I was young and stupid, and believed that these kinds of things had no strings attached, so I eagerly accepted the money. I used that seed money to invest in my software, and it blew up to what it is now. So PassportMed was funded on borrowed drug money." I blow out a breath and so does Amelia.

"Evan, you got a loan from a shady guy. That doesn't make you a bad person, and it doesn't make your accomplishments any less admirable."

"No Amelia, that's exactly what it means. I have no integrity. I was surrounded by your family during the holidays and heard their struggles, real struggles. From immigrating to a new country, learning the language, dealing with racist pricks, having to retake medical exams and work their way back up the totem pole with no guarantee that it'll work out in the end, just so that they can try and provide a better future for their children. That is integrity, that shows the character of a man, and I am no better than my father for taking the easy way out. "

"Evan, stop," Amelia pleads.

"I'm actually worse than my father, now that I think of it. He at least paid for his crime. What did I get? Huh? I became insanely rich. It's a fucking joke. I've spent the last decade trying to downplay my finances to your family because I know I don't deserve them. And now, after all these years, it's finally caught up to me. And you're what's at risk." My eyes burn with fury.

"What do you mean Evan? Did you ever pay him back?" Amelia asks, her face wrangled with worry.

"Of course I paid him back. Six months after he gave me the loan, I paid him back with interest. It was basically all the money I had just made off of it. I got more investors once my software gained visibility, and a year after that I gave him fifty thousand more as a thank you, and told him to consider it as a gift for his mom, who I knew was sick. He seemed to appreciate the gesture, and I assumed that would be the end of it for us, until this summer happened."

"What happened this summer?"

"I was on the cover of Forbes magazine with my team. The company net worth was printed, along with our projections for what we expect to make once our international deal goes public. Billions. He reached out to me for a meeting, which I felt I couldn't turn down due to our history. If he spoke to reporters, it could blow up this deal and I could not stand the thought of seeing thousands of our employees losing their jobs, not being able to feed their families, due to a scandal. So against my better judgment, and that of my security teams, we all met."

"What did he want?"

"He wanted fifty million dollars."

"What?!" Amelia shouts.

"Yeah. My thoughts exactly. Says he deserved it since he was my first investor. Said he could retire out of his 'enterprise' with that kind of money and move to the Caribbean. I shut him down and left. I knew that any money given to him would be traced and would be just as bad if he outed our original loan setup. I didn't think about it again, until after we got back from the cabin."

Amelia visibly stiffens at the mention of the cabin. "What happened after the cabin?"

"Remember when I had to leave you after your holiday party because LC called me?"

She nods.

"Well, dad's been working as a PI, and he stumbled on some information. One of Mr. Valentine's patsy got drunk at a bar and started blabbering about a job Mr. Valentine had him do. Take pictures of a rich tech guys' cabin up in the Berkshires."

Amelia's hand covers her mouth. "Does that mean ... that's what I saw. Out in the backyard?"

"Yes. My team set up a meeting with Mr. Valentine. He had the pictures. Pictures of us, at the cabin. And now his old deal was off the table, and he had a new one. Twenty percent stock in my company. He seemed much angrier this time and not as cocky. I offered the fifty million, but he spat at my feet at the notion. I told him I would bring it up to my board, but I knew there would be no way in hell that would happen. He's a well known drug lord. There is no way he would have a seat in corporate America. And I knew he'd known that as well, so I had no clue what he was playing at. Until your birthday."

"Oh God," She says, eyes brimming with tears.

"I left your party because he set up a meeting with me. He said he would drop all the threats under one condition. I stop dating you. Stop seeing you completely."

"Me?!" Amelia screeches. "What does this have to do with me?"

"Nothing baby. It's another one of his mind games. He wants control. He can't have my money, so he wants my happiness. In his sick mind he must think that we're even if I'm not able to be with the one woman I love."

"You can't be serious, Evan. Please tell me you're not going to let us go because of a psychopath!" Amelia digs her hands into my thighs.

"I was. After your birthday party, when you weren't answering my calls, I thought that maybe it was for the best. At least until things cooled down with this Valentine guy. As heartbroken as I was, at least I knew you were safe."

I lean down and wipe the tears off her face. "But then you came back to me. And I don't care if I have to move us to Fort Knox or a deserted island, I'm never leaving your side again, baby." I kiss her gently and she pulls herself onto my lap. Holding onto me as her tears subside.

"Okay is that the end of the story now or is there more? Because if there is, I'm going to have to dump this lukewarm tea out for a chilled shot of tequila." She sniffles into my neck.

I run my hands up and down her back. "That's all of it. So now you know everything. Now you can take the information and make a decision on how you want to move forward."

She leans back. "Move forward?"

"With us. That's a lot of information and a lot of baggage to take on. You need to give yourself the opportunity to—" Amelia jumps off my lap. She wipes her tears away ferociously and towers over me on the couch.

"Mira Evan, you listen and you listen to me real good." She points her index finger at me. "The only thing this changes, is that now you have a partner to help you take this bastard down. You are never doing life alone again, do you hear me?"

I stand up to hug her, but she surprises me by pushing me back on the couch with one hand. Hard.

She bolts to the kitchen and makes good on that promise of getting tequila. She pours us two generous shots and comes back to hand me one. I can tell she's raging inside.

"Who the hell does this Mr. Valentine guy think he is? What a stupid name anyways. Plus, you have more money than God, we can just have security until things cool down, or better yet, we can take him down! Yeah, that's what we'll do. We'll gather evidence on him, and send him to prison, then *poof* problem solved." She tips her glass in my direction to cheers, fully content with herself for seemingly coming up with a plan for us.

I pull her back down on the couch. "How about we save your master plans for tomorrow, and tonight you just let me hold you?" I kiss her shoulder.

Amelia takes a sip of her tequila, then slowly settles herself onto my lap again after a couple of calming breaths, letting her nails gently caress the back of my neck. "Evan, we're going to get through this. But I need us to be on the same page. We're endgame. No matter what happens, we're in it together. Got it?"

I smile like a fool.

"What are you smiling at! I'm laying down the law here Evan!" she scolds.

"I've spent forever trying to figure out how to convince you to love me, and now you're threatening me with your love. Ain't that some good shit." I chuckle.

She pushes my shoulder playfully. "Shut up, let's get to bed. I have a war to plan tomorrow." She makes an attempt to move off of my lap, but my hands keep her in place.

"Yeah, but before we do, what's this waxing situation you were speaking of earlier?"

40

AMELIA

IT'S EIGHT AM AND I'M AWOKEN BY EVAN'S PHONE ringing.

The screen says **Security**. I ask him to put it on speaker. No more secrets.

"Good morning Mr. Cooper, we have an Officer Antonio Nuñez down here. Says he has breakfast plans with you. How would you like us to proceed?

Fuck.

"Um, yeah. He's a friend. I'll call him and tell him I'm busy today," he stammers while rubbing his eyes.

"Actually, tell him he can come up," I say into the phone as I get out of bed and head to the bathroom to brush my teeth.

"What?!" Evan hisses at me as he bolts out of bed.

"What's it gonna be boss? Let him up, or no?" The security guy chuckles.

"Yes, please. Maybe one of you escort him up. Just to be safe," I yell from the bathroom.

Evan looks at me as if I've grown a second head.

"Hold on a sec. Tell him I'm taking a shit. I'll call you right back," Evans says into the phone while staring at me.

I'm moving quickly through the closet. Pulling a sweater and leggings off of a shelf.

"Care to let me in on what you're doing," Evan says.

"Not living in fear. You should try it sometime, babe," I tease.

"You think now is the time to tell Antonio? After you've spent the night?" Evan pulls at his hair.

I finish getting dressed, then place my hands on my hips. "Evan, last night you told me there's a psychopathic drug lord trying to keep us apart. I've got bigger fish to fry than worrying about my older brother's reaction to me dating his best friend. Call back now. Let him up. Put on a shirt."

He stares at me blankly.

"¡Ahora!" I clap repeatedly.

"Si señorita," Evan mumbles to himself. "Nice knowing ya. Just remember I want to be cremated, not buried." He rolls his eyes as he calls security to let Antonio up.

I make my way to the kitchen and start a pot of coffee.

Evan comes up behind me, dressed in a black sweater and dark jeans. "So what's the game plan? How are we breaking it to him? Do you want me to start, or do you start?" he says while wringing his hands together.

I start laughing. "Amelia, why are you laughing for fucks sake, your brother is on his way up here right now!" he says, panicked.

"I've just never heard you ramble before. It's quite adorable." I stand on my tip toes and place a soft kiss on his lips. "I got this baby, don't worry."

We hear a knock on the door.

Evan groans. "What does that mean, Amelia?"

I walk to the front door with Evan hot on my heels. Then he takes a giant step back, as if that will help the situation.

I swing the front door open and smile widely. "Good morning big bro. Want some coffee?" Antonio stares at me then over to Evan. Antonio is still in his officer uniform. He probably just got off from working the graveyard shift.

Antonio's mouth drops, but I cut in before his brain catches up to what his eyes see.

"Antonio, you see those two big dudes behind you?" Antonio looks back at them and then back at me, his jaw slightly slacked. "They're highly trained security officers. I need you to remember that information for what I say next."

Antonio shakes his head in an attempt to process what he just walked into. "What the hell are you doing here Amelia?"

"Evan and I are dating. Not only dating, but we're in love. If you want to come in and talk about it like a grown man, I've made some coffee. If you want to throw a tantrum and start swinging at Evan, then I urge you to remember the two security guards standing behind you." I nod behind him.

Antonio stares at Evan over my head. "What?!" he shouts.

I point my finger into Antonio's chest. "Option one or option two, Tony?" I glare at him. I can feel his chest rising under my finger, so I push it down harder.

"Coffee," he barks.

"Good choice. Go sit at the dining table and I'll bring you a cup," I say sweetly.

Antonio walks into the apartment while staring at Evan.

"We good here?" security says, clearly amused.

"Yeah, all good." Evan nods as he shoots me a look.

"Evan, can you grab your own mug, I'll carry mine and Antonio's."

"What fucking twilight zone did I walk into?" Antonio asks while his eyes bounce back and forth between Evan and me.

I sit at the head of the dining table, with Evan on my right, and Antonio on my left.

Evan beats me to it before I've fully settled into my seat. "Antonio, I'm in love with your sister. I'm sorry I kept this information from you, but we've been trying to figure out our feelings before we started telling people." Evan holds my hand over the table, and Antonio looks at where our hands touch in disgust.

"Telling people? You can't be serious. How long has this been going on?" he spits out.

When it comes to Antonio, I usually let a lot of shit slide when he plays the overprotective big brother role. And I've given him even more leeway ever since mom died. But seeing the way he's reacting to my happiness snaps something inside me.

I shoot up out of my seat, sending the chair flying behind me. Startling both men. "Mira Antonio. I'm going to let your initial reaction slide, because I know this is surprising. But I need you to pull your head out of your ass for a second and listen to what we're fucking saying. We're in love with each other. Do you know what that means? It means we make each other happy. If you give a shit about me or my happiness, then these feelings should matter more than whatever bro code that prohibits Evan from touching me," I scold.

Antonio crosses his arms over his chest and looks down at the table, but I don't relent. "What would mom say about your reaction right now?"

Antonio slumps lower in his chair, but stays silent.

I pick up my chair and take back my place at the table. "Antonio, I know this sounds stupid, but I think mom had a hand in getting Evan and I together." I take Evan's hand back in mine and smile at him.

"That snowstorm named Anna. It came out of nowhere. It forced Evan and I to talk about our feelings for one another. This isn't something we're doing on a whim, and we're not going to stop loving each other because you're upset, but I would love it if my big brother would give us a chance and get on board."

Antonio's eyes finally meet mine, and he lets out a sigh. "So, you're saying that you're happy?"

My eyes soften. "Yes, I am." I say, squeezing Evan's hand in mine, and Evan lifts it to kiss it. Antonio watches this interaction with less disdain.

"I guess I can skip the part where I threaten to kill you if you hurt her?" Antonio deadpans to Evan.

"Wouldn't dream of it, man." Evan holds eye contact with Antonio, and Antonio nods.

"Alright then. Guess that's that. But please no kissing or PDA until I leave. Give me a grace period. This is too weird for me right now," he murmurs.

I jump up and wrap my arms around him. He keeps his arms crossed over his chest and rolls his eyes, but there is a hint of a smile in there. "Have I told you you're the best brother ever?" I squeeze him harder.

"Yeah, yeah. You guys gonna feed me or something? I came here for breakfast, not this lovefest.

"Actually, you and Evan have some other pressing matter to talk about, I can order some food so you can discuss over bagels."

Evan shoots me a warning look, and I give him one right back.

"Do you guys already have a secret language? God, I didn't know I would need a drink this early in the day." Antonio complains.

"Evan, I know you come with baggage, but so do I," I say pointing to my brother. "And my baggage happens to be an NYPD officer, so we aren't keeping any more secrets."

"Amelia—" Evan starts.

"No. More. Secrets." I stare at Evan, not leaving room for discussion. He waves at Antonio, letting me know he concedes, then proceeds to run my brother through the whole story.

"Wait, what the fuck are you talking about? You're in the crossfire of a drug dealer, Amelia?" Antonio shoots forward in his seat.

"Well technically I think Evan called him a drug lord last night. Anyways, we'll probably need your help."

"What the fuck have you've gotten my sister involved with Evan?" Antonio snaps at Evan.

"I'm handling it. Hence all the security," Evan says while pointing at the front door.

"Fucking hell." Antonio starts pacing the apartment.

"Why don't you guys put your heads together and come up with a solution? I'm going to head out to my apartment to grab a few things," I say.

"No, you're not," the men say in unison.

Great. Now they're in cahoots. That took long enough. "Don't worry, I'll take one of your beefy security guards with me." I wiggle my eyebrows in an attempt to lighten the mood.

"Until we get to the bottom of this, you're not going anywhere. Besides, what's so important that you need to go to your apartment right now?" Antonio asks sternly.

"Well. I need my work laptop, so I can work from home here, and some other stuff. I'll be in and out in ten minutes, you can time me!" I say quickly.

"I can send someone to get your laptop later Amelia, you're staying put." Evan waves for me to walk to the couch.

Well, I did ask for no more secrets...

"I need to go get my birth control," I say matter of factly.

Both men stare at me for a moment, so I continue.

"I finished my old pack while staying at Antonio's, and I can't remember where in my apartment I stored my new monthly supply. So yeah, I need to go get it, unless you guys plan on bringing a baby into this mix." I circle a finger between the three of us.

Evan's face is beet red and Antonio is back to looking disgusted, but at least it worked.

I am now being escorted by four bodyguards to my apartment, flanked like I'm the President being walked to an awaiting SUV. I'm driven the short distance to my apartment and only allowed to leave the vehicle once two of the men have searched my place for the boogeyman.

Once inside the building, two men stand guard at the entrance of the building, while two others follow me to my apartment.

"We'll be out here in the hallway and we're leaving your front door open. Let us know if you need any help carrying anything miss," says the lead bodyguard.

"Thanks, I'll be quick." I wave as I head into the tiny studio apartment.

I grab a tote bag, since I might as well bring a couple of my old comfy clothes with me, it seems like I'm moving in with Evan for the foreseeable future.

I hear some noise in the hallway and look out my front door. It's Mrs. Camacho, my elderly next-door neighbor pestering the guards with questions. She's known for being nosey. I giggle to myself and focus on the task at hand.

I head into my bathroom and collect my toiletries, tampons and pads. Lucky Evan. Then I look in my medicine cabinet, looking for my birth control. No luck. I make a mental note to be more organized with my pills now that I expect to be having a lot more sex. I smile like a goof to myself.

I hear more noise out in the hallway, but ignore it, Mrs. Camacho will still be there when I'm done here.

I open the cabinet under the sink, and bingo! My birth control is here and ready to go. I should be good to leave. Anything else I need is probably already at Evan's or can be easily delivered to me.

I open my bathroom door and notice that Mrs. Camacho is no longer there. Actually, no one is at my front door. Maybe she convinced the men to help her out of the building. The lady is also a flirt. I'm shutting off the bathroom light when I notice a man casually stroll into my apartment.

Wait. This isn't right. Is that...

"Hello there Amelia."

"Julian. Hi. What are you doing here?" I ask while trying to compute how Julian Vazquez is now here. In my apartment.

He smiles mischievously, "Just here to drop these off."

I look down and see him carrying a bouquet of black roses.

"W-why are you bringing me roses Julian," I say trying to lighten the tense mood. It's like my body knows it's in danger, but my brain hasn't caught up yet. "The Julian Vasquez I knew never bought girls roses. I pegged you as more of a chocolates guy." I force a smile.

"Yeah, well a lot has changed since we last hung out, Amelia. I now like to go by Julian Valentine."

My heart stops.

Mr. Valentine.

Julian is Mr. *Fucking* Valentine.

Julian smirks. "By the look on your face it seems like your boyfriend may have already told you about me. I knew he'd run and snitch to you. But I'll worry about him later. Right now, you and I are gonna take a stroll down memory lane," he says while touching a rose petal.

My body is humming with panic as I eye the door, searching for the damn guards.

"The guards are busy taking a little cat nap Amelia. They're not coming," he taunts with a smile on his face.

My eyes widen with fear.

"Don't worry, they'll live. But we gotta get going sweetheart, before they wake up and they're all groggy."

"I'm not going anywhere with you Julian," I say in a slow drawl. Anger taking over and pulsing through my veins.

Julian cocks his head to the side. "Yeah, I'd figure you'd say that. Which is why I have one of my buddies in the waiting room of your dad's hospital." He taps one finger over his temple while he squints his eyes at me. "Third floor, suite 352, office of Dr. Nuñez." He opens his eyes fully now and grins. "I got it right, didn't I?" He smirks.

I feel my throat tighten. "You stay the hell away from my father," I barely manage to whisper.

"I will, as long as you come with me. Just for a chat, mi amor. I wouldn't harm a hair on your head." He reaches his hand out to me.

At that moment, I needed to make a decision. Dateline should have prepared me better for this.

I know it's more dangerous to go to a secondary location with your captor. But if I don't go willingly, he'll probably take me anyways since I'm defenseless here, and I would be putting my father's life in danger.

I can't fight him. This man is clearly deranged. He brought me black fucking flowers. He thinks this is flirting. I can't interrupt the fantasy. I need to play along. I need to fucking survive. For me. For Evan.

So I slip my hand into his. "Where to Mr. Valentine?"

41

EVAN

"So, who is this guy? I need a name so I can ask around and see what kind of danger we're dealing with," Antonio says with his cop stance.

"He goes by Mr. Valentine now. I used to know him as Julian Vasquez back in the day."

"You've got to be fucking kidding," Antonio yells.

"What is it? You know the guy?"

"Of course I know the guy! My parents knew his mom. She was nice, but my parents found out what her husband did for a living and forbade me from hanging with Julian. But not before he gave Amelia her first kiss."

First kiss?

My blood begins to boil.

"What are you saying Tony?" I shout.

"I read her diary once. Save the judgements for later. She wrote about her first kiss at the neighborhood laundromat with a kid named Julian and I knew it was him. He was always following me around, but I guess it was actually to be closer to Amelia." Antonio kicks a chair. Then his eyes widen, realization seems to overcome him. "Amelia's birthday. He came by the pub and talked to Amelia. I stood by her, so he didn't get any ideas, but the fucker was clearly flirting with her. It happened after you left."

After I left Amelia. He was able to get to her once. He will try again.

I'm going to kill this man.

"I'm going to call Amelia to come back. This whole thing isn't about getting back at me, it's about getting to Amelia." I run to the kitchen to get my phone when Antonio's cell starts ringing.

"Nikki is calling me; she's never called me before," Antonio says before he picks up the call and puts it on speaker. "Is everything ok?" Antonio asks.

"Tony! I just called the cops. There are four guys passed out in the lobby, and Amelia's door is wide open. There are black flowers scattered everywhere. I think something bad has happened to her. She won't answer any of my calls!"

Antonio goes pale, and I'm sure I do too. He goes straight into cop mode.

"Did you already walk into her apartment?" he starts.

"Yes! Are you listening to me?! There are black flowers everywhere and a tote bag filled with her makeup and tampons, this doesn't make any sense!" Nikki yells.

"Okay, so you've already contaminated the crime scene. Listen carefully. Do you see a note by the flowers, or anything that would indicate where she's gone?"

"Give me a sec to look," she says.

I text Rocco that his team has been compromised, and that Amelia is missing. I'm not sure why, but I forward the same message to my dad.

"I found a card! Oh God," Nikki whimpers.

"What does it say Nikki?!" Antonio barks.

"You never forget your first."

"Officer Nuñez to dispatch, please be advised that I am en route to a potential hostage situation at a laundromat on the corner of Ninety Sixth and Amsterdam Avenue. The suspected kidnapping victim is my sister, Amelia Nuñez. Suspect Julian Vazquez, AKA Julian Valentine, is considered armed and dangerous. All nearby vehicles please respond," Antonio says into the patrol car's radio as we speed down Amsterdam Avenue, sirens blaring.

I've updated Rocco and my father, and they're on their way. Rocco's team is gathering all surveillance near Amelia's apartment building and my dad is pulling favors from everyone he knows to get information on Julian's whereabouts.

"Are you sure they're gonna be there?" I ask Antonio.

"Of course not! But this sick fuck is reminiscing about their first kiss, so this is the only place I can imagine him taking her. Fuck!" He slams the steering wheel as pedestrians try to run out of his path.

"This is all my fault, Tony. I'm so sorry." My voice cracks.

"Stop that shit right now. We can throw around the blame later, but right now I need you to focus. You're gonna have to be my partner when we get in there, okay?" he says as he looks over to me.

"Okay." I nod.

"Dispatch to Officer Nuñez, please move over to station twenty three, your Captain is on the line."

"10-4. This is Officer Nuñez."

"What the hell is this I'm hearing about a hostage situation? And it's your sister? What the fuck is happening?" his Captain demands.

"Just like you heard it, sir. I'm two minutes out and I have a civilian riding along with me," Antonio states.

"Hardly a time for a joy ride, Nuñez. Who's riding with you?"

"His name is Evan Cooper. He's ... He's my best friend and my sister's boyfriend."

"For fuck's sake, it's already a family affair. Look, a lot of my officers are dealing with a protest gone sour by Central Park, so we don't have many officers available, but I'll funnel as many as I can. But don't you dare go in there until we have confirmation that she's there and you have backup. Even then, once you have eyes on her, wait for the hostage negotiator. You know the drill."

Antonio bares his teeth. "With all due respect sir, that's not happening. That's my sister in there. I will follow protocol to the best of my ability, but if I get in there and I have confirmation that she's alive and well, I'm going in."

"Nuñez. Stand down and wait for backup. That's an order. Need I remind you that your detective badge is on the line until you're sworn in after the new year?" his Captain barks.

"Yes, sir," Antonio responds, then turns off his radio.

"We're not waiting for backup, are we?" I side eye him.

"Not a chance."

42

AMELIA

I TRY TO REGULATE MY BREATHING AS I STAND SHAKILY while wiggling my wrists. Julian has tied them behind my back with zip ties, and they are already digging into my skin.

I quickly try to take in my surroundings, but there's no use since Julian hasn't turned on any lights. I know we're in a basement, because we used the sidewalk cellar doors to get in here, and all of New York City sounds muffled above me.

Julian flips on a light switch, causing three bare light bulbs hanging from the ceiling to flicker on. Still not much light, but at least I can make out a large desk in the center of the room, two walls lined with tools and other business supplies, and a small table with two chairs next to me. Julian opens a drawer from the large desk and takes out a small knife.

"Amelia, Amelia, Amelia. Alone at last," Julian says as he slowly makes his way towards me. "Do you even know where I've brought you, mi amor?" he asks with hopeful eyes.

"The Four Seasons?" I croak.

Julian's chest swells, followed by a deep laugh. "Ah, I've missed that sense of humor of yours. One of the many reasons why I knew I had to do everything in my power to get you back in my life," he says as he skims my arm with the knife with featherlike strokes. I stiffen at the feel of the cold metal. "Don't worry, I'm not gonna hurt you. Unless you give me a reason to. Plus, this is just my grandfather's lucky dagger. I'm not much of a gun guy. It's so impersonal if you ask me. And unnecessarily loud." He grimaces.

"Where are we, Julian?" I ask, hoping to refocus him.

"Oh, right. Well, you probably can't tell since we're in the basement, but we're back where it all started, the laundromat where we had our first kiss." He grins. "You see, for years I've bought and owned laundromats. It's a good cash business for my type of entrepreneurship. And once I saw that *our* laundromat was put on the market, I just knew I had to have it. I bought it for you, cariño." He places the knife under my chin and lifts until my eyes meet his. "You see, I've been doing a lot of things for us lately, for our future. Because I believe that fate has brought us together. Actually, I think our mothers had a hand in our rekindling."

The mention of my mother almost makes me head butt him, but I essentially have a knife to my throat, so that wouldn't be ideal.

"What do you mean by that?" I ask instead.

He smiles. "This summer, before my mother passed away, she told me she heard some neighborhood gossip about your fiancé cheating on you, therefore breaking up your engagement. I hadn't seen my mother light up while telling me *chisme* like that in years, since the cancer had made her so weak. She was always fond of you and your family, and once she found out that you were single, she told me in a not so subtle way, that I should settle down with a woman like you. Even better if I managed to actually woo you myself. Then I let her in on our little secret. The fact that I was the one to give you your first kiss. I told her how I found you sitting by yourself at this very laundromat as all of the older kids played out on the street without you. You seemed so sad, so I made it my mission to make you smile and forget about those losers you and your brother always hang out with. And how when you mentioned that you'd never been kissed, I didn't even hesitate before I laid one right on ya." He smiles fondly at the memory that now feels like a poison in my mind. "So when I found out that your mother had also passed away from cancer, I thought I would reconnect with you. But being a romantic at heart, I knew I needed to know more about you before I walked back into your life. I got locked up a few months ago on a silly technicality, and you're all I could think about when I was in prison. My lawyer eventually got the charges thrown out and my plan was back in action. Before I could start romancing you, I had to get to know you better. So naturally, I had you followed." He grabs me by my shoulder and slowly turns me to face the wall behind me, and I almost fall back into him when I realize what I'm looking at.

Hundreds of pictures of me. Grabbing coffee, walking to brunch with Nikki, leaving work late at night. It's all there. My every move in pictures for the last six months.

"Amelia, I now know your coffee order, how often you visit your dad, how late you work at the office. All the things you can't learn from a silly first date."

"So you've been following me since *before* the cabin?" I ask dumbfounded.

I hear him sigh behind me, then he points to a picture on the wall. It's a photo of Evan and I on the night when he showed up to the club to take me home. We are fighting in the picture; this was probably moments before I threw up on the sidewalk. "You can imagine my surprise when this weasel showed up on my surveillance. I thought that I had nothing to worry about, since you clearly had no issue telling him off, but then you went to the cabin with him. Alone." He tsks three times. "That's where fate steps in. A storm named Anna released her wrath. I took it as a sign that your mother was unhappy with you being holed up alone with Evan all weekend. So I made it my mission to speed up my timeline, and re-enter your life. I had already sent you flowers to your father's house the day after I saw you with Evan. And I had planned on revealing myself sooner to you, but Evan insisted on taking up all of your time. I had a weak moment on your birthday. I needed to see you in person. More importantly I needed you to see me. The way you looked at me told me everything I needed to know. There was a chance for us, and I just needed to stay the course. I gave Evan the ultimatum to leave you alone, or risk your safety. So imagine my surprise when I pick up the newspaper this morning."

He turns me around, then walks back to the desk. He picks up the newspaper and holds out the front page so I can see the picture and read the headline.

New York's most eligible bachelor is now a taken man. Evan Cooper locks lips with mystery beauty at his company's holiday party, sending all single ladies in New York into a weeping tailspin.

The headline is accompanied by a full page photo of Evan and I kissing, wrapped in each other's arms like a scene out of a movie.

Julian then throws the newspaper on the ground. "It's not fair Amelia. After all I've done, he got to kiss you. But he's not your first, I am." His voice becomes harsh and demanding. He places the knife on my chest and starts to draw small circles with it. "Tell me Amelia. Was he a better kisser than me?" He leans in closer, inches from my lips.

I freeze. My body is more repulsed by the idea of kissing him, than the cold knife pressed to my chest. I need to stay alive, but I don't know how much longer I can keep my hot head in line. Before I answer, I hear someone whistle. Julian and I whip our heads in the direction of the doorway and that's when I see him.

LC.

Luke is here.

"Sorry, didn't mean to interrupt. But the laundromat's front door was open, and I let myself in. I have quite a bit of laundry to do, but the coin machine is locked. Any chance I could get change?" Luke smiles at Julian.

If Luke is here, that means help is on the way. This nightmare is almost over!

Julian hides the knife behind his back and forces a smile towards Luke. "Sure thing. Just a second." While Julian walks towards the large desk, Luke sends a quick wink my way. Relief starts to wash over me. And just as I start to visualize my rescue, all hope is diminished with a loud bang.

I fell to the floor, startled by the noise. When I look up, I see Julian holding a gun, and Luke laying on the floor on his side.

Nooooo!

Julian lets out an animalistic sound. "I said I don't like using guns! Why did he make me use one?! He ruined our moment Amelia!" He makes his way back to me and sits me up on the ground. His right hand holding the gun and his left holding the knife.

He stares at me, looking deranged as ever. "Now or never Amelia. I can have a plane ready for us to leave in twenty. We'll go to a country with no extradition laws. We can finally start living the lives our mothers had hoped for us." His eyes are frantic. His hand gestures erratic.

My eyes are filled with tears, barely able to focus on Julian's face when I hear a familiar voice.

"NYPD. DROP YOUR WEAPONS. HANDS WHERE I CAN SEE THEM!" Antonio shouts.

I throw myself back on the ground, creating as much space as possible between Julian and me.

It all happens so fast.

I hear more shouting, then gunshots. I immediately feel the weight of Julian collapse on top of me, making it hard to breathe. My hands are still tied behind my back so I can't move him. The adrenaline running through my body is making it almost impossible to get a full breath in.

And then I see him.

Evan is here.

He rolls Julian off me.

But he doesn't seem happy to see me. That's odd.

Then I see Antonio mirror the same expression.

Next, I hear a beep from Antonio's radio. "I need the EMT's in here ASAP. We have a thirty-year-old female stabbing victim, knife still lodged in her abdomen. Get them down here NOW."

And that's the last thing I hear before it all goes dark.

43

EVAN

I'M COVERED IN AMELIA'S BLOOD.

By the time she was put on a gurney, her blood had started to pool around her.

I stayed by her side the entire walk to the ambulance but wasn't allowed on. Antonio calls me over to ride back to the hospital with him, and that's when I notice my dad.

"It's a flesh wound. Bullet went right through. Go to Amelia. Now!" he shouts as he sits at the back of another ambulance, getting gauze placed on his bullet wound.

I nod and jog over to Antonio's patrol car. The siren is already on by the time I get in, and we take off to the hospital.

Thankfully it's a short drive, and we're right behind the ambulance as they arrive.

When they pull Amelia out the ambulance, a small female EMT is riding on the gurney on top of Amelia doing chest compressions on her. "Take us straight into the OR, this is Dr. Nuñez's kid. Let's go, let's go, let's go!" The male EMT shouts as he sprints with a team of ER doctors behind double doors.

Please live Amelia. Please live, baby.

Four hours later, Amelia is still in surgery.

We're all sitting in a private waiting room. The entire cousin crew, spouses, kids, and the doctor wives.

Julian's death is all over the news, and so is Amelia's kidnapping. It doesn't help that we were on the cover of the New York Times today, therefore creating a media frenzy outside.

Everyone in the room leaves me be. They know now is not the time to ask me about our relationship status. My knees shake uncontrollably and my eyes are bloodshot. I have Amelia's dried blood all over my hands, but I refuse to wash it off. No matter how many times Antonio has told me to.

Amelia needed multiple blood transfusions. That was the last update we got an hour ago. Dr. Nuñez, along with all his doctor friends, were already working at the hospital when we arrived. Therefore, she's gotten the best medical care possible. But it still doesn't seem to be enough, because we haven't heard any updates.

Finally, a nurse comes into our waiting room and I bolt out of my seat. Antonio meets me by my side, and I hold my breath.

"Hello everyone, I'm nurse Pooja. Amelia made it out of surgery, and is now in recovery, as we prepare to move her over to the ICU. The surgery went well. It was a bit touch and go there for a moment, but we got the bleeding under control, and the knife wound wasn't deep enough to damage any organs. We'll be keeping her under observation for a couple of days, to make sure there's no more internal bleeding, but if all goes well, she should be home by Christmas Eve." She smiles warmly.

The whole room releases a deep breath, and then we're all blindly hugging one another.

Dr. Nuñez arrives and all of the women flock to him. By the time all the hugs and kisses subside, his watery gaze meets mine.

What do I say to the man whose daughter I almost got killed?

Luckily he's a better man than I'll ever be, and he holds his arms out for a hug.

Dr. Nuñez is barely an inch taller than Amelia, but I swear I feel like he's a giant keeping me up during the hug. He pats me on the back, then finally speaks. "She's asking for you, Evan."

I wipe away the tears I didn't know were there, then nod profusely. "Can I go see her? Please?" I ask warily.

"Yeah, you and Antonio come with me. Everyone else, go home. I'm sure Amelia will appreciate all the cake and food you're all about to make her." He chuckles to himself. They all nod and say their goodbyes. "You can't stay long. She needs to rest, and is heavily medicated." I make a face, but Dr. Nuñez raises a hand dismissing my frustration. "As soon as she's moved out of the ICU, you can stay with her. Usually a father knows his daughter has a boyfriend before allowing him to sleep in her room, but I guess these are extenuating circumstances." He gives me a stern look, which in turn makes me feel like I'm a teenage boy about to take his daughter out on a date. I nod in understanding, and he leads us through multiple checkpoints that need his key card access.

We finally reach her room, and Dr. Nuñez gives us more warnings. Don't make her emotional, keep things light, and leave after a few minutes.

They enter the room before me, and I trail behind.

When my eyes finally land on her in the hospital bed, she's already smiling at us. "My men," she rasps.

My tears immediately threaten to overflow again, when nurse Pooja walks in to check on Amelia's vitals. We're all quiet in the room, until Amelia breaks the silence again. "Nurse Pooja, you've got a nice rack. Can I touch them?" She squints as she tries to lift her arm.

We all erupt into laughter, and the nurse turns to us. "It's the meds. Makes everyone a little loopy and extra chatty.

Dr. Nuñez smiles. "Please excuse my daughter, Pooja. Wish I could say she's much more reserved than that, but I'd be lying."

"Oh no need to apologize. She said much worse when she was being wheeled into the recovery room." Then she eyes me, and blushes. "I'm assuming you're Evan?"

Antonio interrupts before I get a chance to answer. "Oh God, spare us the details. I'm still coming to terms with them dating." Antonio groans as he squeezes Amelia's foot over the covers, which causes her to smile.

She raises her hand to me, and I walk over to her side and take it. My body finally receiving the much needed relief of Amelia's touch.

"I'm so sorry, Amelia. I put you in danger. I will never forgive myself—"

"Your dad, is your dad okay?" her raspy voice interrupts.

"Yes, he's okay. He was flirting with the nurses in the emergency room while you were in surgery." I offer a weak smile.

"He has a type." She chuckles softly, which turns into a cough.

"Okay, I think that's enough for now. Amelia can call you later tonight or tomorrow." Dr. Nuñez motions towards the door.

"Wait Papi. I need to say something first." She tries to sit up a bit, but struggles. Nurse Pooja adjusts her bed and Amelia takes a deep breath.

"This can wait, mija," her dad states softly, but she shakes her head.

"No. It can't. Plus it also counts as official police business, and Antonio is already here."

We all perk up and focus on Amelia.

"Julian." She winces, but continues. "He's had me followed since I broke up with Sebastián. Way before we started dating, even before you saw me at the club. I'm sure you'll see all the photos he had plastered on the wall of that laundromat basement. All the evidence is there." Antonio and her dad exchange a confused glance, but remain quiet.

"How is that possible?" I say. "I thought he was after you because of me."

She shakes her head again. "His mom wanted us to date for years apparently, so Julian was carrying out his mother's sick dying wish. It had nothing to do with you, Evan. You were just an obstacle in the way. By me being with you, it probably kept me more protected if anything. Made his access to me that much more difficult. He was never going to let me go. He was planning on flying us out of the country." She squeezes my hand. "He also said he had someone in the waiting room of this hospital with eyes on dad. Said he would hurt him if I didn't leave my apartment with him. I'm so sorry guys." She starts to tear up and I kiss her hand.

Then I'm all over her. I gently kiss her cheeks, her forehead, and then her lips as I wipe away the tears. "It's okay baby. You're safe now. He can't hurt you anymore."

"Wait. So is he ..." She pauses.

"Dead," Antonio offers. "And we'll track down all of his associates. They're all scrambling now. We cut the head off the snake and everyone is already rushing to make deals with the feds since their ring leader can't protect them anymore. This is over now, Amelia. I promise you that."

Amelia takes a deep breath and closes her eyes. She really is exhausted and needs her rest. I give her one final kiss on the forehead, and stand to leave, but she squeezes my hand. "Does this mean you're going to take me out on a real date now Evan Cooper?" She smiles as she lazily reopens her eyes.

I bite down on my smile while I look at her father and brother. "You're lucky I have more respect for the men in this room. If not, I would forgo asking for their blessing and ask you to marry me right now, Little Miss Amelia."

Her dad sports a surprised smile while Antonio rolls his eyes, although I can tell he's holding back a smirk.

"And Mami. Don't forget to ask for her blessing also," she whispers as she seemingly falls asleep.

"Don't worry, baby. I got that covered too," I whisper back to her.

44
AMELIA

APPARENTLY, ALMOST DYING REALLY TAKES A TOLL ON your body. Luckily, I had Evan by my side the whole time I was in the hospital. My dad was able to pull some strings and managed to get him access to my room. I moved out of the ICU after a day and a half, and into a normal room. Which meant every single person I know was visiting me around the clock.

Poor Nikki clung onto me the longest. She was the one who found the guards knocked out and the sinister flowers sprawled all over my apartment. And to add insult to injury, her and Justin had broken up moments before I was taken. I was sad to hear, but happy to talk about another subject besides *Julian Valentine*.

His drug ring came crashing down after his death. Police were given a warrant to his home after he kidnapped me, and had enough evidence to arrest most of the people involved in his enterprise.

It's Christmas Eve, and I'm finally allowed to leave the hospital. My incision doesn't hurt much since I'm on pain meds, but walking is another story. I wobble more than walk, but I'll take that over being bed bound.

Somehow, Evan convinced both my dad and Antonio that I'd

be better off recovering with him. I'm pretty sure he hired an around the clock nurse for me, so that seems to have done the trick.

Although my dad really didn't have to go into detail about the medical repercussions of having *sexual intercourse* before I'm fully healed.

Thanks, Dad.

Teddy picks us up at the hospital, and is holding a bouquet of flowers for me. I shudder at the memory of Julian's bouquets. Evan notices and takes the flowers for me. "She's more of a balloons and chocolates kind of girl now, Teddy." Evan smiles tightly.

Teddy looks mortified. The details of Julian's terror have been all over the news, but he must have forgotten that little nugget.

"Oh, I'm so sorry—"

I stop him. "Thank you, Teddy. I'm not going to start hating flowers now because of one little ol' psychopath." I chuckle. "But in the meantime, just buy me a slice of pizza. I'll appreciate it more." I wink at him as I take the flowers back from Evan.

We settle into the car, and Evan can barely sit still.

"I'm fine Evan. Why are you freaking out over there?" I ask, grabbing his hand.

He kisses the back of my hand and smiles. "Just excited about your Christmas present." He smirks and kisses my hand again.

"Hate to be the bearer of bad news, but I was a bit too busy not dying to get you a gift. Does that make me a bad girlfriend?" I tease.

"All you have to do is accept my gift, and we'll call it even." He bites down on his smile, then looks out the window.

Oh God.

Is Evan proposing to me right now?!

I mean, absolutely yes. I want to spend the rest of my life with this man. But is this really happening right now?!

I take a few breaths to calm myself, and then notice that we've arrived at our destination. But it's not Evan's apartment building.

I get out of the car slowly, and realize we're standing in front of the brownstone Evan was thinking of purchasing.

"You bought the brownstone?" I gasp.

Evan laughs and slowly leads me up the stairs to the front door. "Our names *are* on the deed," he says casually. My jaw drops, but before I can say a word he guides me through the front door. Once inside, we shed our coats and Evan starts turning on lights as I stand in the foyer.

The pictures did not do this place justice.

It has all of the character of an old New York institution, with all the design and kitchen upgrades to make any HGTV designer drool.

"Your gift is upstairs," Evan whispers into my ear. "Do you think you can make it up the stairs slowly if I carry most of your weight?" he asks cautiously, but I'm already walking past him without an answer. "Okay, slow down there, speedy Gonzalez." He laughs.

We make it upstairs and he guides us to the master bedroom.

"Uhh, Evan. I know I put up a good front, but I think we should listen to my dad and not have sex until my stitches fully absorb." I smile nervously.

Evan rolls his eyes, not finding humor in our celibacy I suppose. He opens the door, and holds my hand as he leads me inside.

It takes me only half a second to realize what I'm looking at.

His bedroom at the cabin.

The distribution of the room is different, but the furniture, wallpaper and even the wood paneling is the same from his bedroom at the cabin. I turn to him confused, shocked, yet thrilled.

"You turned your bedroom ... into the cabin?" I squeal.

He shakes his head. "No, I turned *our* bedroom into a replica of the cabin. This is where I want us to call home." He leans down and kisses me gently. "We made a silly little pact a while ago, not sure if that rings a bell for you." I laugh, but he continues. "And in that pact, we made a promise. *Within these cabin walls, you are mine and I'm yours.* I want our bedroom here to always remind us of the beginning, of the first time we allowed ourselves to love one another. Plus, it will guarantee that no matter what craziness we deal with on a daily basis, we can always come back to this room, where our only desire is to love one another." He places a kiss on my forehead. "So, what do you say? Will you move in with me, will you make this place our home?" he asks eagerly.

I pull him down to me and answer between kisses. "Yes, yes, yes!"

He carefully hugs me close to him, aware to stay clear of my right side. I start laughing uncontrollably into his shirt.

He lifts a suspicious eyebrow. "What's so funny? Did you take your meds today?" He teases.

"Yes, I did. I just thought that you were proposing to me today. I got all worked up in the car. But this is amazing. Even better than a proposal, if you ask me! It's property in New York City!" I snort, followed by a cackle of laughter.

That earns me another playful eye roll from Evan, but then his face turns predatory. "Like you said, best if your stitches heal before we get ahead of ourselves."

How can one sentence make me giddy and horny all at the same time?

45

AMELIA
ONE MONTH LATER

TODAY IS THE DAY.

The one year anniversary of my mother's death.

I've dreaded the idea of this day for so long, but in true Mami fashion, she had already coordinated a *celebration of life: anniversary party*, for when this day came.

It's hard to think that in one year, my mom has already missed so much of my life. Hell, the last few months alone are enough to write a full telenovela.

I know that I need to be grateful. I almost lost my life. And instead of dying, I ended up moving in with Evan into our dream home. But I can't help thinking that I was robbed from experiencing more life moments with my mother's presence. With her love and her approval.

I allowed myself the morning to grieve, be sad, and shed some more tears for my mother.

Now, I'm on my way to my father's apartment to celebrate my mother's life. Just like she's requested.

In a way this is also a do-over for Christmas, since I spent it on bed rest at Evan's apartment. We decided to put off moving into the brownstone until I was fully healed, so I could handle the stairs.

I'm now six weeks post-op. Fully recovered for the most part, but definitely have some nerve sensitivity near my scar.

Even so, Evan refuses to let me carry anything heavier than my purse into my father's apartment. "¡Papi!" I shout as soon as I enter the apartment. I give him a quick kiss on the cheek, then head into the kitchen. "Can you tell Evan that I'm healed now, and he can stop acting like I'm a delicate flower." I cross my arms over my chest as I lean onto the kitchen counter.

They exchange a comical glance. "Stop complaining. In a few weeks you'll text me saying that he has you doing manual labor at the new house." He waves me away as he brushes past me to grab a beer from the refrigerator.

Rude. Since when did these two become *buddy buddy*?

Quickly, the rest of the crew shows up.

Music is playing throughout the apartment and there is enough food to feed all of my father's neighbors. There are a dozen small framed photos of my mother placed around the apartment for décor. She picked the photos and the frames. It makes me laugh how she made sure we were not left to our own devices when picking out photos to remember her by. All of the pictures are flattering, in good lighting, and from her best angles. The woman's a genius.

There are even a few new faces at this party. We invited Luke and Maribel. One saved my life, and the other helped me get my man back. Maribel has also lost a spouse, so she was delighted to see us celebrating my mother's life. Something she hopes to do for her late husband with her own kids.

Maggie is also here, and it's nice to see Evan mingling with both of his parents after all of these years.

I'm about to get a refill on my wine, when one magically appears before me. "Truce?" Priscilla shrugs.

"Wine is better than an olive branch in my opinion." I take the glass from her and smile.

Over the past month, Priscilla has sent over food, flowers and even offered to help clean our home, but we haven't really spoken one-on-one since our blowout on my birthday.

"Look. I'm sorry ... For being an asshole and all." She laughs. "We're too grown for this shit, and life is clearly too short to be fighting over literally nothing. I'd like to get a chance to know the grown up version of Amelia. The one I've been too busy filling in the blanks for. That is, if you're also willing to get to know me. I'm a lot more versatile than you think. I don't even date married men anymore." She nudges my shoulder. "Which by the way, was a complete misunderstanding, but everyone was too busy sensationalizing it to listen to my version of events." She sighs into her glass.

"Well I would love to hear the story if you ever want to chat about it. Over brunch maybe?"

She quirks an eyebrow. "Make it a boozy brunch, and I'm in."

"Is there any other kind?" We clink glasses and laugh.

I feel an arm snake around my waist and squeeze my hip. "I swear this is only six ounces of wine, Evan. I'm sure I can hold up the weight of this glass just fine," I playfully tease.

Evan shakes his head. "Yeah, yeah, c'mon. We're going to play a few home videos now," he says.

I still. "Do you think that's a good idea? Last time we did that for dad's birthday he got choked up."

Evan kisses my head. "Don't worry, your dad knows all about this video." He winks, then guides me to the living room.

My dad is sitting on the center of the couch, looking a bit too giddy. Is he tipsy already? I take a seat next to him.

Evan calls everyone over, and they all sit in mixed matched chairs and stools. Nikki comes and sits on the floor near me.

She and Antonio have been acting weird ever since Evan and I convinced them to take that one-week vacation that Nikki and her ex, Justin, were supposed to take together.

Antonio got a paid two-week suspension after he rescued me. "Optics" is what his Captain claimed it to be. Either way, he was sulking about his promotion to detective being delayed with nothing to do, and Nikki was sad after her breakup. So Evan and I figured they both deserved a vacation over New Years Eve, regardless of the fact that they can barely stand each other.

But now they seem to be acting even more off than before. I make a mental note to remind myself to grill Nikki about it after she's had one too many glasses of wine.

I'm pulled from my thoughts when I see Evan standing in the middle of the living room, by the TV.

"So, as some of you may remember, we tried to watch some home videos for Dr. Nuñez's birthday last time we were here. But the poor man was still watching them on VHS." Everyone laughs.

"I finally got the time to convert everything to digital, and I thought today would be the perfect day to share a certain clip with everyone, in honor of Anna's celebration of life." He smiles, then presses play. He stays standing beside the TV while the video starts.

It's actually the same exact clip that we cut off last time we tried to watch.

It's my mother in the kitchen...with Evan. I'm pretty sure this was his first Christmas with us, so he must have been fifteen at most.

My mother spots my father recording her and turns towards the camera. "¡Hola! Mira Evan, turn around and smile for the camera." A shy Evan half turns and waves.

My mother looks so happy, she's glowing with life.

"Look mi amor, Evan here has been helping me in the kitchen all night! I swear to you, by the time I'm done with this young man, he's going to be a better cook than any of the women here, mark my words." She smiles down at him, and he beams at her.

My eyes are watery, witnessing this exchange between Evan and my mom. I look over to Evan, and he mouths *I love you* to me.

The video has been edited because now it cuts to a different year. Evan looks at least eighteen and it's now New Year's Eve. He's cooking in the kitchen with my mother. She turns and waves to the camera as Evan is hyper focused on the chicken he's sautéing on the stove.

"Evan turn around and wave to the camera! Say 'Happy New Year!'" my mom says as she does a little dance. She then turns her attention back to the stove and it's hard to hear what she's saying, but I can tell she's giving him instructions on what to do next with the chicken. My heart swells seeing them interact this way.

The video cuts once more, and now Evan seems to be in his early twenties, most definitely in college. He's again in the kitchen, but this time surrounded by all of the Tías. Everyone is drinking while he's focused on not burning the tostones.

"¡Feliz Navidad!" All the women cheer. Then my mother grabs Evan by the shoulders and playfully turns him around to face the camera. "Look everyone. Say hi to Evan! Did you know that he helps me cook at every family event? I've taught him everything he knows!" All the women laugh as they look at Maggie, Evan's mother.

"I'm not going to correct you, cooking is not my thing! Keep teaching him so he can keep feeding me the good stuff!" Maggie laughs. My mother hugs her playfully, then goes back to Evan.

"Evan is such a sweetheart, and so handsome. Maggie you can suck at cooking given that you've raised such an amazing young man." Evan blushes as my mother gives his arm a squeeze.

"Mira, escúchame," my mother continues. "Mark my words," she starts, pointing to the camera. "The woman who ends up marrying Evan will be the luckiest woman on the planet! This one right here, just give him a couple of years, but he is husband material, ladies." She pinches one of his cheeks and he finally turns away to pay attention to the plantains on the stove. My mother laughs hysterically and pats him on the back. "I'm sorry to embarrass you, but you're like a son to me, it comes with the territory!" She smiles and tips her champagne glass towards the camera.

The screen goes black.

Only now do I realize that I've been holding my breath this entire time, and that everyone is staring at me.

"Amelia, care to join me up here?" Evan asks with glassy eyes.

Nikki must catch his words before I do, because she is on her feet and lifting me off the couch in a second. I make my way over to Evan and I'm pretty sure I'm starting to realize what's about to happen.

He takes my hands in his and kisses me on the forehead. Oh how I've learned to love these forehead kisses.

"Amelia, I have loved you for a very long time. And recently, my opportunity to love you forever was almost taken from me. I know that today is a somber day. A day in which we will always take a moment to grieve and remember your mother. But I also want today to be something else. The day you remember as the one where your mother gave me her blessing to marry you." He gets down on one knee and the women in the apartment release a collective screech, as the men quickly hush them.

"Little Miss Amelia." He grins. "I never thought I'd actually see the day." One of his hands goes into his jean pockets and pulls out a small black velvet box.

My knees are already wobbling with anticipation. This is such a formality when I'm already dying to say yes and promise to love him for the rest of my life.

"Amelia Nuñez, would you do me the greatest honor ... will you marry me?" He opens the ring box quickly. I'm about to ignore the ring completely just so I can jump into his arms, but then freeze.

The ring.

It's a massive radiant cut diamond. And it's stunning. But that's not what catches my eye at first, shockingly.

The huge diamond is placed on a thin gold band.

My mother's wedding band. The one I took off of her myself a year ago, today.

A piece of my mother forever intertwined with a piece of Evan. *It's perfect.*

"For Christ's sake Amelia stop ogling the ring and tell the man yes already before I have to start performing CPR on the poor bastard," Antonio teases from the couch.

"Shit. Yes! Yes! Of course, a thousand times yes!" I yell.

Evan quickly slides the ring on my finger and raises to his feet to kiss me.

The whole apartment erupts into cheers and tears.

Nikki is walking around topping off everyone's drink for a toast and Antonio has turned the music back on, but my eyes stay locked on Evan's.

Last year, taking this ring off my mother's finger, marked the saddest day of my life. One year later, Evan slipping the same ring onto my finger, marks it as the happiest day of my life.

A true celebration of life indeed, Mami.

"You know what this means, right?" Evan whispers under his breath.

"Umm, that we're getting married?" I respond comically.

He licks his lips and leans into my ear so only I can hear his words. "You're about to become Mrs. Amelia *Fucking* Cooper."

My forehead falls to his chest. "Ughh is this one of those 'live long enough until you become the villain' bits?" I moan. He pinches my good side. "No, but seriously. How. How did you—I don't even know what to ask you first!" I laugh while I bury myself into his chest.

His smile stretches across his face. "Your mother is the person who taught me how to cook. I remember our times together in the kitchen during the holidays. But when your father started playing one of those clips during his birthday, I vaguely remembered your mother saying something about me and marriage. That's why I requested all of the tapes from your father. I knew then exactly how I was going to propose to you." He grins.

"What?! But that was before the cabin! That was when you

were walking around this damn apartment with my stupid thong in your pocket!" I slap his chest while laughing hysterically.

He scratches the back of his neck. "Yeah, that part doesn't seem very romantic now, does it." He chuckles as he pulls me closer. "But there was never a doubt that it would be me and you. We were always destined to belong together, Amelia. I may have been your first crush, but you were always my forever."

EPILOGUE

Evan
Ten Months Later

"ONE, TWO, THREE, PUSH! ALMOST THERE BABY!"

"Evan, I don't think I can do this!"

"Well that's what happens when you drink wine and shop online. We end up with a five hundred pound chest that you refused to pay delivery fees for," I complain. "C'mon, one more push and we can leave it by the window."

"The delivery was the same price as the chest, that's just outrageous Evan! Okay whatever, just leave it there and I'll have it returned. I refuse to push anymore, I need a break after that workout."

I finish setting up the chest by the window and laugh to myself. I'm pretty sure Amelia didn't push the chest one bit, but I'm perfectly happy with being roped into any of my wife's wild shenanigans.

Yes, wife.

Amelia and I got married over the summer at the cabin. We tried to keep it as small and intimate as possible, but with her family from the Dominican Republic alone, we were only able to cut the guest list down to one hundred.

I was floored when I saw Amelia's wedding dress. She looked like an angel. My angel. To know that she picked out that dress with her mother, made the moment even more special. I was also taken aback when Amelia revealed that this dress was a variation of the one she wore at last year's holiday party, and that just solidified what I already knew. Amelia and I were always destined to be together.

Which is why the decision to step down as CEO of Passport-Med was a no brainer.

Right before the summer, I was officially inducted into the billionaire's club, since we acquired a new deal in Tokyo. I had more money that I could burn through and I would give it all back and then some to spend every waking moment with Amelia.

So before work ramped up to eighteen hour days, long business trips and high stress meetings, I promoted my CFO and remained as a silent partner and board member. I still own majority shares, and any big decisions need to be approved by the board, but I no longer deal with the day to day logistics.

My departure made a big splash in the tech world, but I never created my software for my ego, I did it for my mom. And now that I have a wife, and hopefully a crew of cute curly haired kids soon, I wasn't going to allow myself to fall into the trap of trying to juggle it all. I wanted to be present. I wanted to be a good husband and father. And the fact that we were financially blessed beyond measure made it an easy decision.

But that doesn't mean I stopped working all together.

I created a non-profit called **LC's Project**.

It's an all-in-one drop in center for kids who have a parent incarcerated. We provide counseling services, as well and homework prep. We also keep kids from missing out on their childhood because of the prison system. So if a child wants to participate in a sport, but can't afford gear, uniforms or fees, we have it all covered.

If single parents need free child care while they work or interview for jobs, we've also got their back.

We also teach classes to teenagers, for things that their parents would usually teach them if they weren't locked up, like how to tie their ties, how to do simple home repairs, and how to cook for themselves. I even teach that last course a few times a month.

My dad has signed on as a mentor for the kids and parents who are re-entering the world post incarceration. Offering advice and guidance as to how to rejoin the workforce, and catch up to a world that may look completely different than when they were sent away.

It's been a real bonding experience for my dad and I, and hearing the stories of other parents who were separated from their kids gave me a better appreciation for what my dad went through, no matter how I feel about his past crimes.

I can't remember the last time I was this passionate about work. I traded in meaningless corporate meetings for afternoons with inner city kids who were excited about making pasta.

Venturing into the nonprofit world gave me renewed purpose. A way to make tangible changes in others lives, which in return surprisingly managed to heal some of my old childhood wounds. I am now able to give these families a do-over of what my life had been after my father was arrested. I was able to help rewrite the ending to their story, and not allow them to slip through the cracks of the broken incarceration system. And to think that it was all due to a random idea Amelia had that stuck one night when we were babysitting Abby and Vanessa's kids.

Amelia had always been buried deep into my soul, and the moment she fell in love with me, I began to bloom.

Which is why I find it kismet that once she saw the work I was doing, she decided to quit her corporate job as well. It wasn't an easy decision by far, especially since Amelia struggles to understand that she herself is now a billionaire as well. But after I had our lawyers draw up an agreement that clearly stated her physical assets (the cabin and our townhouse fully, and half of my other numerous properties) Amelia was able to fully comprehend her net worth, and walked away from her corporate job.

To others that may seem silly, being a billionaire and worrying about walking away from a nine to five, but I understood. Once you're poor, you work as hard as you can to never put yourself in a precarious situation in which you could be struggling again. And since it's not like we manage cash from day to day, I could see how the billionaire status seemed as if it was made believe.

Amelia being Amelia, she jumped in full force and created her own non-profit and now we both work from home most days, coming up with ways to better our communities.

Her non-profit is called **Anna's Angels**, and it aims to help the Hispanic community learn financial literacy. She and her team help immigrants and Spanish speakers understand how to create healthy financial habits and how to manage their credit scores. She creates classes that help explain the financial world and how to create generational wealth.

She has attorneys that help her clients understand their rights, regardless of their immigration status, and arm people with knowledge, so that they don't feel like they have to hide in the shadows, and therefore forcing themselves to make financial decisions that would keep them there indefinitely.

Amelia was tired of feeling like the diversity hire at her old job, so she decided she wanted to help others learn how to climb the corporate ladder, so that there would be more people that look like her at the top, and I couldn't be prouder of my wife.

It's now the day before Thanksgiving, and we're supposed to be relaxing before our trip up to the cabin with the family and cousin crew tomorrow, but Amelia just can't seem to sit still today.

To think that it's been a year since we made a silly deal to trial date, and now we're happily married and fully immersed in our new careers.

Maybe I need to take her on a vacation. The last time we took a trip was our honeymoon to the Amalfi Coast and the South of France. It was also the second time I feared for Amelia's life, because we ran into Andy Cohen at Cannes, and I was certain that Amelia would pass out. Luckily, she was able to keep it together and only badger him about Bravo and Housewives over the course of one cocktail.

I try not to think about Julian and how I almost lost her, but every time I see the small scar near her hip bone, I'm reminded of how strong and resilient my wife is. It's a reminder that life is short, and each day I have with Amelia is a gift I never knew I could be worthy of.

Life is good.

And now, as I watch Amelia mischievously trying to record me on her phone, I know that I will never be happier than at this moment, at home, with my wife.

Mrs. Amelia *Fucking* Cooper.

Amelia

I finish recording Evan from my stealth location in the kitchen, and quickly send it to Hayden. He promised he could add this short clip to my presentation with a turnaround time of ten minutes, so I'm hoping I can keep my cool until then.

Evan eyes me suspiciously, but being up to no good is my baseline, so he can't be onto me just yet.

Hard to believe how many changes I've been through in the last year. Most recently, I resigned from what I thought would be my dream job.

It's funny how things work out. I used to believe that moving to Miami would be the solution to my identity crisis, when in reality, the city never mattered. It was up to me to do the work and figure out who I wanted to be in this world.

I realized most of my imposter syndrome stemmed from trying to fit myself into a box for others to understand me. I noticed that I constantly tried to break my personality down to bite size pieces for others to be able to consume.

Also, almost being killed by a psychopathic drug lord does wonders for self-reflection.

That experience with Julian made me recognize that most of my life, I felt out of control. But prior to being kidnapped, I was the one giving away my control for others to dictate. I allowed the fear of what other people may perceive of me to determine my actions, and second guess my instincts.

And now, I've never felt more connected to my roots while working with the immigrant and Spanish speaking community. Being able to open multiple centers along with Evan's non-profit across New York and Boston.

I feel like I'm constantly evolving into newer and better versions of myself. And another version is soon to come thanks to the love I share with Evan.

I take advantage that Evan seems preoccupied on his phone to use the bathroom quickly, and when I walk out, I am surprised to find Evan outside of the door.

"Spit it out. What are you up to, wife?"

Wife.

I still turn into putty when he calls me that. But now is not the time to lose focus. I have a plan to carry out and I need to keep my wits about myself.

"Just had to tinkle, *husband*. Did you miss me too much during my little bathroom break?" I patronizingly pat his cheek.

He rolls his eyes, "You're up to something. I can sense it. Did you order more furniture? Because if you did, I swear to God Amelia, you need to start hiring home delivery services."

I wave his words away as I bypass him.

"Don't you worry your pretty little head honey, I'm as innocent as they come. Honest." I bat my eyes playfully, to which Evan responds by simply raising one brow. Clearly his signature move.

PING

I look at my phone and see that I have a text from Hayden with a video attachment.

It's showtime.

After promising that I wasn't pulling a prank, Evan sat on the couch for a presentation I told him I made.

"Okay boss. Let's see it." Evan crosses his broad arms over his chest, eyeing me humorously.

I screenshare my phone to our smart TV.

"Okay, so I need to confess that it's more of a present than a presentation. But you're not allowed to make any comments until the video is over, got it?" I say in mock seriousness.

"A present. Oh God. This should be interesting." Evan runs his hands over his perfectly shaped scruff, and I struggle to bite down my smile.

Here we go, time to press play.

I stay standing by the TV as the first text is displayed on the screen.

THE MOMENT WE FIRST MET

A clip from one of my old home movies starts playing, showing Evan's first Thanksgiving with my family. In it, Evan is a tall, lanky fifteen year old sitting awkwardly on the plastic covered couch with loud merengue music playing all around him. He awkwardly waves to the camera when my dad shouts his name, followed by me interrupting the shot by shyly walking over to Evan, and offering him a soda. "Hi, my name is Amelia. My brother is playing Nintendo 64 is his room and he said you could play with him if you want." Evan offers a small smile and nods, standing to meet Antonio.

I look away from the screen to see Evan's reaction, and his heartwarming smile can't be contained as he stares at us on the screen.

THE MOMENT I DEVELOPED A CRUSH ON YOU

The clip moved to a summer street fair in the early 2000's. Antonio and Evan are walking over to my parents and I with freshly baked funnel cake. My dad is recording the street fair vendors, but Hayden was able to slow down the video and zoom into the bottom right corner of the screen, where we see a young Evan offering me a piece of his funnel cake after Antonio seemingly denied me some of his. You could practically see my heart shaped eyes looking up at him in awe.

That earns me a wink from Evan on the couch.

THE MOMENT I THOUGHT I HATED YOU

A sneaky picture that Xioana took of Evan and I mid-fight at the pub where we had our infamous fight is displayed on the screen.

I simply shrug and smile as Evan rolls his eyes playfully.

The next moments came in quicker, flashing countless photos of our memories together.

THE MOMENT AFTER YOU TOLD ME YOU HAD FEELINGS FOR ME

THE MOMENT AFTER WE MADE THE DEAL THAT CHANGED OUR LIVES

THE MOMENT AFTER I TOLD YOU I LOVED YOU

THE MOMENT I SHOWED UP AT YOUR HOLIDAY PARTY (LOOKING HAWT)

THE MOMENT YOU PROPOSED TO ME

THE MOMENT WE BECAME HUSBAND AND WIFE

Then the screen went dark for a few moments, making Evan think the video was over.

"Honey that was so sweet, what's the occ—"

THE MOMENT BEFORE YOUR LIFE CHANGED FOREVER

The video I had taken minutes before, showing Evan eyeing me as I recorded him from the kitchen started to play on the TV.

Evan looked visibly confused. Poor thing wants to act like he knows what's going on, but he's clearly drawing a blank.

"Husband, can you please look for something between the couch cushion beside you?" I ask as my voice cracks and tears start to well in my eyes.

Evan instantly looks concerned, but does as I say.

When he pulls out the positive pregnancy test, it takes him a second to register what I just pulled off.

And with perfect timing, the video screen shows a final picture of a sonogram taken today, of a tiny baby the size of a rice grain.

Under the sonogram a *Hi Daddy!* is spelled out.

Now tears are fully flowing from my eyes, to the point where I didn't see Evan shoot up from his position on the couch and charge towards me.

He holds onto my arms, seemingly to steady himself, rather than me.

"You— you're pregnant? We're having a ... baby?" Evan croaks.

I bite my bottom lip and nod incessantly until I feel my feet lift off the ground and Evan spinning me in his arms.

"WE'RE HAVING A BABY!!!" Evan shouts as he parades me around the living room as if we've just won the Super Bowl. "Oh crap. I need to put you down. Are you okay? Is the baby okay? When did you find out—"

I'm not sure if I'm sobbing or laughing. I can already tell that these pregnancy hormones are gonna be a doozy, but I stop Evan from his barrage of questions by pulling him in for a kiss. "Baby and I are perfect. It's still early so we need to be cautious, and I peed on a stick yesterday and was able to have Lucy book me a last minute appointment with her husband Bill to run a blood test this morning and have a sonogram taken two hours ago. Perks of having doctors in the family." I wink.

Evan lets out a deep breath, then pulls me closer. "So we finally made it. We're living the crazy life we've always dreamed of huh."

I lean back to look at him, and a cheeky grin spreads across my face. "You know what this means right?

Evan cocks his head. "Um, we're going to be parents?" He chuckles.

I giggle before I say, "After all this time, we're finally gonna get to play that *daddy* game Mr. Cooper."

Our house is filled with laughter and tears as we continue to hold one another. Basking in the joy of living out one of the best parts of all rom coms.

The '*And they lived happily ever after*' part.

The End

ACKNOWLEDGMENTS

Oh my God I wrote a book.

I have so many people to thank for helping me along this process, because it takes a team to make a dream come true. First and foremost, I want to thank my husband, Hugh, for being my rock. Not only is he my Rom Com dream come true, but he is also the reason I was able to write this book. By taking on extra parental duties and supporting our family on one salary so that I could explore this opportunity to the fullest. I never thought I would have a best friend who pushed just as hard, if not harder for my dreams. And luckily for me, I got to marry him. Hugh, thank you for being the best dad to our son Beau, and for cheering me on as if this win was your own. I love you endlessly.

Mis padres! Ay Dios mío. This is the part that I got to keep short and sweet so I can get through it without crying. (Who am I kidding, I'm a crier and this will be no different). My parents share the same immigrant story as millions of others. Coming to the United States in search of the American Dream. Without them, I wouldn't have been afforded the endless opportunities that have led me to the life I now live.

Immigrating was just the tip of the iceberg. They instilled in me the value of my culture, and reminded me that regardless of the geographical location of where I lived, I was always going to be a strong Latina who could take over the world if I ever decided to do so. Gracias Mami y Papi, sin ustedes nada hubiese sido posible.

To the Kris Jenner in my life, my friend Kelly Olson, thank you for pushing me and keeping me on a deadline. And by deadline, I mean asking me for new chapters to read, the second after I emailed you my current work. There were so many moments in which I almost backed out of writing a book out of fear, and I am so glad that I had you by my side (even though you live in Boston) to help keep me focused, and entertained with your commentary on my writing. Sorry, I'm still not giving you that 15%, but I promise to take you out to dinner next time I'm in town!

Like I said, writing a book takes a village, and I had no idea where to start. So thank God for Instagram... I mean bookstagram for introducing me to my favorite all female small business owners. Huge thanks to Britt Tayler (@tropic.bookclub), who not only edited my book, and made it look legible, but for also being a sweetheart and reassuring that my imposter syndrome was unfounded. Sam Palencia (@inkandlaurel), you are insanely talented, and I would have finished the book cover process regardless of if I had finished this book or not, just to be able to own a piece of your work. Thank you for your incredible creativity and patience for every time I emailed you asking for updates, you're a saint! Lastly, I must thank Kristen Hamilton (@kristenreadswhat) for taking me on and quickly formatting my book for me. I had no idea I was earning a friend and massive cheerleader in the process!

And for the real hype team, my beta readers! Brenda Morales (@latinabibliophile), Carolina Capunay (@carosbooknook) and Amanda Squires (@mandy.squ) are the people who gave me the feedback I needed to make my book better, while also letting me know that my book didn't suck. They're truly the sweetest humans on this planet, and I'm so glad I get to call them friends now.

And finally, to my real life Dominican family, real and surrogate. Thank you all for playing such crucial roles in my life, and for being fun inspirations for the characters in this book.

Amo mi cultura y amo a mi gente. Siempre pa'lante, pa'trás ni pa' coger impulso.

CPSIA information can be obtained
at www.ICGtesting.com
Printed in the USA
LVHW081147271022
731543LV00013B/472

9 798218 087791